SIT. STAY. PLAY DEAD.

SIT. STAY. PLAY DEAD.

LILY ROCK MYSTERY BOOK SEVEN

BONNIE HARDY

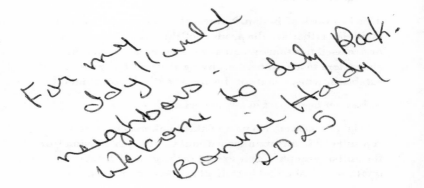

For my idyllwild neighbors - Welcome to Lily Rock.
Bonnie Hardy 2025

ON THE OTHER HAND BOOKS

EPIGRAPH

"Happiness is a warm puppy."

Charles Schulz
1922-2000

CHAPTER ONE

Olivia Greer stood in front of the kitchen sink. Michael, engrossed in his phone, sat across from her. The wide island counter made her feel like it was difficult to communicate without raising her voice. She sighed.

The new house challenged her every day but never more than in the morning. The vast size of the island made everything feel distant. It took several steps and a long reach just to refill his coffee mug.

"Here you go." She patted his shoulder after stirring in his preferred fixings. "Lots of cream and sugar just the way you like it." He didn't look up.

Over the past few months, flecks of gray had grown at his temples. He looked more distinguished and less boyish, even more pleasing to Olivia. She inhaled, appreciating his citrus and pine-scented aftershave early in the morning.

Michael looked at his mug as if surprised. *He didn't see me do the refill*, she thought. *Haven't we become the cozy couple.* Finally he looked up. Steel-blue eyes softened as he raised his mug in a good-morning salute.

"Good morning." She smiled.

His eyes drifted back to his phone as he took a sip.

Olivia stood frozen as she watched the water pour from the faucet. It came on automatically when her hand activated the sensor. *What a waste*, she thought as it continued to run. Even though she knew one more wave of her hand would instantly stop the water, she still felt disgruntled. "Not like my old faucet," she muttered under her breath.

Her eyes drifted to the massive dining room table dominating the space between the kitchen and the living area. Designed to hold twenty side chairs in total, with a larger head-of-table chair at each end, it looked like it belonged in a hunting lodge for burly people. *Maybe a medieval feasting table*, she thought. *Big enough for a king and queen, and all the other land owners.*

She waved her hand in front of the faucet to stop the streaming water. *That's better. Sounds like Niagara Falls. Not like a decent sink, like the one in my other kitchen.*

Olivia wore cotton pajamas. Somehow her bare feet felt underdressed. *I'm not fancy enough for this place.* She tugged at her falling messy ponytail. *I need a new morning wardrobe to go with the kitchen.*

For a moment she imagined being filmed for a lifestyle video for the rich and famous. How a hairstylist would sweep in to fix the loose tendrils, and someone else would powder her shiny nose to look better for the camera.

Michael had gone to great pains to include her in every decision about their new house. She'd agreed with his vision every step of the way. But now she felt adrift. Fortunately she'd not confided in him but kept her feelings to herself.

She also kept her secret from anyone else who asked, "Do you love the place Michael built? He did it for you..."

She'd told everyone the same thing. "Our house is beautiful; he's already getting attention for the architectural design.

Architectural Wonders of the West Coast took photos. The house has been selected for an award." And then she'd abruptly change the subject.

Feeling ungrateful made her crabby and restless. All she could hope was that Michael wouldn't take it personally once he found out. Which he would. Because it was his project and he'd done everything right. And eventually he'd sense her lack of authentic enthusiasm, and then, as they say, the jig would be up.

Olivia walked across the room to drop her wet towel into the laundry chute. She made her way back to the kitchen, past a massive double-sided stone fireplace. Granite boulders had been sourced at Michael's request. The structure rose to the height of the room, the chimney lifting farther to the peak of the roof.

He knows who he is, she mused. *A gifted architect and designer. But who am I? We've been together for over four years and I'm still confused. I still feel adrift. Oh well. Maybe I will never be satisfied.*

Spotting dust on the glass-top table, she reached for a clean kitchen towel. *Gotta dust.* The oversized leather sofa and two enormous leather side chairs looked lost in the room. Surrounded by open windows looking into the woods, she shivered. The room felt chilly, even with flames from the fire licking against the stone interior.

Shadows flickered overhead. Early morning sunlight shone through the uppermost branches of the pine trees. A bright glare reflected against the glass. She blinked. *Is there such a thing as too much light?* This thought surprised her.

"Bellemare's vision of a cabin in the woods is captured in his latest design. Enormous in scope, intimacy is achieved by the indoor-outdoor abidance of the natural surroundings." That's what one reviewer wrote in an article.

Is there such a thing as too much light and space?

She remembered her old sink. When she washed a dish, she looked out the window. She'd often have her best ideas there, and relive her best memories. *No window behind the new sink. Just that gigantic quartz counter.*

Stop comparing, she chided herself. *You're acting ungrateful. Stay present. No use thinking about what was...*

She poured herself a cup of coffee. And at that precise minute she remembered, *I haven't seen Arlo for awhile. He'd understand what I'm feeling.* She could always tell Arlo when she was uncomfortable, and he'd listen without judgment.

He'd known her since she'd first arrived in Lily Rock. Arlo had so many issues back then, what with Cayenne's medical challenges and his business. *Arlo knows defeat. And how to pick himself up and start again. I wish I could talk to him.*

Her mind raced. *Now I remember. The last time I saw him was at Village Hardware. He was in such a hurry.*

"Can't talk now, Olivia," Arlo had mumbled, dropping his money on the counter.

Then he took his can of WD-40 and rushed out the door before she could call after him.

Olivia kissed Michael's ear. "I've been so busy unpacking boxes with this move, I just realized I haven't seen Arlo in a really long time. I'm kind of worried."

Michael's dark blue-gray eyes appeared thoughtful. "Arlo's being Arlo. Most of us can't predict where he'll be or when," he reasoned. "Don't you have a pub gig coming up soon? You can check on him then."

"True," she said. "Arlo booked Sweet Four O'Clock months ago. I guess he was part of the first annual Woofstock planning committee."

A sharp scratch came from the back door. "Mayor Maguire. He wants breakfast." The labradoodle bounded past her feet. His tail waved a greeting as he headed directly to his food dish. Finding it empty, he nosed it across the floor in the direction of the walk-in pantry. Then he sat and looked up at Olivia.

"I'll get your kibble." Olivia ruffled his ears.

She called over her shoulder to Michael. "I have a funny feeling Arlo's in trouble." Unable to ignore her instincts, Olivia admitted.

Michael glared at Mayor Maguire. The dog had planted his front paws on Michael's chest. Maguire nosed the last bite of toast Michael held in his hand.

"Down, Maguire." Once on all fours, Michael gave him the toast anyway. "Now that you mention it, the last time I saw Arlo was by that new inn around the corner from the hardware store. He stood outside talking to a guy I didn't recognize. I said hello, but he didn't hear me. Oh, and Arlo had a dog with him," Michael added, a note of surprise in his voice.

Maguire looked up, a string of drool dripping from his left jowl. The dog's eyes focused on the fresh slice of toast Michael held in his hand.

"Arlo had a dog? That's strange. I didn't think he likes pets. What breed?" Olivia stood across the counter.

Mayor Maguire nosed Michael's knee. The labradoodle had a keen sense of when the conversation was distracting anyone who held food, and he wanted a bite of toast.

"One of those brindle-colored flat-faced Frenchies. Kind of surprised me. I thought if Arlo ever got a dog or a cat, he'd adopt. I've heard Frenchies cost a bundle." He broke off a piece of toast and tossed it to Maguire.

As Olivia stacked dishes in the dishwasher, she called to the dog, "M&M. Enough begging. Want to go for a walk?"

No dog appeared by her side. She only saw a few crumbs

on the floor by Michael's stool. M&M wasn't in the dining area either.

"Maguire," she called again. When he didn't appear, she patted Michael's shoulder. "What happened to the mayor? He was just here a minute ago."

He pointed. "The back door's open."

She groaned. "I must have left it open when I let Maguire in." Pine needles and dust blew inside. But still no dog. Her phone pinged at the same time Michael's phone chirped. He was the first to speak.

She ignored his conversation to shut the door against the breeze.

"Gotta go. There's an emergency at the dog park," he called.

A tingle ran down her spine.

"Anything you can tell me?"

"Can't say right now." His tone sounded serious.

Since Michael was a Lily Rock volunteer first responder, she was used to him leaving unexpectedly. After the incident was handled, he'd fill her in, but not before. Need-to-know basis, she'd heard from him and Janis Jets often enough.

He stopped to kiss her cheek.

Once he'd gone, Olivia held her phone to her ear to listen to her message.

"It's Janis. I need you at that new dog park. We've discovered a dead body."

CHAPTER TWO

"Olivia, over here!" Jets looked official in her usual navy blazer and tan slacks, her white shirt tucked in. The Lily Rock cop hadn't changed much since they first met.

Michael and another first responder hovered close by. Right then, an ambulance pulled to the curb. Michael and the other volunteer hurried over to talk to the driver just as Olivia crossed the street.

She waited while Janis finished typing with the on-screen keyboard on her tablet. Only then did she notice the bulge at the back of the cop's blazer, designed to cover her weapon. Janis would be the first to say that her uniform was her best weapon in most cases.

"On the one hand, as the solo cop in Lily Rock, my uniform sets me apart from everyone else. My presence and sparkling personality deter most people from their bad behavior instantly. But on the other hand, if that doesn't work, I have this." She'd pat the bulge of her blazer.

Olivia waited for the cop to look up and acknowledge her presence. When she did, Olivia's heart jumped. Janis's eyes were puffy and red. Olivia inhaled quickly, preparing herself for a shock. "Who is it?" she asked. "Who's the dead guy?"

"You're not gonna like this." Janis sounded grim. She slipped the tablet into her backpack and then nodded toward the entrance to the dog park.

Olivia gasped. On the other side of the chain-link, she saw the body of a man sitting on a bench. He wore jeans and a hoodie, and he was slumped over at the waist.

Olivia feared the worst. *Is it somebody I know?*

"Change of plan. Stay put," Jets insisted. "Give me a minute."

Olivia steadied her nerves by reading the sign displayed on a post: "The Frenchie Connection." Underneath, a warning had been written boldly in dark script: "Only AKC French bulldogs permitted to use this privately owned dog park."

"Not my first problem with The Frenchie Connection dog park," Jets commented dryly. "A complaint came across the constabulary desk just last week. A report that some employee of The Frenchie Connection—the inn, not the dog park—booted out a wiener dog because he wasn't the right kind." Jets grimaced. "I'm not a fan of long low dogs with pointy noses, but I'd never say he couldn't come to my dog park."

Olivia wasn't paying attention. Her eyes focused on the slumped-over body in the distance. Her eyes widened. "I suppose that means Mayor Maguire isn't even allowed."

"Yep. That's what I'm sayin'." Jets glanced away. She said softly, "I've already identified the body. I wanted to give you a heads-up. Brace yourself, Nancy Drew."

"Do I know the victim?"

"It's Arlo," Jets said, her voice dropping. "He's been stabbed. Dr. Martinez is having a look right now."

A roar rose in Olivia's head, then a rushing sound. Her

body's way of blocking out an unpleasant truth, always too late.

Since the death of her friend Marla a few years ago, she'd seen her share of dead bodies. But no one she called a friend had passed since then—until now. "Are you sure it's Arlo?"

"Do you think I'd kid about something like that?" Jets snapped. "It's him all right. And what a mess. Lots of blood. Take a quick look for yourself."

One look revealed a scraggly ponytail that stuck out the back of a faded blue baseball cap. The gray hair matched the thin beard, which barely covered his chin. Arlo's skin looked gray, his mouth slack. Olivia felt numb.

One hand lay at his side, the other in his lap. The worn jeans and the familiar Grateful Dead sweatshirt brought tears to her eyes. "It's him. I'd know that sweatshirt anywhere."

A keen memory appeared from nowhere. How Arlo had leaned out of his truck to offer road assistance that first day Olivia had run off the road in Lily Rock. He'd worn the same dusty-blue cap. His hair wasn't as gray then.

Olivia never quite trusted Arlo, but that hadn't stopped them from becoming friends. Plus his wife was her mentor. They'd become close over the years, meeting at the labyrinth for meditative walks.

"Has anyone contacted Cayenne?" Olivia asked.

"Not yet. I was hoping you'd go with me, since you know Cayenne better than anyone," Jets said.

She heard the reluctance in Janis's voice. *Not just another crime scene for her either. She's sad and trying not to show it.* "Sure. I'll do what I can."

Jets looked down at her feet as if at a loss for words. "Probably one of his drug connections gone wrong," she said softly.

"But he's legit now," Olivia insisted.

"So everyone tells me. I'm not convinced. Plus sometimes

your past catches up with you." Jets looked toward the body again and shook her head.

"Who found the body?" Olivia asked.

"That guy over there with the short shaggy beard who looks like he belongs in a *Scooby Doo* cartoon. He called the constabulary and 911. Claims he's The Frenchie Connection dog trainer. Every morning he arrives early to walk a dog and pick up the leftover poop."

A thin man leaned against the fence on the opposite side of the dog park. Gray hair over his ears stuck out from a faded baseball cap. The gray beard made his chin appear pointed and narrow. Olivia put him in his mid to late fifties.

Sniffing at the dirt and then at the man's worn running shoes, the dog jumped to one side, then the other as if he'd come upon something worth investigating. He used a front paw to poke at the dirt, then jumped back to watch the thumbnail-sized beetle he'd discovered.

Jets growled. "That has to be the stupidest dog I've ever seen. Playing with a stink bug. Just eat the damned beetle already."

She looked at Olivia and said, "Why don't you wait over there? I don't want you to contaminate my crime scene. When I'm done talking to Shaggy Rogers and his not-too-smart dog, I'll be back."

"I loved *Scooby Doo*," Olivia commented. "He does resemble Shaggy."

Jets walked away, her shoulders slumped.

Olivia watched from the other side of the fence. She felt restless. *I'm the only one without a real job to carry out at this crime scene.* She inched closer to the body and the first responders chatting with the local doctor.

Luis Martinez hovered closest to the body. He was the only one to glance Olivia's way. She raised her chin in greeting. Michael and Jeff Grossman stood side by side, both with their arms folded over their chests. Finally Michael gave her a quick nod.

Olivia's stomach clenched. Looking at Arlo this closely, she saw red stains on his clothes that spread across the bench, puddling on the ground. She edged closer. Martinez spoke to Michael.

"A sharp object, probably a thin knife, five inches or so, maybe a stiletto..." the doctor reported. "Shoved into his armpit. I'd say off the top of my head the blade hit an axillary artery, which caused a hemorrhage. That would account for all the blood. Of course my assessment will have to be confirmed by the coroner down the hill."

"A terrible way to go," Michael muttered.

"He bled out. Happened fast," Martinez stated flatly.

"So what's next?" Jeff Grossman asked.

"You guys can pack him up and take him now. I'm done here." Martinez turned to close his medical bag.

Michael looked away, his hand covering his eyes.

"Michael," Olivia called to him.

He walked closer.

She explained, "I'd go home, but Janis wants me to go with her for the notification." Tears filled her eyes. "This is so awful."

Michael's jaw tightened. "You're too close to this, Olivia. It's Jets's job to make notifications, not yours."

Michael had made it known in the past that Olivia's involvement in solving murder cases wasn't to his liking. He'd been tolerant for years, mostly busy with his own work. But now, with another dead body, he doubled down.

Olivia knew he had a point. Helping out Jets had increased from one murder to the next, each one with its own complications.

Jets had openly disagreed with Michael right to his face. "Olivia has a gift," she'd told him. "Not official or anything, but helpful to me. It's her face or her big eyes. Especially when she sings, that's when it's most noticeable. People just spill their guts to her. She can get a confession faster than I can. It's kinda spooky. So butt out, Bellemare. Let the ladies do their job."

Unsure if it was a gift or not, Olivia would say, "I like helping Janis," whenever the subject came up. She'd told him more than once.

When he refused to be convinced, she compared her civic volunteer police work to his civic volunteer first responder job. "I'm a first responder just like you. Only with the cops. You can't tell me that I can't fulfill my civic duty."

But now the look on his face made her realize the full extent of his disapproval.

"I think she asked me as a friend this time," Olivia explained. "She seems unusually upset. I mean, Arlo was an Old Rocker.

Michael's jaw tightened again. "We can talk more later. I have to help with the stretcher. I'll see you back at the house."

"You're angry..."

"I just want you to be safe. It's hard for me to watch you being so upset around a scene like this." He leaned over to kiss her forehead. "Sure you're okay?"

"Not yet," she admitted. "But I want to be there for Janis and Cayenne."

"I get it. We can talk later." He walked away, his eyes cast downward.

They loaded Arlo's body onto the stretcher. Olivia blinked as a sob rose in the back of her throat. She held her hand over her mouth.

Wiping away tears, she looked for Janis.

The officer stood across the park, making notes. Right next to her, the brindle-colored Frenchie rolled in the dirt, his lead getting tangled around his body and legs. "Yip!" The dog leaped to all fours. He freed himself from the leash and trotted closer to Janis, then circled her boots, creating a noose around her feet.

Janis raised her boot and kicked at the leather. The dog tugged again. Janis lost her balance, tablet in one hand, arm flung to the side as if riding a surfboard. Finally she righted herself.

"Dude, curb your dog," she called to the Shaggy-looking man.

"Fifth, knock it off." He picked up the end of the leash. "Sorry about that." He reached to untangle Janis's other boot. Held in both arms, the dog looked him in the face. "Yip!" The Frenchie shoved two front paws against the man's chest, and he placed the feisty animal back on the dirt.

"What kind of a name is Fifth?" Jets mumbled, walking away. "It's a number, not a name. Fifth of what? Gin, maybe?"

Olivia offered another possibility. "A science fiction film called *The Fifth Element*. Came out in 1997. With Bruce Willis. Maybe the owner is a fan..."

"Whatever. People and their dogs," Jets huffed. "Makes me sick."

"So what did you find out?" Olivia prodded.

"The guy's name is George Quigley. He works for The Frenchie Connection Inn. He's worked for the man mostly, for several years." Jets opened her tablet. "Uma and Eldred Whitlock. He's a breeder. She runs the day-to-day of the inn.

"Anyway, they hired George over there to walk and train their dogs. He also walks and trains the dogs of those who stay at the inn."

"So Fifth—is he a boarder or one of the owners' dogs?"

"The owner. I guess Fifth is some kind of super stud. Whitlock told me more than I wanted to know about breeding the mutt. Between you and me, George almost sounded envious when he was telling me the details."

"Ick," Olivia said.

"Ah come on. Don't tell me you're not thrilled imagining dogs doing it." She sneered at Olivia's shocked expression. "Just so you know, according to ol' George over there, breeding Frenchies avoids actual physical contact. I mean the stud is a stud in name only, if you get my drift. Kinda stupid from my point of view. What kind of fun is that? Anyway, the mutt looks like a big dummy to me. Did you see him wrap that leash around my feet?" Jets scowled.

"Fifth is important enough to have his own full-time trainer," Olivia insisted. "What else did you learn?"

"So George came over here for an early morning romp with Fifth and he saw someone slumped over on the bench. Part of his job is to keep the animal riffraff out of the park. He didn't even act embarrassed when he told me. I guess separating dogs in his world is natural.

"Like I was saying, it's a collateral job for George to enforce the dog park rule of only allowing in pure-bred Frenchies, and the other rule. No one can loiter in the park without a pure-bred Frenchie. That's why he spotted Arlo. He occupied a bench without a mutt." Jets sighed.

"George claimed that he didn't recognize Arlo. That he thought the man was a hobo and maybe asleep. But when he looked more closely, he saw the blood on his shirt and the bench. In his exact words..." Jet opened her tablet. "That guy on the bench—well, he wasn't playing dead."

"Arlo's gone," Olivia mumbled. "I just can't wrap my mind around any of this."

"Yep." Jets shut her tablet. "No time to think about feelings. Before we notify Cayenne, I have a couple of things to do."

"Does that mean I'm still supposed to tag along anyway?"

"Why not. I need to stop at the constabulary. I have to relieve my assistant of his temporary assignment. You might as well find out. He's babysitting."

"What!" Olivia glanced at Jets. "Is that why you have circles under your eyes and look so terrible? Did you adopt and you're not getting enough sleep?"

"My eyes are just fine." Jets scowled. "In fact, *I'm* just fine. Oh sure, it took me aback when I realized the victim was Arlo. But now I'm on track. It's a cop's duty to stay detached."

"You're not fine," Olivia insisted. Jets scowled again, making Olivia wish she'd kept her mouth shut.

"See here, Nancy Drew. I know your little tender heart is worried that I'm not myself. I can see it in your face. But stop worrying. Like I said, I was shocked. It takes a beat to adjust to the idea that a friend has been murdered in your patch, on your watch.

"A blow to my ego, if you must know." Jets's mouth drew a straight line. "Enough introspection and jibber-jabber. Meet me at the constabulary. And don't bring him." She pointed to the street right as Mayor Maguire rounded the corner at a fast trot.

"Bork!" Maguire called. He bounded across the road, straight toward Olivia. He came to a skidding halt at her feet, his tongue hanging out of one side of his mouth.

"M&M," she said in a low voice. "You disappeared this morning..." She scratched behind his ear.

With a quick turn of his head, he licked her open hand.

She kneeled down to wrap her arms around his neck, burying her face in his soft fur.

CHAPTER THREE

When Olivia walked through the door of the constabulary, she found Janis talking to her assistant, Brad May, who sat behind the reception desk. A gray bundle of wiggling fur sat in his lap. Brad grinned as soon as he saw Olivia.

"Like I was telling the boss, he's doing great. We had a walk and a poop—"

"I don't want the details," Jets groaned. "He's alive. That's what matters. Now stop coddling him and put him down."

The puppy leaped from his arms, disappearing under the desk. Olivia heard scratching against the wood floor. The dog scurried from underneath the desk to stand at Janis's feet. "Yip," he said.

Jets stared at him, a puzzled expression on her face.

"Yip, yip, yip."

"Oh, okay." She lifted him with both arms. Using both hands, she held him away from her body. Stubby back legs dangled in the air.

She pulled him closer to scold. "Stop squirming. What did I do to deserve you? I could kill that man."

"What man?" Olivia asked.

"Cookie Kravitz. He can bake a to-die-for shortbread cookie and he's a wonder in the sack, but he has no clue what makes me tick. Thinks I need a dog to care for."

"'He'll soften your otherwise surly attitude'," Jets said, imitating her partner's gruff voice. "That's what he told me. The nerve. I'll soften him," she grunted, placing the puppy back on the floor.

"So may I assume that having a baby is no longer being considered?" Olivia winked at Brad behind Jets's back.

"No human ones for sure," Jets muttered. "I disabused Cooks of that notion months ago. It took some persuading, but I thought he understood. We're too old to be having babies. I'm nearly fifty.

"But then he brought home that lump of potato as his consolation prize." She pointed to the puppy, who proceeded to lift a hind leg and pee against the desk. "Stop that!" Jets roared. "Uncivilized beast." She picked up the dog again.

The puppy snugged a flat nose under Jets's chin and began to lick.

"What's his name?" Olivia asked.

"Tater Tot," Jets mumbled. "Because he looks like a small potato."

"But he's gray, not brown," Olivia objected. "Potatoes are brown."

"Stop being so literal. And have a look." She held out the squirming dog, his feet dancing in the air. "The body shape," Jets explained. "He can't run two feet without falling over. I wanted to name him after my uncle, but Cookie said no. So Tater Tot he is."

"A Frenchie, maybe three months old," Olivia observed aloud. "An interesting shade of gray." The puppy's short coat appeared dark gray on the surface, but upon closer inspection she could see a lilac-blue undertone.

"Yep," Jets said. "The mutt cost Cookie a fortune. You don't want to know how much. I can't believe that man." She turned her chin aside to avoid Tater Tot's vigorous licking.

"Take the mutt, would ya?" Jets handed the puppy back to Brad, who smiled from ear to ear.

"Will do, boss," he said politely.

"Don't call me boss," she retorted, adjusting her shirt collar over the wet spot left by puppy kisses. "Okay, so I'm done here. Checked on the fur baby. We can go see Cayenne." Jets sounded more official now that she wasn't being showered with doggie kisses.

Olivia had to admit watching Janis and Tater Tot had lifted her spirits. The entire morning had gone from terrible to a whole lot better within minutes. Olivia couldn't help but feel more hopeful watching Janis Jets try to act like she didn't care about her new puppy.

"Stop looking like that," Jets grumbled.

"Like what?" Olivia said innocently.

"Like you've been witness to the resurrection or something. You're to blame for all of this. Cookie thought your niece was so cute. After that, he wanted his own baby. It's all your fault that I have this dog."

"Technically, Sage is to blame," Olivia reminded her. "I'm just the auntie."

"And on top of that, I already have a pony," Jets remarked.

"I didn't know that. Since when?"

"It's not like I'm proud of it; more like I got stuck. Before you showed up in Lily Rock, I was regifted Sparkles. A full-bred Shetland who is the most useless animal on four hooves. She's ill-tempered and eats her weight in oats.

"I pay for her board and for someone to walk her around.

She's too small for an adult to ride—I've been told that often enough. So she needs to be walked like a dog." Jets huffed under her breath. "Not like I'm going to start a pony show for children just to keep Sparkles from being bored."

Jets glared at Tater Tot. "And now a puppy. What's the matter with Cookie? Is it such a surprise that I'm not an animal person? I don't even like people that much."

Olivia tried to catch Brad's eye, but he'd ducked his head under the desk.

"Maybe I can meet Sparkles some time," she suggested. "You know Star will be ready to ride her first pony soon. Talk to Sage. You could work something out."

"Sure. When I have time. Which is never. I'll handle my menagerie just fine by myself without your suggestions. Wait for me out back while I instruct my assistant in the finer points of police work."

Then she yelled at him, "Get out from under that desk and show some respect!"

"Talking to me, boss?" Brad's head popped up, his eyes wide with feigned innocence.

"Who else is my assistant," Jets retorted.

Brad's grin widened, which nearly made Olivia giggle. He winked at her and then said, "I'll get you coffee, boss."

"That would be appropriate," Jets muttered.

"See you outside." Olivia hurried toward the exit.

She stopped at the door for a quick backward glance. Janis held Tater Tot nose to nose with her as the puppy's back legs flailed in the air. "Who's a good doggie," Jets said in a teasing voice. Then she pulled her pet in for a hug.

"You sit shotgun while I drive," Jets directed.

Buckled snugly in, Olivia gritted her teeth. Not a careful

driver on most days, she anticipated Janis's mood might make her driving even worse.

Jets slammed her foot on the pedal as the truck lurched backward. She shifted and sped forward toward the main highway. Olivia nearly bit her tongue as Jets came to an unexpected screeching halt.

A deer and her fawn stood in the road. "Move it, would ya!" She bumped the horn. When the deer didn't move or even look her way, she leaned out the window. "Get going. I have a job to do."

The deer lifted its head. Her tail swished. But she didn't budge.

"It's a mom and her baby," Olivia explained. "Be patient. You of all people should understand, now that you have a fur baby." She kept her face straight.

The deer dropped her head to nudge her fawn. She gave a backward glance at the truck and then trotted across the street. The fawn followed.

Jets lowered her boot on the accelerator, passing the deer at the side of the road. She took the first curve on the mountain road way over the speed limit. Olivia gripped her seat and stared through the windshield. Instead of focusing on her fear, she thought about Michael.

He'd touched a nerve when he'd questioned her involvement at the crime scene. She knew that he'd been less critical for the past several months because he was busy, knee-deep in house plans and construction. Since their move to the new house, he'd gone back to his earlier objections.

Though she argued for equality, Olivia wasn't convinced that he didn't have a point. She'd gotten into some sticky situations in the past playing amateur detective. She'd thought it would only be that one time. But the universe seemed to have other plans. So many dead bodies... She shuddered.

It turned out that Lily Rock had more than its share of murders. In fact, she'd begun to compare Lily Rock to Miss Marple's Saint Mary Mead. Or even Jessica Fletcher's Cabot Cove.

Though she loved figuring out puzzles and getting confessions, Olivia didn't like being compared to the older sleuths. *I'm more like Nancy Drew. I have a car. Okay, it isn't a fancy convertible roadster. But it still runs. I have chums. I call them friends, but I do have them. Nancy had a friendly housekeeper, Hannah. And instead, I have the crew from Mops R Us. They stop in every two weeks.*

All comparisons aside, Olivia felt stuck. *Michael hates that I work with Janis. But if I don't help out, I'll need to find another temp job to keep occupied. The last thing I want is to be waiting for him to come home and tell me about his day.*

She consoled herself with one last thought. *At least Sweet Four O'Clock will be up and performing again, though we don't have another gig planned after that.* Since Sage was fully employed at the music academy and raising her baby as a single parent, she no longer seemed interested in touring.

Janis spun out of the last curve. "Yeehaw," the cop yelled, pushing her foot harder to the pedal. "Hang on! We're almost there."

Jets screeched to a halt at the top of the hill. The truck bumped over the dirt road onto a gravel driveway. The Lily Rock nondenominational chapel appeared at the end of the drive. Jets slowed the truck, giving Olivia a chance to remember her first impression.

Constructed on a knoll and surrounded by a forest of oak and pine, it looked like something from a picture book. The white clapboard siding and peaked roof loomed ahead. The steeple jutted toward the sky. The church gave the impression of being transplanted from a coastal town on the eastern seaboard.

Olivia knew that the chapel's traditional appearance was deceptive. One only needed to step inside to be surprised. The first time she thought there would be the usual items one found in a church. She expected an altar at the front, with a communion table. Maybe a cross at the center. She'd expected to see a pulpit and an array of fake flowers in an urn and maybe a banner flung over the front. One to match the altar cloth.

But the chancel of this sanctuary was empty. No pulpit or decorations. Not even a table. The farthest wall had been constructed with a large plate-glass window, framed with darkly stained wood. When she'd looked past the window, she'd gasped. Surrounded by pine trees, a weathered ten-foot wooden cross took her breath away.

Unprotected from the elements, the cross had stood the test of time. Worn with splinters and discoloration, the base was held down by boulders and river rock. At the time, Olivia knew various faith groups used the sanctuary for meetings and occasional services. It was probably reasonable to leave the Christian symbol out of doors so as not to offend others.

Janis's truck juddered across the gravel, her front tires hitting potholes; Olivia's teeth rattled. As Jets parked behind the church, Olivia faced her dread by closing her eyes. She heard the slam of the driver's side door. Then she opened her eyes to look toward the clearing. Nestled in the trees was Arlo and Cayenne's cabin. Olivia bit her bottom lip to hold back tears. There was no welcoming smoke rising from the chimney.

Standing on the path she heard a crow call out. When she turned to look over her shoulder, she caught sight of the labyrinth. Constructed out of river rock and boulders, Cayenne and friends had laid the spiral design years before.

It didn't take long for news to spread that Lily Rock had a labyrinth open to the public. People from out of town would come up for spiritual retreats to make their way on the journey to nowhere. It was supposed to symbolize the inward path, one that began and ended at the same place.

Olivia's heart sank. "I don't see Cay. She's not walking the labyrinth today." She looked to Janis for confirmation.

Finally Jets cleared her throat. "This is new to me—doing a notification to a friend." She nodded toward the cabin. "I thought I'd done everything on this job, but I guess not. Notification to a friend about her husband... A real challenge."

Olivia exhaled slowly. She felt unnerved. Janis was expressing the unthinkable: her feelings, the vulnerable ones she rarely admitted.

"I think this is more than a challenging circumstance," Olivia said slowly.

Janis's face had turned to stone in an effort to hold back her feelings.

Olivia kept talking. "What if you don't pursue this case? The county could send another temporary cop, one who doesn't live in Lily Rock."

"I could do that. Inform my boss," Jets admitted. "But I feel responsible for Arlo's death. It's tricky. I think I'm pretty good at what I do, and I want Arlo and Cayenne to have the best investigation we can offer. Get some answers and justice. I'd be letting them and myself down if I didn't at least try."

"So you know you're the best, at least in these circumstances." Olivia felt a pang of envy. She wanted to feel that kind of certainty in her life. That she had a talent and that she would be paid to use her talent to help other people. Like

Michael and Janis and even Sage, who managed to direct an entire high school and be a mom.

"Pretty arrogant, I admit." A slight smile came to the Janis's lips.

"Calling yourself out for being arrogant. Is this the new and improved Janis Jets?" Olivia dismissed her own sense of inadequacy to support her friend. She kept her voice light, hoping to lift the cop's spirits.

Jets pushed her shoulders back. "Okay, I am the best. No use denying it. I have a job to do and you're here to help me figure out who killed Arlo. No more looking back."

Underneath the introspection and bluster, Olivia heard Janis's competence return. Olivia pointed toward the cabin. "We have to notify Cayenne before we can gather any more information. You don't want her to hear from someone else. So do you have any instructions for me before we knock on the door? You know, cop stuff."

"No smoke from the chimney," Jets observed aloud.

"I noticed that myself," Olivia said. "Anything else?"

Jets shrugged. Then she coughed, hiding her face in her arm. By the time she looked back at Olivia, she'd regained her composure.

"On the one hand, no smoke coming from the chimney— not so surprising. Not like Cay is one of those homebody types, sipping tea in front of her fire, petting a kitty cat. She has her Mops 4 Us cleaning business to attend to. But on the other hand..."

Jets strode with determination toward the cabin's front porch. Her "on the other hand" was lost the farther she stepped away.

CHAPTER FOUR

Side by side on the front porch, Jets pointed. "Look at that. Someone's jimmied the door."

Scraps of wood lay across the door's threshold, and deep gashes had been made against the metal plate surrounding the knob. There were dents in the door as if someone had kicked it open.

Jets pulled out her phone and took a quick picture. "I want this for evidence just in case." She put the phone back in her pocket and then reached back under her blazer for her weapon. Holding it in the air, she used her other arm to shove Olivia behind her back.

"Stay here. I'm going to have a look around. Don't move until I say so." She gave a stern look.

"Understood," Olivia muttered.

Janis inched the door open. Hinges creaked as she stepped inside. "Hello. Anyone home? Police," she loudly called out.

Olivia shivered. Taking a step backward, she leaned against the wood siding, waiting for further instructions.

She could hear Janis's boots clomping across the wood flooring. She'd visited Arlo and Cayenne on any number of occasions, so she had no trouble picturing the interior of the cabin. *She'll try the mudroom first. Then she'll stop in the hall to check out the bathroom...*

To her surprise Janis reappeared at the doorway. "Okay, Nancy Drew. I think the coast is clear. No one's hiding inside. You can come in."

"What about Cayenne?" Olivia asked.

"I said no one, that includes Cayenne," Jets snapped. "I would have mentioned her right away."

Relief flooded through Olivia. She wasn't sure what she would say to Cay, and now she need not worry. But for a brief second, considering the looks of the break-in, she was afraid that Cayenne might have been found inside, attacked.

Not likely, Olivia now realized. *But I'm jumpy, I have to admit.*

The A-frame was not unusual in any way. Many cabins on the hill were constructed with a similar floor plan. Olivia only knew this because Michael had explained when he was drawing the plans for their new home.

"I want to create something unique for us," he'd explained. "An element of surprise around every corner, along with a spaciousness." His face lit up as he told her, eyes bright. She'd not really understood at the time.

Nor had she ever considered that an architectural masterpiece might not be a place she wanted to live in or call home.

To be honest, Olivia would have been very happy in a simple A-frame. But that was before. Before she'd moved in with the love of her life, the famous Bellemare architect. Up until now she'd been able to keep her feelings to herself.

She stood in the mudroom. A narrow hall connected it to the rest of the cabin. There was a bedroom across the hall and a bathroom on the right. The kitchen was to the left. Then the dining area. And finally the living room with windows lining the center of the wall.

Two levels of glass were framed by paneling. The lowest level of glass included sliding doors with windows on both sides. Unreachable without a ladder, two large picture windows opened up to the blue sky and treetops beyond.

A squirrel chattered as he stood on the railing, his tail twitching and swaying over his back. Another squirrel scurried up the bark of a tall pine tree. He carried a nut in his mouth, racing ahead to the next higher branch. He turned and chattered at the one behind, now holding the nut securely in his little hand-like paws.

Like me and Janis, Olivia chuckled. *She leads with her nut and calls back to me to hurry up.* She sighed. *Maybe that's who I am. The one who follows other people but never leads.*

She turned her attention to the dining area. The farm table held two cereal bowls with spoons hanging over the side. A ring of milk curdled at the bottom of each. Olivia sniffed, the sour smell accosting her nose.

She glanced toward the kitchen. The sink was filled with dirty dishes, pots, and one blackened frying pan. Utensils lay on the counter next to open takeout containers.

Craft beer bottles rattled when she opened the refrigerator door. An unappetizing and uncovered open can of tuna fish sat on the top shelf. She turned away to block the smell.

Under the main part of the fridge were two drawers. One was already empty. A strong odor emanated from the other. She turned her head again. *What is that terrible smell?*

Fingers clamping her nose shut, Olivia inspected the contents of the other drawer. A pouch labeled The Farmer's Pet lay open, half full of meat and what looked like decaying carrots. She read the label. *Gourmet dog food good enough for humans.*

"Maybe a week ago," she muttered under her breath, shoving the drawer closed.

Jets entered the kitchen and peered over her shoulder. "What's that horrible stink?"

"A package of not-so-fresh gourmet dog meat," Olivia mumbled. "And an open tin of tuna. Check out the counters. It looks like Arlo and Cay have been living off of takeout and not cleaning up after themselves." She stepped away from the kitchen, rubbing her nose with the back of her hand.

"I looked in the loft," Jets said. "Papers everywhere, along with more food containers. I'll open some windows to get the smell out. Then I'll get a warrant and have forensics look the place over."

"A warrant..."

"Until we find Cayenne, we don't know who broke in or why. Not like Arlo's talking." Jets looked around. "On the one hand, Arlo may be a terrible housekeeper. But on the other hand, Cay runs and owns a housekeeping service. I can't imagine her settling for this mess. Maybe another person, a guest or family member, added to the mess. I'll know more once the local guys gather prints. It could take a few hours. I'll make that call.

"But now I'm going to have a look at the fireplace ashes. With all the papers around, I wonder if someone broke in to destroy and maybe burn some sort of evidence. Why don't you check the loft one more time. Maybe you'll see something I missed."

Olivia took each step slowly. She stopped to look at each of the photographic prints on the wall. One was a photo of Lily Rock, the town's namesake. Sunrays reflected off the granite. *Must have been photographed in the morning light,* she thought.

There was a blank area on the wall, dark as if a print had been removed. And then a photo of Arlo standing at a microphone. *I remember that night. A town council meeting.* Arlo held his faded blue cap in his hand, his eyes looking earnestly at the audience.

Arlo had made a confession to everyone. It led to a new beginning for him and a reconnection with Cayenne. *No matter what life threw at them, they always got back together.*

Olivia shifted to look back at the blank space between the two framed photos. "One of their wall photos is missing," she called out to Janis.

"How do you know?" came the reply.

"There's a shadow where it used to hang."

"Do you remember the photo?" Jets asked.

"I don't remember," Olivia admitted.

"Good detective *you* are," muttered Jets.

Olivia stepped onto the landing. She confirmed Janis's impression of the break-in with one glance. *This place is a mess.*

She wrinkled her nose at the overflowing ashtray reeking of stale cigarette smoke. Not just cigarettes, she realized. *He's been smoking his own product.*

An old television sat across the room, tucked under the eaves. A-frames were known for providing a spacious loft along with slanted walls. That's why people placed furniture and beds toward the center of the room—to avoid hitting heads when anyone attempted to stand.

Natural light came from the skylight above, with a view of the blue sky and the pine trees overhead. But unlike most A-frame lofts, there was no cozy reading chair. No casual array of throw pillows and soft blankets tossed over the sofa cushions.

She looked around the room and sighed. Without the customary tucked-away vibe, this space felt more like the one-bedroom neglected apartment of a college student.

Her glance drifted toward the low bed shoved under the eaves. Next to the bed there was a tension rod that had been suspended between two beams. Only two empty hangers remained on the rod. The rest of the clothing and hangers had tumbled to the shag carpet.

Olivia knelt to look at the clothes. A puffy coat with a hole in the sleeve. One flannel shirt that Arlo wore in the photo. A wool blanket. And a pair of faded jeans. *All men's clothes.*

Three flat pizza boxes had been abandoned on the shag carpet. Olivia sniffed again. She eyeballed the decaying slice of pepperoni pizza left in one box.

This place looks like it hasn't been tidied up in months. The carpet has holes. There are flies in the window.

Olivia leaned over the half wall to peer down at Janis. "Nothing up here. Except a bad smell."

Jets closed the door to the fireplace insert and looked up. "So I didn't miss anything. No dead bodies..."

"I'm beginning to suspect that Cayenne didn't live here. The kitchen was the first hint. Plus she's a professional cleaner who owns her own business. She would never leave an overflowing ashtray. Nor would she leave old pizza boxes on the floor with a leftover pepperoni slice—she's a vegetarian."

"And there's no sign of any female clothing. Just Arlo's stuff. Cast off and kinda..." Olivia rubbed her nose. "Icky. Disgusting really."

"Before we jump to any conclusions, let me have another look in the bedroom and the closet," Jets snapped.

"Okay." Olivia turned around for one more look. A box

labeled Express Printing caught her eye. She read the flier on top. *Welcome to Lily Rock's first Woofstock Festival.* Her eyes drifted to the words on the bottom. *Sponsored by Arlo Carson and the Mountain Herbs Dispensary. We grow with love and share with joy.*

She wasn't surprised that Arlo planned to promote his weed business by extending the well-known Lily Rock hospitality. A celebration of dogs for an entire weekend felt very Lily Rock.

Woofstock. Surprising someone hadn't thought of that sooner. She knew plenty of people in town loved harkening back to the original sixties event. Some even claimed they were there.

Olivia thought about the one time when Arlo made a special point about how Woofstock resonated with Lily Rock's vibe. Their vision of a welcoming community. Meadow McCloud summarized it best: "It's Woofstock around here every day. Why not invite some visitors to join in? Good for business too."

Afterward the town council granted him a permit. The peace and love vibes, along with the potential for small business revenue, had brought unanimous approval.

Jets made her way up the stairs, still talking. "I checked the bedroom. A few pieces of clothing, all male. One entire half of the closet has been cleaned out. Just empty hangers. The bed's not made. No female stuff anywhere."

"It's looking more and more like Arlo lived here alone." Olivia pointed to the empty spot between photos on the wall. "Now that I think about it, that was a wedding photo. I remember talking to Arlo the last time I was here. Remarking how happy they both looked. Of course Cay was male then. We laughed together.

"Have a look," she continued as she moved into the loft.

"There's a pile of papers by the sofa. Fliers. All about Woofstock."

"That entire festival was Arlo's idea," Jets said.

"Will it be canceled now, since...you know..." Olivia frowned.

Jets's eyes narrowed. "I think Meadow will pick up the pieces. It might be nice to go on, as a tribute to Arlo if nothing else. I wish we could talk to Cayenne. She'd know what to do for sure."

"I think Cayenne took her stuff and moved out. I don't think there's any doubt. Just look at the mess," Olivia said.

Jets rested her hands on her hips. "Okay, so we've got some investigating to do. Cayenne may be our number one suspect. Until we find her, we can't rule that out."

"No matter how good of a friend," Olivia added quietly.

"And then there's this break-in. I mean, we don't know if it was before or after Arlo's death. Nor do we know if this chaos was caused by Arlo or an intruder looking for something."

Olivia sniffed. "Do you smell dog?" She looked around.

"I smell old carpet." Jets grimaced. "I'm warning you. Keep your mouth shut. Until we get a warrant and some answers, don't say anything to anyone, not even Michael. We have to proceed with caution. I don't want people to jump to conclusions and assume Cayenne killed her spouse."

A chill ran down Olivia's spine. "Have you tried Cayenne's business phone? Maybe she's at work."

"I tried once. Went to voicemail. Let me give her another ring." She tapped and held her cell to her ear.

"Cay, would you give me a call? ASAP. This is important."

She hung up, then turned to Olivia. "We'd better get going. Whatever's happened, I want to find her first."

By the time they were seated in the cab of the truck, Jets's phone sounded a message. "Looks like we've got permission to do an official search of the cabin," she said. "They're waiting for my okay." She held the phone in her hand as if trying to decide.

Then she put it in her pocket.

A dead body. Cayenne is missing. Evidence of their home being broken into. *What does all this mean?*

She shuddered. She hated to think that Cayenne had anything to do with Arlo's death. *Incomprehensible.*

CHAPTER FIVE

Olivia sat across from Janis. A whine came from under the desk.

"Be quiet, you dumb mutt." Jets reached into a grease-stained paper bag to remove a large fry. Waving the fry in the air, she said, "Sit."

A prolonged whine accompanied the command.

"How about stay," Jets bargained. She dangled the fry lower.

The whine was followed by two yips and an odd snorting sound.

"We've been through this, Tater. No food until you follow the command." Jet glared. Then she lowered the fry again.

"Yip, yip," called the dog. Then he gurgled with a growl.

Olivia's eyes widened. *Such an odd sound for a dog to make.*

Jets tried one more time. "You don't want to sit and stay. Well play dead then. You know you want this fry. I'll give you this one and another for being good..."

If Olivia closed her eyes, she was certain she'd think that

Janis was coaxing a child to eat more vegetables rather than a dog to do a trick and take a fry.

So far Tater Tot had not made an appearance. She heard nails scratch as he began to negotiate from underneath the desk. Next came a snuffle and then a guttural growl. Then a paw appeared, followed by a, "Yip yip."

She held her breath to stop from laughing.

"Okay. I give up. No tricks for you. But you're still a good doggie. Here you go." Janis tossed the fry in the air. The sound of moist chewing and a burp met her ears.

"I see you're in full control with the dog obedience," Olivia observed dryly.

"He doesn't like being bossed around," Jets admitted. "But when it's his idea, he's brilliant at sitting and staying. He did play dead one time for Cookie. It might have been the bacon. But you should see how cute he is lying on his side with his four legs sticking out. Just adorable." Janis's face took on a soft and misty look.

She suddenly ducked under the desk. When she sat up, she held Tater Tot in her arms. Drool dripped from the dog's chin. The dog stared back at Olivia with shiny black eyes.

"I can come back later," Olivia offered.

"Just keep talking. We're listening." Jets dug her fingers around Tater Tot's leather collar. "Sit still," she ordered.

Before Olivia could ask about the investigation, the door opened and Brad walked into the room. "Hey, Olivia," he greeted her. "What's up, Tater Tot," he added. "Riverside called. They're still waiting for your okay to start collecting evidence."

Jets waved her fingers in the air. "Whatever. Leave the forms."

Brad dropped the papers on the corner of the desk. He

closed the door, but his laughter could be heard as he walked down the hallway.

Jets addressed the dog. "Aren't you the little sweetie. Okay, off the lap. Have to get back to work."

As soon as Jets placed the dog on the ground, he began to whine. Jets spun her chair toward her computer, reaching a hand into her drawer. "Here you go, baby." She tossed a dog biscuit in the air. Olivia heard the *chomp chomp* of loud chewing. She braced herself for the follow-up whine, only to be overcome by a noxious smell.

Olivia rubbed her nose. "Did you get a whiff of that?"

"Stop being so fussy. Frenchies have digestive issues. Most of them are lactose intolerant." She leaned over. "Fart all you want, Tater. She's just being overly sensitive." Jets tossed him another dog biscuit.

"He's gonna get fat if you keep feeding him every two seconds," Olivia cautioned.

"Frenchies are supposed to be chubby. It's part of their allure," Jets assured her.

Not exactly the word I'd use to describe a dog who looks like a baked potato on four legs. But if she thinks he's alluring, who am I to argue?

"Okay, here we go," Jets announced. She began to read. "The renovation of The Frenchie Connection Inn was finished nine months ago. They started taking in customers a week later. Right here on the website I see the owners, husband and wife, Eldred and Uma Whitlock, along with George Quigley, the guy we met in the dog park. The one who first discovered the body. He's listed as an AKC-trained dog handler and trainer."

"Are we going to the inn for our next interview? I want to see inside."

"You sound like Bellemare," Jets complained. "This isn't an

opportunity for an architectural tour. We're on a murder investigation. But yes. We have time today to head over and interview George again, and hopefully find out more from the new owners.

"By the way, the fingerprints were all Arlo's. No other person. Not even Cayenne."

"So we were right. She's not living with him anymore."

"Looks that way," Jets said. "As much as I hate to let her go, I want to focus on other potential suspects. Since Arlo's body was discovered on the Whitlock private property, they may know something."

"What about the weapon? Obviously it was a sharp blade. From what I could see, there was a lot of blood."

"Yah, that might take some time. We'll know more once forensics completes their assessment. But I agree. Looks like a stabbing. We'll wait for confirmation." Jets clicked back to her screen saver and stood. Not before Olivia saw the large photo on Jets's laptop background of Tater Tot wearing a bright blue T-shirt saying: Me + Mom vs. whoever wants to lose.

"You have shirts for your dog?" Olivia used her most innocent voice.

"Yep." Jets dropped the lunch sack into the trash. "Let's get outta here. I'll put a lead on Tater Tot. Maybe he'll ease the way at the new inn, being a Frenchie and all."

With Tater Tot marching between them, Janis and Olivia exited the constabulary. Passing in front of the library, Meadow called out the open window, "Yoo-hoo, dears. May I have a word?"

"I suppose," Jets said. "I guess you heard about Arlo."

Meadow's eyes quickly brimmed with tears. "Yes, dear. I've already heard. A tragic situation. Unthinkable. I wanted to talk to you about Arlo if you don't mind. Bring Olivia and come inside." And then, as an afterthought, she cast her eyes to the dog.

"You can bring him too. I have dog toys to keep him busy. They're usually reserved for the mayor, but he won't mind sharing."

After they made their way inside, Meadow invited Tater Tot behind her desk. "Come here, little one." She used the voice she reserved both for children under five and for her friend, Thomas Seeker. And since she was Thomas's only friend, no one seemed to mind.

Tater pulled on his leash to investigate behind the library counter.

Meadow reached over to take the leash from Janis. She turned and said, "Sit." The Frenchie immediately lowered himself to sitting, staring up at her with his intent round eyes. Meadow opened a drawer, bringing out a cookie shaped like a dog bone. She examined it carefully, taking her time.

Tater Tot sat as if frozen, his eyes on the treat.

Meadow held the cookie in front of her waist-high. "Stay," she commanded. Using a flat palm as a hand signal, she backed away one step, then another.

Tater Tot did not move. The dog watched the treat but did not budge. He was a vision of stillness, eyes on the prize.

"Play dead," Meadow commanded. She lowered her voice and her palm.

Plop, the dog fell over, his four feet sticking out from his round body. Flat on the carpet, he looked like a tiny beached whale. Olivia giggled.

"Good boy!" Meadow clapped her hands. She leaned closer to deliver Tater Tot the much coveted dog treat. He chomped down on it and looked up for more.

"Meadow has a way with dogs." Olivia smirked. "Three

tricks for one bone. Kind of inspiring actually. You could learn from her example."

"Give me a break," Jets muttered. "Don't forget Meadow's like a professional. She trained Maguire long before you got here."

When Tater Tot had finished his cookie, he sniffed the carpet, looking for crumbs. "Go to your place." Meadow pointed to the corner toward a large dog bed. "Mayor Maguire" had been embroidered on the outside in dark blue letters. Tater Tot trotted right over and then jumped in. He flopped onto the cushion, his head hanging over the side.

Meadow took her eyes off of the dog to face Janis Jets. "I thought you'd like to know something about Arlo and Cayenne. They separated, you know. Months ago."

Olivia's heart sank. The confirmation of the breakup came as sad news.

"Do you know when that happened? A month or even a date?" Jets asked.

"Let's see. This is April. I'd say nearly five months ago. Near the holidays. I know it was around the time Star was born. Arlo came over to tell me the news. He was quite distraught. In fact, that might have been our last in-depth conversation."

Meadow's bottom lip trembled. "We were friends, you know, Arlo and I. Even after those difficulties with his licensing and the dispensary, we managed to patch things up. Last year was the only time he didn't come for my Christmas Day open house."

"Did he tell you any reasons for their separation?" Olivia asked.

"As everyone knows, those two had been through a lot. But he seemed to think that Cayenne didn't want to be with him anymore. She'd get home from work and head right to the labyrinth. Sometimes she slept outside in a tent rather than in their cabin."

"Interesting," Jets mused. "Your information confirms what we discovered. No sign of Cayenne at the cabin. Not even fingerprints."

"The place was a huge mess," Olivia admitted. "Trash everywhere." She wondered if Jets would mention the break-in to Meadow.

"I suppose Arlo was quite depressed," Meadow said. "I thought planning Woofstock might cheer him up a bit. When I came back from lunch on Monday, I found fliers tucked behind the counter. He'd left a note asking me to hand them out to friends of the library and everyone who checked out books.

"I've talked up the event to everyone. But now I'm not sure if we shouldn't cancel, what with him being dead and all."

Tater Tot's head rose from the bed. When Meadow didn't turn around, he dropped his chin back to his paws.

Jets spoke. "This is helpful. But before we go. Do you know anything about that new inn and dog park?"

"You mean the owners of The Frenchie Connection." Meadow's face set in a scowl.

"Yep, that's the one."

"Eldred Whitlock and his wife, Uma, own the place. Both in their fifties. Did you know they only allow AKC Frenchies in their dog park?" Her chin jutted out. "Even the mayor has been banned. He's purebred by labradoodle standards, but he's not a French bulldog. I think the council may have to weigh in on the discrimination policy. It's on the agenda for next month."

"The Whitlocks own the land," Olivia objected. "Can't they invite anyone they want? I mean, it's not like dogs are people. You can't take them to jail for breaking fair housing laws."

Meadow's cheeks flushed pink. "Of course dogs are like people. This is Lily Rock. It's our civic duty to uphold the highest standards for the acceptance and inclusion of all."

Olivia knew better than to argue with Meadow when it came to Lily Rock. She'd seen this testy side of Meadow before, in the early days when they first met. Not sure what to say, whether to object or remain silent, Olivia chose silence. She looked to Jets, her eyes pleading for help.

"I agree," Jets stoutly affirmed. "If you need someone to sign a petition, I'd be happy to add my name. Anyway, we have to move now. I'm still on the lookout for Cayenne. So text me if you see her. Let's go, Tater Tot."

The dog opened one eye, looked at Janis, then Meadow, and then rolled over to face the wall.

"Go along, Tater Tot." Meadow used her librarian voice.

The dog popped up. He shook himself off and trotted to sit at her feet. She reached into her drawer and then tossed him a dog cookie.

Jets sighed, picked him up, and made her way toward the exit.

CHAPTER SIX

The Frenchie Connection lobby looked like any other upscale boutique in Lily Rock. New finishings, plank flooring, high-end overstuffed furniture placed in a conversational setting in front of the massive fireplace.

The leather sofa and matching occasional chairs were arranged in a horseshoe shape, reminiscent of a ski lodge. Olivia wished she could sit down against the array of cushions. *This has been such an exhausting day.*

Tall palm trees planted in large cobalt-blue pots stood on each side of the discreet reception desk. The oversized fronds cascaded over each end of the counter. Olivia read the welcome sign on the front of the desk: "The Frenchie Connection. A boutique home away from home for you and your Frenchie pet."

Two identical glass jars stood side by side on the far end of the counter. Each labeled and filled with dog treats shaped like bones. One had a sign that said "Homemade with Fresh Ingredients." The other said "Keto." Olivia turned to Janis. "Those look familiar. Is Cookie supplying the inn with Thyme Out dog treats?"

"I guess he is," Jets said. "You gotta admit Cookie makes a great dog cookie. The main ingredient is peanut butter. Tater Tot loves them. Don't you, sweetie..." Janis used her baby voice and then bent to give her dog a quick scratch behind the ear.

A man appeared from around the corner. "May I help—" He didn't finish his sentence. One glance at Tater Tot and his face tightened into a disdainful expression.

"You can't stay here." He pointed to Tater Tot. "We require proof of his certification. We only accept AKC-certified French bulldogs at The Frenchie Connection. You'll have to find other dog-friendly lodgings."

Janis narrowed her eyes. She didn't speak but made a move for the badge she kept in her pocket. She flipped it open.

The man brushed past her to make his way to the exit. He opened the door. "I'm not up for any discussion. Have a nice day." The tone in his voice suggested anything but.

Olivia felt a pang for Tater Tot. He didn't seem to understand that he was being dismissed, nor the harsh words. Ignoring the interchange, he sniffed the cobalt-blue clay pot on the right, tentatively lifting a leg.

Jets pulled him back. "Not now, Tater." She dragged him toward her and then bent to kiss the top of his head.

"I'm holding the door," the man yelled, stating the obvious.

Then a woman from behind the reception counter called out. "Stand down, Eldred. I'll handle this. Can't you see they're cops?" She drew a fake smile across her lips, shaking a finger. "Close the door now. You're letting the air conditioning out," she said between clenched teeth.

Jets stepped closer for the stranger to read her badge.

"These women are not here for a room," the woman announced. "They're here on official business." One look at

Janis's grim expression made her add, "I can see I'm not mistaken."

The man named Eldred frowned. He let go of the door right as Janis squared her shoulders. Ready to confront him, she stood taller, her mouth in a tight line. Expecting a barrage of words, Olivia felt surprised when none came.

She's speechless. And fuming. Janis slid the ID back into her pocket. Then she inhaled deeply, her face an angry shade of red.

"We are here on police business." Jets's voice sounded deliberately calm. "I want to interview the owners of The Frenchie Connection dog park. I assume that's you two." She looked back and forth at the couple.

"I'm Uma Whitlock and this is my husband, Eldred. We own the inn and the dog park." Uma's voice sounded overly sweet and thick with politeness. Like a cupcake with too much buttercream frosting.

Olivia waited for Janis to make a smart remark. To her relief none came. She blinked and then observed Eldred Whitlock. He wore a T-shirt with The Frenchie Connection logo. Underneath was a superimposed photograph of a French bulldog. The brindle-colored Frenchie stared back at her, his round soulful eyes melting her heart.

That must be a high-class AKC not-the generic-kind-of-Frenchie, she thought. *Look at his skin rolls and those large jowls. So he's the breed standard.* His enormous bat ears stood at attention, accenting the flatness of his face and nose.

As for the rest of Eldred Whitlock, she judged him to be in his late fifties. Wrinkles burrowed next to his mouth and at the corner of each puffy eye. Eldred's eyes looked as if they'd seen too much of life, or perhaps too many hours indoors.

She averted her gaze, knowing instantly what kind of a

person he was on the inside. *He uses his strong opinions to get his way. A bully.*

Olivia brushed off her uneasiness, mentally distancing herself, coming to her own conclusion. *If you're a kid and want to wear your dog's picture on your shirt, that's one thing. But that shirt on a fifty-plus-year-old. Kinda off-putting.*

Firmly grounded in her own thoughts, she felt safe. She sent Eldred a direct stare. This time he dropped his gaze first. She made a point of blinking. Then she let her eyes linger on his belly, which protruded over the belt holding up his baggy jeans.

Uma Whitlock watched nervously from behind the desk. She tapped a finger against her chin. Tall and slim, she held herself with certainty. Olivia didn't have to make eye contact with her to make an initial assessment.

Everything about the woman felt controlled. Starting with her light brown hair, intentionally coiffed, tucked behind her ears, with bangs expertly shaped to cover her forehead.

I wonder if she goes to the salon and gets it styled like women did back in the day. A standing appointment to trim each hair so that it never looks too long or too short.

As soon as Uma appeared, Olivia suspected who was top dog in the Whitlock relationship. The woman gave off the impression of instant preparedness, exuding efficiency in her matching pink track suit. Unlike her husband's more sloppy attire, her partially zipped jacket fit her snugly, revealing a trim figure. *I bet she doesn't wear a dog photo printed on her shirt.*

Olivia took a deep cleansing breath. Bracing herself for a series of withering remarks from Janis, she took a step backward. To her surprise, the cop had resumed a more relaxed stance. Janis appeared disinterested and partially tuned out. The calmer she seemed, the more agitated was Eldred.

Once Janis returned Tater Tot to the floor, he took advantage of the moment. Pulling against his lead, he sniffed, moving forward as if on a mission. Finally he nosed the cobalt-blue pot. Finding it satisfactory, he turned to lift his leg to finish what he'd started earlier. Pee ran down the side of the pot and into the carpet.

Eldred was the first to object. "Stop that instantly!"

Uma hoisted herself to look over the counter. Tater Tot put his leg back and smiled up at her. "What a sweet doggie," she said in a very calm voice. Then she turned to her husband. "Clean it up, Eldred."

Tater's ears lowered at the tone in her voice. He looked toward Janis for her approval. Jets reeled him closer, giving his head a pat. When she didn't scold, Tater Tot turned his chunky body around. Nose down, he made his way back to the planter.

Olivia took matters into her own hands. She snatched the lead from Janis. "Come on, Tater. Let's go." She half tugged and half dragged him toward the exit. But Tater resisted. The more she pulled, the more he leaned back. His back legs and bottom dragging along the floor.

"Okay, air jail for you." Olivia picked the dog up in her arms. She made her way toward the door as Janis followed close behind.

"Do you believe that?" Jets pulled Tater Tot from Olivia's arms. "My dog has been attacked and marginalized. Just for being himself. Why wouldn't he be AKC certified? He cost enough. Cooks spent five grand for this little guy." She gave Tater Tot's head a kiss and handed him back to Olivia. "Hold him a little longer. I have to text Brad. I'm not going to subject Tater to such judgmental behavior."

Did I hear her right? Five thousand dollars. Why wouldn't Cookie adopt a dog from Paws and Pines, already neutered and chipped, for ten bucks with a free collar and leash to go?

Done with her call, Janis reached for Tater Tot. She buried her face in the folds of his neck. The pup squirmed with delight, his tongue inching out to lick her chin.

While Janis and Tater snuggled, Olivia did an internet search on her phone. Something did puzzle her. Mostly the classification of the American Kennel Club when it came to French bulldogs.

"I've got it right here," she announced. But she stopped, interrupted by Brad's arrival. He pulled his truck next to the curb.

Janis kissed the top of Tater Tot's head again, handing him into Brad's open arms. It wasn't until he secured the puppy in the back seat and drove away that Olivia continued.

"You can get papers for pure-bred French bulldogs, but only certain colors have been qualified as American Kennel Club acceptable."

"What colors? Tater is beautiful. Even you said so yourself. The blue and lavender undertone. That's what cost Cookie the extra money. His coat."

"I've got the breed history right here." Olivia scrolled. "There was some controversy about round ears versus bat ears. The English, French, and Americans got their tails in a twist over that one." She grinned. "Get it? Tails in a twist."

Jets scoffed. "What are you, a Frenchie expert now? Not all Frenchies have a twist in their tails by the way. Some have stumps or very small almost tails. Tater Tot has a stump. I find it very attractive. Cute, in fact. What else have you got? What about the colors?" Jets waited.

Olivia continued. "There are only a few acceptable AKC colors. They actually have assigned code numbers for each. Brindle, fawn, white, cream, and brindle and white among a few others. The fur patterns also matter. Here are the numbers."

"I don't want to know the numbers. Sounds like some kind of scam."

"Did you want to show Tater Tot? Is that why you're so bothered?" Olivia asked. "Doesn't he need AKC papers for that?"

"He's got papers. What do you take Cookie for, an idiot? He paid five grand for a cute dog who was specially bred, with papers." Janis rattled off her dog's background as if she had practiced for an interview with a prestigious preschool.

"Don't give me that look. Tater Tot is officially registered as a full-bred French bulldog, from a breeder," Jets added firmly.

Olivia expected her to whip out the paper and photos of his breed line at any moment. But before she could ask, Janis continued.

"I'm not a show dog kind of woman. I don't even like dogs, remember. But I want to know my dog can be accepted anywhere he chooses to go. He's not going to be disrespected by some boutique inn owner who thinks he gets to diss my little baby because of," she stumbled over the right word, "his fur tone."

Olivia raised an eyebrow.

"I took sensitivity training, remember? Three times. Got refreshed at the request of the town council just a few months ago."

"I remember," she said. Janis was sent to sensitivity training when one of the Lily Rock Music Academy students was a suspect in an investigation. The teen insisted on using the personal pronoun "they," which made Janis quite annoyed.

She deliberately made fun of them until the council

insisted she get training. Though Janis didn't talk about it, she'd changed her behavior. But Olivia suspected she had not changed her opinion.

But she hadn't heard any more about sensitivity training since.

"Are you ready to go back inside?" Jets demanded. "Because I am. I think one of those people, or maybe the Whitlock couple, killed Arlo. They've got guilt written all over them."

"You never were partial to pink," Olivia said, referring to Uma Whitlock's attire.

"Never mind that, it's time to interview them separately. And before you try to calm me down, I have no intention of being nice. These fancy people make me sick." Jets re-opened the door to the inn with a flourish.

Caught off guard, Olivia stopped to think. It wasn't like Janis to jump to conclusions before she'd gathered more evidence. *And now she's determined that one or both of the Whitlocks are suspects just because they insulted her dog.*

Following Janis into the lobby, Olivia felt her heart race. *This case is different. Not only do we both know the victim, but now Janis is convinced she's already found the killers.*

I may be an amateur, but even I know that's the wrong way to begin an investigation.

CHAPTER SEVEN

They stopped short once inside the lobby. Two men waited at the reception desk, looking remarkably alike in stature and style. The one on the left watched Uma with a fond expression, as if he found her amusing. The other man was the first to speak.

Olivia slid closer to the window to be able to listen while going unnoticed.

Those two look like partners, she thought. *Maybe here for the weekend.*

Janis Jets tucked one hand in her front pocket and sauntered toward the fireplace. She sat down and bounced on the leather sofa cushion. Lacing her fingers behind her head, she sat in repose. Olivia continued to take in the room from her vantage point.

The large low table in front of the sofa was covered with magazines and merchandise, coffee mugs with the face of a Frenchie on the front. Placed next to the mugs were candles in glass containers with gold trim. The Frenchie Connection logo prominently printed in bold letters. Next to the candles was an array of matchbooks, casually arranged in a fan shape.

They also had The Frenchie Connection logo printed in gold.

Janis leaned to pick up a matchbook. Then she tossed it back with the rest. She raised an eyebrow in Olivia's direction.

Olivia rejected the unspoken invitation. Instead she returned her gaze to the front desk and the men checking in.

The one man still had eyes for Uma. His face held a wistful expression. *Maybe she reminds him of someone*, Olivia thought. *His mom or grandma.*

He looks so boyish. Probably older than his hair might indicate. Dark brown styled in waves, each strand held in place to look windblown and casual. One unruly curl drifted over his right eye. He moved the hair aside with a toss of his head.

The self-conscious gesture made her wonder. *Is he a model or does he think everyone is looking?* The odor of pungent spice with a floral undertone met her nose. *He's a walking advertisement for a Beverly Hills salon.*

Olivia leaned closer, her instincts heightening with each observation. *His skin glows with health. I'd call his skin gingerbread color. Definitely spends time at the spa getting treatments.*

She ducked her head as he looked over.

And his eyes—wow. Light green with dark flecks. Maybe there's something to that old saying: the eyes are the window to the soul.

Even his gaze is childlike, she mused. *Probably enhanced with permanent eyeliner and the arch of his professionally styled brows.* She waited for him to look away before raising her head.

"You're here for the entire week," Uma confirmed. Slipping her glasses from her head, she perched them at the end of her nose to stare at the computer. "You registered and left a credit card in the name of Sydney Ayers. Is the information still current?" She looked up as Sydney nodded. "And you also registered your Frenchie named Juicy Fruit. Let's start with her first. I'll need to see a photocopy of her AKC papers."

Olivia watched as Sydney's partner, maybe tired of being ignored, fidgeted. He stepped nervously from one foot to the other. "Excuse me," he said in a timid voice.

Uma raised her glance and blinked with a smile. "Hello," she said softly. "I didn't see you there." She reached her arm over the counter to extend her hand. He took it in his, staring into her eyes. A flush traveled up his neck before he released her grasp.

"I've got this, Shelly." His partner sounded annoyed. He turned to Uma. "I already sent Juicy Fruit's paperwork in an email attachment."

Now Olivia had time to take in Shelly's appearance. Like his partner, he looked recently coiffed. Tinted light brown hair, shaved on the sides and back of the head, longer strands on top. Each arm looked slightly muscled, accented by a short-sleeved shirt, which had been tailored so the sleeves ended right at the broadest part of his bicep. Tucked into slim-fitting jeans, he gave the appearance of sporty but elegant.

The couple matched. As if they used each other to mirror their best qualities.

Uma continued to search her computer as Shelly called out, "Here, Juicy."

Only then did Olivia look for the dog.

A cream-colored Frenchie stuck out her head from behind the potted fern. She sported a pink rhinestone collar. "Good girl," Shelly told her, handing over one of The Frenchie Connection's free dog treats. She began to crunch as he closely inspected the other merchandise displayed on the counter.

He picked up a matchbook from the basket and shoved it

into his back pocket. Then he lifted the dog into his arms. Not finished with the display, he lowered his nose to inhale the scent from The Frenchie Connection candle. "Do you want a sniff?" he asked the dog.

When the dog turned her head away, he returned the candle to the display.

Juicy Fruit seemed bored. She pushed her back legs against Shelly's stomach, pummeling and kicking.

Shelly held her firmly, back legs dangling in the air. Then he gave the dog a quick kiss to her nose.

Now that's quite a family, Olivia thought. *They somehow fit. Expensive and fidgety. The dog matches her people. They're a couple*, she concluded. *And Juicy Fruit must be their fur baby.*

Uma tapped at the computer keyboard. "Oh yes. I have your reservation right here along with the appropriate paper-work. I must have overlooked it the first time. You are Sydney," she confirmed and then raised her glasses to stare at the other man. "And who would you be? Your name, sir?" She tilted her chin slightly, a soft smile at her lips.

"Shelton Ayres. People call me Shelly."

She flushed and then turned to type, eyes focused on the computer screen once again.

Shelly gripped Juicy Fruit closer. He addressed his part-ner. "You didn't put my name on the booking. I've told you about that. I want to be included." His bottom lip trembled as he turned his head away.

Sydney reassured, "Honey, don't fuss. I'll remember next time." His face looked conciliatory, but the tone of his voice sounded slightly condescending. "This is my husband," he explained loudly to Uma. "I want him to be listed on the reser-vation. And we need two key cards."

"Not a problem." Uma slipped her glasses back into place.

Jets picked herself up from the sofa and made her way across the room to stand next to Olivia. She whispered under her breath, "Are you listening to this?"

Olivia nodded. She lifted her finger to her lips.

"Oh please, we don't have to play footsie with these people." Janis took out her badge and marched to the desk.

"I'm Officer Janis Jets. That woman over there," she said, pointing in Olivia's direction, "is Olivia Greer, a police consultant. There's been an incident in town connected to this inn. I'll need to take your names and occupations."

Shelton turned first, his eyes wide in surprise. He still held the dog, who also stared at the cop. Her stump of a tail began to quiver. Sydney gave Janis a once-over and then turned his back. "Give me a minute," he said. "I need to sign this paper."

Jets extended her fingers toward the dog. Tickling under her chin, she used her baby-talk voice. "Who's the cutie? Such a good girl." She bent closer to make a face at the dog, giving it a chance to sniff her lips in return.

After a thorough licking, Janis swiped her mouth with the back of her hand and then wiped the drool onto her pants leg.

Sydney turned from the counter, displaying perfectly aligned white teeth. "I'm Sydney Ayers. This is my husband, Shelton Ayers. And this is our fur baby, Juicy Fruit." He took the dog from Shelton's arms.

Juicy Fruit began to wiggle and squirm. Sydney placed her on the floor. "She wants to do her business outside," he explained. "That's your job, remember?" He glared at his husband.

Shelly gripped the leash. "Come here, Juicy," he said sweetly.

Sydney now gave his full attention to Janis. "Are you investigating the murder that happened this morning?" The question made it clear that he'd already heard and that the murder wasn't news, at least to him.

The assumption ruffled Janis. She retorted, "Obviously the word is out. But what I don't know is why you care. Don't you want us to think you're here for a cozy weekend? A romantic getaway with the hubby? Time for two athletic, in-shape dudes like yourselves to take a hike while your baby gets her nails clipped and a bonemeal body wrap?"

She ignored his surprised look, taking advantage with a few more choice words.

"I bet the murder changes your plans now, doesn't it? Not the idyllic stay you imagined." She placed the back of her hand to her forehead, mocking her shock.

"I can hear you both now. 'What have I gotten myself into? There's a dead body spoiling our stay.' Is real life too inconvenient for you?" Jets scowled.

Sydney's mouth tightened. "Actually I'm a journalist here on assignment. I caught up with the Lily Rock breaking news on my way up the hill this morning. I make it a point to research before I begin an assignment. You lost a town local, I believe..." He leaned closer to Janis's face. Not one bit intimidated.

"We did." Janis looked him up and down. "So what was that? A journalist, you say?"

"Like you assumed, we're here on vacation. But I'm on company time too. Been assigned the first annual Lily Rock Woofstock festival."

"Who exactly do you work for?" Jets took out her tablet to make a note.

"I write for *It's a Dog's World.* An independent online publication for canine fanciers. You may have heard of us."

"Nope." Janis dismissed him with a wave of her hand. "I do have a dog though. A male. About a year old. A Frenchie like yours." A glint came to her eye. Her voice drawled, "Not exactly like yours. What's-her-name is purebred, right? AKC registered. So they're exactly alike, purebred, only yours is AKC registered and mine is AKC second class."

The resentment in Janis's voice made the hair on Olivia's neck stand up. She braced herself for a full-on self-righteous confrontation about dog discrimination. Fortunately, Juicy Fruit interrupted with a whine and a then a noise at the back of her throat that sounded like she was gargling with mouthwash.

So different than Mayor Maguire, Olivia realized. *When he barks, it's not a suggestion but more a demand. This dog, Juicy Fruit, sounds like a dog who expects to have her mind read. I wonder what happens if...*

As if to prove her point, Juicy Fruit tugged on her lead, straining toward the exit door. Shelton dropped the lead and turned to Janis Jets. "I'm Shelly, I'm a licensed social worker and family therapist." His voice sounded smooth and deliberately pitched to deescalate the situation.

"Yip," Juicy Fruit called from the door.

Jets's right eyebrow rose. "Juicy has to poo," she stated in a calm voice. "Like I said, just like my dog. Same needs."

"You need to take her outside," Sydney interrupted, his tone impatient. "Don't make me ask again."

Shelly shrugged and glared but didn't move. Then Sydney turned to Janis.

"I don't mean to offend you or your dog. Let me explain. Our fur baby daughter is very special. Not that your dog isn't...special. Not for me to judge. But I bring Juicy Fruit to exclusive inns that cater to AKC Frenchies so that she can associate with dogs of the same high caliber."

Olivia felt the color drain from her face. *What's Janis gonna do now, arrest him for making her mad?*

Shelly tried to smooth things over again. He explained in a calm voice, "You have to understand, Officer Justice. Juicy is family. You know how you'll do anything for your child when it comes to her education." Lips curved into an endearing little-boy smile as he waited for her reply.

Jets cleared her throat. "My name is Officer Jets," she said calmly. "Thanks for the info. Since you'll be in town for Woof-stock, I know where to find you. I want to keep track of people who come and go from this so-called exclusive inn. Consider yourselves important to my line of inquiry."

Sydney resisted. "We weren't even here when the death occurred. Isn't it unusual to treat us with suspicion?"

"Everyone is under suspicion until I tell you otherwise," Jets snapped. "Have a nice day." She brushed past the two men to lean over the counter. "I want a copy of those papers," she told Uma.

A sharp yip came from the exit door.

Olivia sniffed.

"Juicy Fruit, how could you!" Sydney turned to Shelly. "You need to get some paper towels and disinfectant spray, and a poop bag. Juicy had a boo-boo." Uma ignored Janis and handed a roll of paper towels over to Shelly without a word.

Once the mess was cleaned up and the men had departed with their dog, Jets confronted Uma again. "I want the papers and a word."

"Of course. I'm happy to see you didn't bring your mongrel back." Uma's eyes widened with superiority.

Olivia watched Janis with fascination. *Did she dare to call Tater Tot a mongrel?*

Jets stretched herself to her full height, eyes blazing. "Tater Tot may not be AKC certified, but we have a bill of sale that proves his heritage is as good as anyone staying at this inn.

So I'll remind you to be polite. I consider what you're saying, the way you say it, as hate speech."

Hate speech. That's a good one. Maybe arrest-worthy, but hate speech...

Uma spoke primly. "Just to make myself clear, people like you think you can come along with your special-colored dogs and change the time-honored standards of the American Kennel Club. In the past, all dogs not registered were considered mongrels.

"But now, due to this climate of ridiculous political correctness, we added a limited registration status. We call them All American. Only if they have papers from accredited breeders, of course. The dogs are registered but cannot be bred."

Janis scowled. "Whatever. I've had about enough with you. I changed my mind about the interview. Where's that husband of yours? I need to talk to him. But don't forget, you're both still under police investigation."

CHAPTER EIGHT

Jets held her badge in front of Eldred Whitlock's bulbous nose. "Do you want to sit down somewhere private or should I ask the questions right here in your lobby?" She pinpointed her best beady-eyed stare into his pale blue eyes.

Whitlock coughed into his fist. "Sorry, allergies," he explained. When Jets kept staring, he added, "Do I need my attorney present?"

"Up to you," she drawled. "Got something to hide?"

She put the badge back in her pocket. "How about your residence. I assume you live on the premises."

"Come this way," he reluctantly offered. There was no further mention of an attorney.

Olivia and Janis followed Eldred past the reception desk, down a hallway to the elevator. He pressed the arrow going up. "Sorry about the dismissal when you walked in earlier. I thought you were someone who booked a room. We make our rules known on the website, but occasionally people fail to comply, in which case I have to make our standards clear as soon as they come through the door."

A small smile came over Jets's lips. "That must be a tough

job, Eldred. Telling people and defenseless dogs they're not good enough. You must have some trouble meeting that challenge. Sleeping well at night, are we?"

Instead of taking the hint, he doubled down with excuses. "You've gotta understand, Officer. I have some people who still try to push me into admitting non-AKC Frenchies. I have to stand up to our mission statement."

"Mission statement?" Olivia blurted. "Why don't you just say it? You discriminate based on genetic selection."

The door to the elevator slid open. He held out his hand for Janis to lead the way. As the door slid shut, he continued to explain. "You are obviously not dog show people or you'd understand. Everything is about standards in the arena. The American Kennel Club has rules. But that's because they want to preserve the breed."

He pressed the button for the top floor. "Not every dog is qualified to show. We know that. That's why we have an alternative category. It's called limited registration. Purebred French bulldogs from reputable breeders, no matter the color, can still qualify. They receive legitimate papers. Of course we insist that they be neutered and spayed. So that the breed is kept pure.

"That allows us to take a stand against puppy mills degrading the French bulldog breed with their filthy kennels and overbreeding of females."

Olivia wanted more clarification. "So you're saying that the AKC rules, the dual registration policies, keep unscrupulous breeders from abusing pets."

Whitlock smiled. He turned toward her and ignored Jets. "That's right. Differentiating between those animals who are show quality and those who are merely pet quality is historical. We've always done it that way. It is what is best for all breeds."

"Separate but equal," Jets mumbled for Olivia to hear.

The elevator door slid open. "This is our apartment." He gestured for them to go first. "We can sit in the living area and I'll continue to answer your questions the best I can." He sounded cordial, especially when he spoke to Olivia.

Eldred placed himself in the middle of the leather sofa. He spread his arms across the back, his right leg crossed over his left. They sat across from him in two identical mid-century-style occasional chairs.

Now that's the posture of a confident man, Olivia thought.

"Like I said, ask away." Eldred directed his eyes to her, a slight smile on his face. *Because I'm nicer,* she told herself.

Jets pulled out her tablet. "Arlo Carson, a Lily Rock resident, was found dead at The Frenchie Connection dog park this morning at approximately 8 a.m. Did you know Arlo, and where were you at that time?"

Whitlock cleared his throat. "I didn't know Arlo, but I'd heard about him. Our trainer, George Quigley, told me that some Lily Rock resident had been hanging around the park for the past couple of weeks. Quigley questioned him at the time. The rules for the park are strictly enforced. No one is allowed to be in the park without an AKC-approved Frenchie, and no non-AKC dog is allowed to run off leash or use the facility."

"Like an exclusive country club," Jets commented.

"There's a good reason behind all of our decisions. We don't want to encourage unwanted pregnancies of our show animals. Frenchie owners of AKC-approved dogs don't take their pet to a private dog park for that kind of behavior.

"Unwanted pregnancies require too much aftercare. The dam's health can be compromised. And the puppies do not bring a good price. So you can understand why we uphold such exacting standards."

Jets made notes in her tablet as Olivia looked at her hands. Eldred's unwanted attention made her uncomfortable. *If I'm understanding correctly, he excludes certain Frenchies from the inn due to AKC rules. He extends the rules to his private dog park. And then he also excludes people who may not agree with his policies.*

They're not invited to watch the Frenchies.

Then it hit her, like a gut punch. *The way Eldred does business couldn't be less Lily Rock.* She pictured the sign over the road, the one she saw that first day. "Welcome to Lily Rock" read the banner.

That first week, she was told about Paws and Pines, their non-profit no-kill shelter. The owners charged a small fee to have each adopted pet spayed or neutered and chipped before they were sent to their forever home.

Her stomach twisted tighter, as the source of tension became apparent. *The Frenchie Connection and Paws and Pines are opposite ends of the dog world spectrum.*

Paws and Pines went so far as to have adopt-a-pet-free days, when they gave dogs and cats away. Generous donors picked up the cost of the spaying, neutering, and chipping. Mayor Maguire was their poster dog. He'd advertise for Paws and Pines by showing up at all their functions to shake paws and receive treats.

The town council, mostly comprised of old-time residents called the Old Rockers, made it a point to include everyone. When they missed the mark, they reassessed and tried again. Take Mayor Maguire, for example.

There was that one time when people objected to his political appointment. And the special privilege of running off leash. "It's not fair to our dogs since they aren't allowed to do the same," one woman exclaimed at a monthly meeting.

Conversation arose over Maguire's breed after that. "A

labradoodle as the mayor of Lily Rock," someone joked. "Not exactly a mutt nor our brand."

But other residents reminded the naysayers that Maguire came to them as a puppy, a gift, and that he was the epitome of the town's motto of welcome. "You can't discriminate against a dog who is bred any more than you can discriminate against a dog who is not," Meadow insisted.

"Declaring Maguire the mayor only elevates his importance, not his breed," was her final word.

No matter how many rules Whitlock had to support the purebred policies of his inn and dog park, Olivia knew that none of them aligned with Lily Rock's identity or their only animal shelter.

She realized she'd been caught between a rock and a hard place. As soon as she realized the difficulty, her stomach loosened. Now she felt more balanced and she smiled at the next insight.

I've been Lily Rocked, she thought. *I believe in the town's promise so completely that I've forgotten not everyone thinks the same.*

She looked at Eldred Whitlock with fresh eyes.

How did he get approval from the town council? Did he tell them only AKC-approved French bulldogs would be welcome? I know Meadow would have immediately objected. I suspect Arlo wouldn't have agreed either, unless there was some financial gain in doing so.

Olivia felt unsettled. *Maybe I don't need to bring that up right now*, she realized. *It might derail Janis's inquiry.* She instead cleared her throat to ask, "Speaking of breeding. I wonder how Frenchies—the AKC fancy ones—are bred. Since you don't approve of the usual way of doing things."

Jets looked up from note-taking. With a slight nod she indicated her appreciation.

Eldred Whitlock pointed to his shirt. "This is Featherington the Fifth. He's sired two AKC best of breeds in the past five years. Sought after for his genetic line and because of his awards. Featherington has made a name for himself worldwide. He's bred with AKC-approved procedures in a sanitary lab, watched over by myself and a qualified veterinarian."

"No female dog in the room then," Jets said. "Just two human dudes and a horny Frenchie."

Whitlock's eyes hardened. He didn't bother to reply.

"A stud known worldwide," Jets said in a matter-of-fact voice. "Good to know. But what's the fun in that if he can't, you know, hook up with a female of his own choice, all by himself?"

Eldred inhaled deeply as Olivia groaned inwardly. *Here he goes. I can tell he's gearing up for more explaining.*

"Featherington," Eldred resumed a professorial tone, "has a good life. For one, he lives in a climate-controlled living room. My wife designed his enclosure as a miniature to ours." When neither woman asked another question, he continued.

"Featherington's abode includes a sofa, armchairs, and is fully carpeted. The walls are also painted the same eggshell blue. A soothing color for him.

"We hired twenty-four-hour, seven-days-a-week staff to take care of the Fifth's needs. The private dog park makes it possible for him to exercise several times a day. He relieves himself, of course. That's also necessary.

"And we provide the most expensive dietary supplements along with his food. Frenchies have notoriously poor digestion. They gulp their food. We have a side line of unique feeder bowls with his label, and we sell them at cost to any dog that resides at the inn. To encourage slower eating habits," he added with a sniff.

"Maybe I can buy one of those fancy bowls for Tater." Jets

used her most sparkly tone. "Or is my money not good enough either, due to his exempt status."

"You can find the bowls in several colors on our website," Eldred muttered. "I'll comp you one as a sign of our goodwill. We have special editions for the Woofstock festival. A logo with Featherington's image."

"Is that a bribe, Mr. Whitlock?" Jets snapped. "You know I'm an officer of the law. I can't take freebies."

Whitlock ignored Janis's insinuation. He continued his speech. "Don't forget, Featherington comes from a line of highly bred Frenchies. He only eats organic, locally sourced fresh food, top quality, delivered four times a week."

When neither Janis nor Olivia responded, he uncrossed his legs as if to end the interview.

"We're not done with you yet." Jets wrote another note in her tablet.

Olivia took the break to ask another question of her own. "I heard that Frenchies have breathing issues, especially in hot climates. And that they are prone to certain eye diseases."

Whitlock recrossed his leg to resume more explanations. "The flat face and short snout contribute to digestive issues." He rubbed his nose with one finger before continuing. "Featherington has no eye problems though. You'd better have your vet check your dog." He glared at Janis. "Blue Frenchies are known to have numerous eye issues."

"I'll make sure to tell my vet," Jets drawled, "now that I've heard it from an expert such as yourself."

Olivia wasn't sure about Eldred's motivation. Either he took himself so seriously he didn't hear the cop's tone, or he refused to be baited. "We take the Fifth to an internist that caters specifically to French bulldogs for regular checkups."

"And that's him." Olivia pointed to Whitlock's shirt.

"That's the dog I saw in the park this morning. The one with his trainer."

Eldred lowered his chin in a condescending affirmation. "Yes, that's right. You saw Featherington the Fifth."

"Who cares about a mutt with a number in his name," muttered Jets. "I've had enough of your *special this* and *better than that*. Plus the last time I saw your champion breeder, he was chasing a bug in the dirt. Not exactly a genius, that one."

Whitlock looked down his nose with disdain. "Your dog may be your personal best in show, but I must remind you again, he's not up to the breed standard. Frenchies, blue like yours, are not invited to compete at AKC dog shows.

"The sooner you get over your hostility, the better. Just treat this as a fact, not something you can change. The AKC is notoriously stubborn about such matters."

Jets clicked the button to turn off her iPad. "Where's the wife? Her turn next. Just so you know, you don't fool me. All this talk about *AKC this and that* is only an attempt to distract me and cover up your involvement in the death of Arlo Carson."

Whitlock looked surprised.

Jets smiled a little wider, as if pleased with herself. "You said you didn't know Arlo. I got that. But you never told me where you were this morning at the time of death."

"I was working with my wife, folding shirts, getting everything ready for the festival this weekend. I unpacked bowls and water bottles for her display at our table," Whitlock insisted.

"And you'll be donating everything you earn to the Lily Rock local shelter?" Olivia asked hopefully.

A look of shock came over Whitlock's face. "We are not non-profit," he said firmly.

The knot in her gut tightened again. She now suspected

that Whitlock deliberately covered up his intentions when he applied for that permit. *Maybe he's trying to take over the town by turning it upside down. He may think Lily Rock is too open and weak to turn him away.*

He stood. "Unless you have reason to press charges right now, this interview is over."

"A wife is not a reliable alibi," Jets stated firmly. "We'll be back with more questions. I'm sure of that."

"You don't know Uma," he insisted. "But I'll go and get her now to confirm my whereabouts, just in case."

Once he'd left the room, Olivia turned to Janis. "You're seeing the problem, right? It's not just about you and Tater Tot. The Whitlocks have set up an inn and dog park in the midst of a town that couldn't be less interested in purebred canines. What are they up to?"

"You bet I see the problem," Janis retorted unapologetically. "But just so you know, he's the guy. And the missus, she may also be the guy. Together they make a couple of interlopers who only want to make money and take advantage of a bunch of unsuspecting do-gooders. I'm gonna bring them both down and use my personal indignation, along with the love of a good Frenchie, to fuel my investigation."

All hopes of Janis assuring Oliva of objectivity evaporated. Now Olivia knew the cop was in trouble. "I haven't seen you do this before. Be so intent at the beginning of an investigation."

"Nobody insults my family and gets away with it," Jets said matter-of-factly.

"You mean your dog that you've only known for...what, two weeks?"

"He's my family, Nancy Drew. An innocent who's caught in the middle of a high-stakes drama that's none of his making. I have to defend him. It's what good parents do."

"But he's a dog, not a child," Olivia insisted.

"Not like you're any different," Jets retorted. "Look at you and Mayor Maguire. You treat him like he can do no wrong. This whole town caters to the mutt and inflates his abilities. I mean how can a dog be psychic, I ask you. People only agree because Mayor Maguire is everyone's fur baby. You know I'm right. Once the word is out about this Frenchie business, there will be plenty of angry residents ready to fight right alongside me. I'll be a town hero."

"Is that what you want? A big Lily Rock rumble!"

"Call it what you will. I'm doing this for our Tater. Cookie's and mine. Tater Tot and all the other mongrels deserve respect."

She's got a point, Olivia thought. *But a crusader for dog rights doesn't make her the best qualified objective cop, especially when she's in the middle of a murder investigation.*

The door behind them opened.

"May I get you a beverage before my interview?" Uma Whitlock stepped into the room, looking cool, elegant, and very pretty in pink.

CHAPTER NINE

Uma sat primly on the edge of the sofa cushion. Her back held straight, she seemed perfectly at ease. Olivia's gaze traveled to her athletic shoes, which were gray with pink soles and pink laces. *She definitely has a preferred color.*

"As Eldred probably mentioned, the inn is solely my business. I run and operate The Frenchie Connection Inn while Eldred takes care of the breeding side of things. We're separate corporations that work under the same roof."

"I see." Jets balanced her tablet on one knee. "I asked your husband and I'll ask you. Did you know Arlo Carson, and where were you around eight this morning?"

"Was Arlo Carson murdered?" Uma fidgeted with the hem of her zip-up jacket. When she looked up, she flinched. Janis Jets's stare had that effect on people.

"I'm asking the questions here, Mrs. Whitlock." Jets corrected her with a stern reproach. "Did you know Arlo?" She separated each word for emphasis.

"I may have seen him in town." Uma folded her hands and sat back as if to think. "He's that tall thin man with the even taller wife. She looks Native, with the long braid and dark hair. An odd couple. Anyway, I saw them when we first moved here. It was months ago. I believe it was at the brew pub. Eldred and I stopped in for a beer."

She doesn't strike me as the beer type, Olivia thought. *But he does.* She remembered his round belly flopping over the waistband of his jeans. *Talk about odd couples...*

"Arlo introduced himself. He was bartending at the time. His wife was helping out."

A wave of sadness came over Olivia. *I'll miss them. Two of my first friends in Lily Rock. When I came for the getaway weekend, how they took an interest in me.*

Their marriage was in trouble then. Cay the silent presence with Arlo making jokes. And then Cay opened up to me. We got closer afterward, when I moved to Lily Rock a year later. She was like a wisdom teacher.

Janis typed with two fingers into her tablet, her mouth tight at the corners. "And that's the last time you saw Arlo," Jets stated flatly.

"We didn't exactly travel in the same circles, in case that's what you're implying," Uma said stiffly.

"I wasn't implying anything," Jets snapped. "Just trying to get an idea about your relationship with the deceased."

"Just so you know, as a taxpayer, I'm disappointed in the local constabulary. I know you're small town, but I have nothing to do with murdering a man I hardly recognized, let alone knew. Are you that desperate for suspects? Maybe you don't deal with serious crimes and murders very often."

Annoyance replaced Olivia's sadness. Uma's judgment felt not only unfair but laughable. *If she only knew*, Olivia thought. *People have been dropping dead in Lily Rock since I arrived. This is a complicated place even for a small town.*

She glanced at Janis out of the side of her eye. The tight mouth had turned into a slight smile. "Yah," Jets replied.

"We're really dummies here in Lily Rock. What would I know being a small-town cop? I basically give out parking tickets all day. You just go on thinking that."

Olivia stifled a smirk just as Jets snorted back a laugh.

Jets covered mouth with her hand and faked a cough. Then she redirected. "So you barely knew Arlo."

"I saw him once." Uma sounded impatient.

"Let's move on. Where were you at eight this morning?"

"I was here at the inn, checking out guests and their pets. Arranging for future stays. With the Woofstock festival this coming weekend, I'm fully booked and taking waitlist reservations."

"Your husband said you were working together at the time of Arlo's death. Something about shirts and dog dishes."

"Oh yes. I forgot. We folded tees and then organized our merchandise for our direct sales. We needed to pull some details together before Woofstock."

"Was your trainer helping out with the merchandise?" Olivia asked.

"George and I don't get along," Uma stated flatly. "He's Eldred's right-hand man but not mine. We occasionally cross paths due to the nature of the business, but I don't welcome his input."

"You have strong feelings about Mr. Quigley," Olivia observed.

"Like I said, I have very little to do with him." She shut her mouth as if finished on that subject.

Olivia chose another line of questioning. "You're catering to Woofstock attendees. Aren't they the exact opposite of AKC members? I mean, any dog is welcome to show up in a costume and join the parade. When it comes down to it, Lily Rock hands out awards for fun, not breeding. That's the whole point. Peace, love, and all dogs are welcome."

Jets turned to Olivia. "Got that right. I bet there'll be plenty of canine hanky-panky during the Woofstock weekend. Dogs getting together with no supervision. Having a grand old time stepping out into the woods while the owners take tie-dye workshops and learn to weave baskets. Make love and score, if you know what I mean."

Olivia chuckled.

This time Jets didn't bother to hide her grin. She shut down her tablet. "That's all I need for now. You say you were at the inn all morning."

"That's correct," Uma confirmed. "And I want you to know I do not hold the beliefs of my husband. I love all Frenchies in every color."

"But you still exclude non-AKC-approved Frenchies here at your inn," Jets reminded her.

"Mostly to keep the peace. Eldred is a difficult man. Our marriage has become an arrangement over the years. Give and take. A divorce would be financially out of the question. I don't want to upset the applecart by taking a stand on something that's unnecessary."

"Speaking of your clients, could you give me the names of the people who have reservations for this weekend? I'd like to know who checked in around 8 a.m. And I'll have to get a look at your computer too."

"Not without a warrant," Uma replied tartly. "I don't want to divulge my guest list. Their privacy is my concern."

Olivia couldn't mask her shock. *It's not like we're in Beverly Hills or a posh resort town catering to the rich and famous. This is Lily Rock. Everyone's life is an open book.*

Olivia thought back to Shelton and Sydney and their dog, Juicy Fruit. *Maybe they're famous and require protection. I'll give her that. They certainly dress the part.*

Janis expressed her doubts. "You're kind of defensive for

an innocent woman. Protecting your people's privacy as if they were some kind of bigwigs or movie stars. Something you want to tell me before I get the warrant and dive into all your business? Every last detail." She sounded threatening.

Uma sat forward, surprise on her face. She made an effort to answer, but the words caught in her throat.

Janis took the moment to insist, "Like you said, Lily Rock cops don't know the ways of the world. By the time I apply for a warrant and get the judge to sign off, you'll most likely cover your tracks.

"I bet you didn't think I'd know that," Jets smiled. "I understand. Why would a small-town cop know anything about computers? Not my expertise. Plus I'm real busy with those parking violations." Now she chuckled, sending a chill up Olivia's spine. *Is she going to tell Uma or do I have to?*

Olivia took the initiative. "Officer Jets worked in Los Angeles before she was hired here. Kinda hardcore in her heart. Knows all sorts of people. When she calls in a favor, people line up to help."

Uma's eyes widened.

Jets blinked provocatively, feigning embarrassment. "Okay, I admit, it's kind of my gift. I catch people lying and I wait for the least opportune time and...I nail them. Janis Jets always gets the guy. Even when she's female." She looked over at Olivia and winked.

"Oh all right," Uma sighed. "I'll print up my reservation list for you as soon as I get back to reception. There will be a time-stamp to confirm when people checked in. And I'll send you their contact information too. As you wish."

"Just send it to the constabulary. That will do for now." She stood, a smile on her face.

Then Jets doubled down. "One more thing. I'll get a warrant for your entire computer. After that I'll have you

73

come to the constabulary for an official interview." Her voice deepened. "You're in my sights, Uma. I'm watching every move at the inn."

She turned to speak to Olivia, knowing full well the words were for Uma. "This one isn't my priority, but that doesn't mean she can't be arrested for obstructing justice."

Jets cast one more superior look over her shoulder toward Uma. As a final reminder, she reached to pat her weapon, watching Uma's reaction.

Did Uma just flinch? I saw her flinch. Yep, that's a flinch. Olivia felt quite certain.

Jets and Olivia sat in the cab of the truck. "Now that may be the most fun I've had in an interview, at least in a while. But now I need to check on Tater Tot. Brad is not a reliable caregiver. Yesterday the nitwit let my dog sit in the passenger seat with no harness. Brad thinks dogs don't require restraint in a vehicle. In fact, do you know what he said?" Janis looked indignant. "That since Mayor Maguire doesn't wear a harness when he rides, why should Tater Tot?"

"That's true." Olivia made her voice sound as diplomatic as possible. "The mayor is free range in my Ford."

"I made Brad install a crash-tested dog seat belt connector in the back of his car and my truck last night." Janis glanced to the back seat. "See? It attaches to a state-of-the-art harness. Have a look."

Olivia didn't want to look, but she gave a cursory inspection to satisfy Janis.

"M&M would feel so confined if I trapped him like that," Olivia said. "How could he hang out the window and watch for squirrels?"

"And you come to a quick stop and what happens then?" Jets scowled. "That doodle flies through the windshield and gets hurt. Or killed. And then we'll need another mayor." Jets's eyes lit up. "Not that I'm wishing anything would happen to Maguire. But Tater Tot could be a public servant. I bet he'd win an election."

"I suppose," Olivia said noncommittally. She was surprised that Janis was no longer Mayor Maguire's advocate. *Tater Tot has certainly changed her*, she mused.

Jets inserted her key into the ignition. "I can't wait to tell Cookie he spent five grand on a second-rate Frenchie. I bet the papers they gave him were fake."

Olivia frowned. "Will he be mad?"

"Oh, he'll be really mad. Fuming. But knowing him, he won't do anything right away. He'll wait and then act. He's like that. I love a man who's slow to anger." Jets's eyes sparkled. "So sexy."

Ugh, thought Olivia. *Too much information*. "Does Cookie hold grudges?" she asked.

"Yep. You don't want to get on his bad side."

"So what does that mean exactly, will he track down the guy who gave him the fake papers?"

"You never know," Janis admitted. "On the other hand he may be just a bit miffed how The Frenchie Connection Inn is treating our boy. Just wait and see." She looked in her rearview mirror. "Since I have things to do, why don't we pick up our interviewing tomorrow morning? I'll have heard from forensics and the coroner by then. At least we'll have a better idea of the weapon used to stab Arlo."

"So you don't need me anymore today?" Olivia repeated.

"Keep your ears open if you hear anything, the slightest suggestion, that may lead to Cay's whereabouts. She's crucial to finding the murderer. If we don't rule her out soon, the investigation loses valuable time and the real culprit will be able to establish a more foolproof alibi."

Olivia asked, "What about Sydney and Shelton? Do you honestly think they are suspects?"

"Nah. Just at the wrong place at the wrong time. On the one hand, I don't want to spread the net to include them. But on the other hand, Sydney may know something. As a journalist he mingles with people in the dog world. I want to keep him close just in case he can shed some light on the why of Arlo's murder."

"So Cayenne first, then you can go after the Whitlocks as person's of interest."

"One of them killed Arlo. I know it in my gut. I'm thinking there may be a money motive. There usually is. I took a good look around the lobby. It's very upscale. All the furniture is new and high-end. The construction spared no expense.

"Only catering to AKC Frenchies and their humans must be more lucrative than I thought." Jets paused before continuing. "I mean, do you know any other hotel, motel, or inn in Lily Rock that has such a narrow clientele niche, who could stay in business and actually make it work?"

She has a point. Olivia searched her mind for a response. "Maybe the Whitlocks see Lily Rock in a different light. As the next weekend destination for Los Angeles people. It's a two-and-a-half-hour drive from the city and forty-five minutes from Palm Springs. The perfect weekend retreat.

"And people can bring their very special AKC-registered Frenchies. That might be an added bonus. That's not an impossible vision. It would open up Lily Rock to a new type of tourist. Less 'get back to nature' and more people looking to escape the daily routine, taking time for expensive self-care." Olivia knew what she said was only speculation. She hoped it would derail Janis from jumping to conclusions about the Whitlocks.

Janis looked puzzled. "That could be. But the dog part feels off to me. Do you actually think French bulldogs certified by the AKC are the targeted population?"

"Frenchies are very popular," Olivia added. "People treat them like children." She waited for Janis to agree. When she didn't, Olivia continued, "If you can afford an AKC-certified Frenchie, you can afford a pricey night or two at the inn."

"That makes some sense." Janis nodded. "I wonder how much Uma Whitlock charges to stay at The Frenchie Connection."

"Don't forget, it's not just the room. There are all the add-ons. I bet they advertise a number of doggie pampering packages. We know they have a full-time trainer and dog handler. He might keep Fido busy and put him through a few paces while the humans go out for a craft beer and dinner. Built-in dog sitting."

"We could use that kind of help," Jets admitted. "Cookie and I have lost sleep since Tater Tot arrived. He likes to play at night."

And back to her and Tater Tot. At least I tried...

"How about kennel training?" Olivia tried. "That would get him on a schedule."

"Nah, that would be cruel. He snuggles between us in bed."

Olivia waited for a self-conscious shrug from Janis, but it never came. So she asked another question.

"From your perspective..." She hesitated, keenly aware of Janis acting more and more out of character. "Are you really thinking the Whitlocks killed Arlo?"

"They did it," Jets promptly answered. "I know they did.

They've infiltrated Lily Rock and are fleecing people with their inn and the rest of their nonsense."

Olivia tried to reason with her once more. "But you said you could use a dog sitter and trainer yourself. Other residents might feel that way. Why would the Whitlocks not see the same and create a brand to make a few dollars helping people out with pets? That's good business, not necessarily a reason to be suspected for murder. And there's one more thing you might want to consider."

"What's that?" Jets asked.

Olivia used a quiet voice. "Maybe with the death of Arlo and your newfound love of Tater Tot... Maybe, just maybe you're jumping to conclusions about the Whitlocks. I mean, I don't blame you after the way they treated your fur baby—"

"So you don't think the Whitlocks killed Arlo." Jets's eyes narrowed.

"I think that maybe you're taking this a bit personally and maybe it's clouding your judgment. Just maybe."

"Ridiculous! I am perfectly clear-headed," Jets retorted. "Now let's get going. I have police business."

CHAPTER TEN

Olivia poured herself a mug of hot peppermint tea. She looked toward the bank of windows that faced the front garden area. Beyond the French doors, outdoor seating beckoned. The patio, constructed around the creek, included a bridge and a path leading to their front door.

All of these features were intentionally designed by Michael. He'd placed local rocks and boulders around the seating area, which gave a hint of privacy but also provided a view through the pines toward the circular driveway in front.

One of Michael's first steps was to apply for a permit that included the creek that ran through the property. He'd moved boulders from the back of the four-acre lot to the front, redirecting the flow of water. And then he'd created the front patio using granite slabs and rough lumber. When people parked in front, they needed to cross a small bridge before arriving at the front door.

Unlike most outdoor seating areas, this one did not have regular borders. The stone, placed in an irregular pattern, appeared haphazard. Of course Olivia knew different. There was nothing in Michael's design that had not been carefully considered and then reconsidered, executed exactly to his vision.

She sighed with appreciation. *Michael has a gift. He's managed to use what's available in the environment to create a habitable space that doesn't stick out or demand attention. Truly inspiring.*

Leaving the French doors open, she sat down to appreciate the morning sunlight. A tree stump with a level flat surface served as a table. One of the first things Michael did before they broke ground for the project was to cut down a ten-foot-tall pine tree. This stump was left over, put to good use.

He'd tried everything he could to leave the tree where it was, but eventually he had to settle for what worked best. "The tree had to go," he'd told Olivia over coffee. "But I think I can keep its memory alive."

He hired a professional arborist to be in charge of the tree's removal. The smaller branches were stacked as kindling for the winter. The needles were scattered at the back of the lot to keep down weeds. Much of the lumber was stored behind the house.

Then he engaged a local artisan to create chairs and a coffee table for the patio. He'd proudly shown her the result. The furniture, made from locally sourced lumber, seamlessly blended with the outdoors. Michael stayed true to his ideal: to use what you have as a primary resource.

"We can use the firewood from the tree for your studio. You know, keep the potbelly burning," Michael explained. It had been his plan to have an outbuilding specifically designed for Olivia and her band. A rehearsal space and room for electronic recording equipment.

"Sounds good," she'd said at the time. Now she knew she hadn't paid close enough attention. His endless zeal for the smallest detail had not engaged her attention for very long. She was polite but checked out. One of her less than desirable flaws.

Maybe if I had paid attention to all of those details, the house would feel more like home.

Olivia looked toward the bridge. No matter how hard she tried she couldn't shake the feeling of displacement. She harbored her lack of gratitude, feeling it take root in her heavy heart and deep sighs. She knew that she was the problem. The truth was she felt disappointed in herself. He'd done everything right, bringing her along, but it wasn't enough. The sheer enormity of the rooms and size of all the furniture made her feel unsteady. *Like I'm in someone else's home.*

Olivia sipped her tea and watched a crow floating overhead. The trickling of the creek soothed her nerves. A tune came to mind. She began to hum.

What song is that? She searched her mind.

"Feels Like Home." Now that's ironic. This house feels anything but...

But she had to admit she felt better. So she sang the chorus aloud. *I don't remember the verses. I'll have to do some research. This may be a song for Sweet Four O'Clock.*

Olivia lingered on the patio. Finishing the last sip of tea, she looked toward the woods. Then she closed her eyes. The scent of pine and earth filled her nostrils, slowing her heartbeat.

The caw of two crows brought both eyes open. Winging from branch to branch, one called louder, as if urging the other bird to come join him. The bird on the lower branch walked toward the tip and bounced. Instead of flying, it soared to another tree, landing a few feet away.

The other bird called, even more insistently.

Olivia forgot about her new house concerns and all thoughts about Arlo's death. She felt the self-condemnation slip away, fascinated with the birds' antics.

Then a sound of tires crunching on gravel brought her back.

A familiar vehicle parked out front. Olivia's heart began to pound. Cayenne Perez sat behind the wheel. Her long black hair framed her face.

From the distance, Olivia could feel her friend's sadness. Of course Cayenne's body language was the first clue. Even in the front seat of her car, her shoulders drooped, and her mouth held a rigid line.

But that wasn't all. Olivia felt Cayenne's sadness in her own chest. Heavy like a boulder weighing her down. Placing her outstretched hand over her heart, she felt slightly out of breath.

Cayenne removed her hands from the wheel and turned off the engine and stepped from the van. With eyes focused on her feet, she walked slowly toward the bridge.

How did she find out? Olivia wondered again. *A stranger in town perhaps. Or maybe Meadow when Cay dropped in at the library. Or did Janis bump into her and have to make the notification by herself without me?*

Cay raised her chin, staring directly ahead.

"Hello, friend," Olivia called out.

Cayenne acknowledged her greeting with a nod. She paused at the highest arc of the bridge to look over the railing to the creek below. Then she looked up toward the mountain range in the distance.

Olivia knew better than to force an unwelcome conversation. She observed her friend with soft eyes. Something she'd learned to do with other private people.

Cayenne gazed at Lily Rock for several seconds. *As if*

asking for guidance, Olivia thought. Her friend seemed in no hurry. So Olivia matched that pace by inhaling slowly to measure her breath.

Michael had once asked her why she got along so well with Cay. "You seem like her only friend. Besides Arlo of course."

She'd tried to explain at the time. "When I'm around Cay I remember I'm not in charge. I can stop worrying and over-thinking. Her calmness overcomes my anxiety. She brings peace with her like an invisible cloak."

"Do you feel that way with me?" he'd asked.

Knowing the answer he hoped for, she hesitated. Then she chose her words carefully. "I feel your steadiness." She'd touched the side of his face with her finger. "It's different than Cayenne's peace."

Now watching her friend approach, she felt something else, an ache near her heart.

"Caw," a crow sounded from a nearby tree.

Olivia broke the silence. "You found our new house. May I get you something to drink?" She wanted to rush forward, to hug the woman, give her solace. But she refrained.

Cayenne nodded. She sat in a nearby chair without a word.

CHAPTER ELEVEN

Two nearly empty mugs of peppermint tea sat side by side on the low table. Olivia waited quietly as her friend leaned over the railing, listening to the rush of the creek.

She willed herself to stay silent. Her thoughts were clear. *Not now.*

Cayenne turned to examine her palms. She looked over toward the mugs.

Olivia searched her mind for words of comfort.

As the silence deepened, she looked up at the sky. A single cloud drifted over the indigo-blue sky. She raised her hand to touch her chest. Then a thought entered her consciousness.

Focus on the space.

The cloud drifted past, but the sky remained.

She made the connection. *All of our words are clouds passing by. I don't have to worry about what to say. I can be the sky.*

Now when she looked at Cayenne, she only felt peace.

"The silence of the heart," Cayenne explained in a quiet voice. "Listen, return, accept. Thank you for joining me here."

"More tea?" Olivia asked.

Cayenne nodded, and Olivia poured from the teapot.

Legs pulled up, she crossed them under her body. Time passed. She listened to the creek and the crows, her breathing easy.

Cayenne began in a soft tone of voice. "You must know by now we haven't been together for months. I moved down the hill."

Olivia nodded.

"We've been having trouble for the last few years. You remember—"

"I do," Olivia admitted.

"I left Mops 4 Us in good hands. Arlo had the cabin. I've been at a Two-Spirit gathering in Montana for the past two months."

"You heard about Arlo while you were in Montana?" Olivia asked.

"I didn't hear exactly. I sensed Arlo was gone. We were connected in deep ways, even if we decided not to live together."

Olivia allowed Cayenne's words to sink in. "Janis and I wanted to tell you. We looked for you at the cabin."

"Am I a suspect?" Cayenne asked.

"Not if you have an alibi. Janis was mostly concerned that you'd hear about Arlo's death from a stranger."

"I didn't. I heard from Arlo directly. Right here." Cayenne laid her palm over her heart. "I'll send Janis the names of the people I was with—that should free her from considering me as a suspect."

"And after that, will you go back to the cabin?" Olivia knew how difficult it was to return to a place previously shared with a loved one, but she still expected Cayenne to say yes.

"I'm not going back," Cayenne said in a reasonable voice. "Arlo and I made our peace. There's no need to return. The remaining stuff, all his belongings, can be donated to the help center. I'll send in someone from my company to handle a clean out.

"We rented the cabin. No need to worry about property or wills." Cay reached into the pocket of her jeans. "I don't know when I'll be back to Lily Rock." She held open her hand. "I wanted to leave you this. For your new home."

She offered a smooth stone to Olivia.

"I painted this for you." Cayenne smiled. "It looks like a Girl Scout craft project, but the symbol holds meaning for me. And us."

On the surface was an outline of an open palm. A spiral had been drawn in the center.

"The labyrinth," Olivia realized instantly.

"That's right. Where we connected." Cayenne nodded. "This is for you, to remind you that not all truth comes from what you see with your eyes. Vision is found within."

"Your last lesson." Olivia closed her fingers around the stone.

"For now," Cayenne said. "You don't need me anymore, not like you did when you first arrived in Lily Rock. Whenever you feel out of balance, you can walk the labyrinth. Then your sight will be transformed to inner awareness, and you can go on."

Olivia sighed. "So once again you comfort me when I want to comfort you. I don't want you to leave..."

Cayenne stood up. "You'll figure it out. You always do."

"This is goodbye." Olivia heard the fear in her voice.

"For now." Cay pulled Olivia into a full embrace. "Be well," Cayenne said and then turned to walk away.

. . .

Olivia left the stone on the kitchen counter to text Janis Jets.

> Cay was here.

> I'll be right over.

> She's already gone.

> You let her get away!

> She didn't kill Arlo.

Olivia picked up the stone from the counter, looking at the symbol. *I've seen this before. At Lady of the Rock. Drawings and jewelry in this same design.* She gently replaced the stone and then picked up her cell.

> Meet me at Lady of the Rock.

> I'm busy.

> I'll tell you more about Cay.

> Maybe. Can Tater come?

> Mongrels always welcome.

She sat outside on a bench across from Lily Rock's New Age boutique. Known for a large inventory of dried herbs and essential oils, the apothecary aka tourist trap attracted out-of-town visitors. Especially since a well-known tattoo artist had ousted the tarot reader two years before.

The artist, named Kari Barber, had become famous overnight. Mostly because he'd been interviewed on a popular Netflix special. After that, people came up the hill specifically to get one of his signature tattoos.

As Olivia scrolled on her phone, she heard Janis huff up the boardwalk stairs. Tater Tot, in air jail, hung over her folded arms.

"He can't walk up the steps himself," she explained.

"Can't or won't..." Olivia commented.

"He refused. He did run out of the constabulary on his own legs. But once we made it to the Fort, he rolled over and played dead." Tater Tot squirmed and then jumped to the boardwalk. Teetering for balance, he fell to his side and then onto his back. His four legs stuck up in the air.

Jets and Olivia chuckled.

"Have a seat," she offered.

Jets clipped the dog's lead on Tater Tot's collar and then plopped herself on the edge of the bench. "So you let my prime suspect get away," she began. "That's an amateur move, Nancy Drew. As soon as you saw Cayenne, you should have texted me. Did she walk or drive?"

At Olivia's silence, Jets sent her a sharp jab with her elbow. "Give it up right now. You're not telling me everything. What did Cayenne say? Did she know about Arlo? Is she hiding from the cops? Where was she when he was murdered?" Each question brought more intensity to her voice.

"Stop asking me all of those questions. I'll tell you everything if you don't interrupt."

Jets clamped her mouth shut.

. . .

"Now you know what I know." Olivia inhaled deeply.

"May I speak now?" Jets sounded irritated.

Olivia nodded.

"So Cayenne's going to send me the names of the people who can alibi her."

"Yes," Olivia said.

"And you don't think she's Arlo's killer..."

"I do not." The very thought of Cayenne killing Arlo was preposterous.

"Are you sad that she's leaving?"

"You never understood my relationship with Cayenne," Olivia sighed.

"I don't believe in all her wisdom mumbo jumbo, if that's what you mean." She softened her voice. "But I don't dislike Cay. I just don't get her."

Olivia knew it was useless to try to explain.

"I just want to say, in Cayenne's defense, she'd never kill Arlo. It's not in her nature. She loved him. Don't forget she values all life; she takes spiders outside as a part of her cleaning service."

"You don't have to tell me," Jets said. "Plus I already know who's on the top of my list of suspects, and that's why I'm not wasting time checking on her alibi."

"You aren't following up leads like you usually do." The words escaped before Olivia could pull them back.

Janis's brow wrinkled. "Not your call," she stated flatly.

And then Tater Tot yipped. Olivia felt relief. She wasn't ready to fight with Janis over her police business.

"What's wrong, Tater?" Janis asked.

He yipped again and then rolled onto his belly, scrambling to all fours. The Frenchie raised one paw and then the other, trying to hoist himself into Janis's lap. When she laughed at his antics, he nudged her hand, demanding a pet.

"You're irresistible." Jets scratched him behind the ear. She kept scratching while she directed another comment to Olivia.

"I bet Cayenne mesmerized you with one of her mind games."

"That is not the case," Olivia promptly replied. "She was very stoic. And quiet."

Jets scratched Tater Tot in front of his tail.

He closed his eyes with pleasure.

"Ever been in that toy store over there?" Jets pointed to the shop next to Lady of the Rock.

"Old Toy Trains? Interesting name. No, I've never been inside."

"The previous proprietor, Betty King, was found dead a few years ago. Crushed by a seven-foot-tall nutcracker. It was before you got here. Anyway Mike and I solved the murder. Turned out ol' Betty had a side gig—one of those women in everyone's business. You just never know about people."

The hair on Olivia's arms rose. *She's changing the subject. I know her tricks. She's using her interviewing technique on me.*

When Olivia said nothing, Jets grew impatient.

"What did Cayenne say about Arlo?" Her stern no-nonsense voice cut through Olivia's reserve.

"Well, she didn't exactly say that much, if you must know." Under Janis's accusing glare, she felt uneasy. "Cayenne didn't say one word. She looked around. She drank some tea. But I'm meeting you here because of this." She held out the smooth round stone.

"Don't tell me. Some kind of wisdom nonsense. A friendship stone or something." Janis dismissed her by looking aside.

"You're being unreasonable," Olivia told her in a firm

voice. "This isn't nonsense. It's a gift from a dear friend. Look at the symbol."

Jets shrugged. "Okay, you're right. But what does it mean? An open hand with an eye in the center. Not exactly original."

"Not an eye," Olivia corrected. "Look again." She opened her fingers.

"Okay, a spiral. I've seen those too. Not as common though."

"So that's why we're at Lady of the Lake." Olivia used her most patient tone. "I know they have lots of similar artwork in the shop. Postcards. Wall hangings."

Jets scowled. "I would have preferred talking to Cayenne myself. Your interpretation only makes things more confusing. Plus you go on tangents with rocks and symbols. In the future, you need to text me when a suspect unexpectedly drops in for tea. That's part of our agreement."

Confused, Olivia asked, "What agreement?"

"Your Nancy Drew amateur sleuth credo."

"There's no such thing," Olivia insisted.

"There is now! Don't you understand certain relationships have unspoken agreements? Ours is that you tell me everything you know, especially about a prime suspect."

"You haven't charged Cay. And you're not even following up on her alibi, so she's not exactly a suspect anymore," Olivia argued.

"And that's where you made the mistake. You should have known I wanted to interview Cay after we informed her about Arlo."

Olivia felt immediately defensive. "That's not fair. I thought you asked for my help with Cayenne. You know, as moral support for the notification."

Jets scowled but remained silent.

"I don't read minds," Olivia stated flatly.

"Yes, you do," Jets said. "You might not know it, but you do read minds. That's why people confess to you all the time. They sense you already know what they're going to say anyway, so why not get it out in the open."

"That's just silly," Olivia replied tartly. "Talk about mumbo jumbo. You know you don't believe that for one minute."

Janis's eyebrows raised. "Whatever you say, Nancy Drew."

CHAPTER TWELVE

Janis and Olivia stepped inside Lady of the Rock with Tater Tot trotting behind.

"Hello, dears," came a familiar greeting.

"Meadow!" Olivia exclaimed. "I didn't know you still worked here."

"I step in when Denise needs to help out with her grandchildren. It doesn't happen often. Just for a couple of hours this afternoon. Any news on Arlo's killer?"

"Not yet," Jets snapped. "It's an ongoing investigation. I can't comment. How do you know it's a murder anyway? No one has confirmed the cause of death."

"George Quigley came in an hour ago. He told me. Plus it doesn't take a genius to know that a sharp knife to the armpit will most likely be murder." Meadow sniffed.

"The Frenchie trainer guy," Jets said thoughtfully. "What would bring him to a place like this?"

"He's friends with the man in back," Meadow explained. "They chat about tattoos. Ink, they call it." She shrugged. "May I give Tater Tot a dog cookie?" She reached for the container on the counter.

"Are they homemade from Thyme Out?" Jets asked. "He only eats the best, made from natural ingredients."

"They certainly are. Cookie makes extra small bones for me to hand out to dogs who drop in. Here, Tater Tot," she called.

The dog came right over.

"Sit," she told him.

His back haunches lowered to comply.

She held up her palm.

Tater froze, eyes focused.

"Okay, play dead."

He lay on his side with his four stubby legs sticking out.

"Does he have to perform for every treat?" Jets grumbled.

"Oh yes, dear. That's how you raise an obedient dog. You never give them any food until they've followed at least one command."

Meadow offered the cookie to Tater, who sat up and immediately gobbled it down.

Removing her eyes from the Frenchie, Olivia asked the question she came for. "I'm looking for information about open-palm symbols." She showed Meadow the stone. "Like this one."

"Don't tell me you're getting a tattoo." Meadow sounded disappointed.

Before Olivia could answer, the curtain in the corner was pushed aside. Sydney and Shelly Ayers filed out. Both had a transparent Saniderm bandage wrapped on their left forearm. "Hello," Shelly said.

"You again," mumbled Jets. "What have we got there?" She pointed to Sydney's arm.

"We got matching tattoos," Sydney announced. "We've been wanting to do this for some time. Haven't we, Shelly?" He nudged his partner with his hip.

"Stop it. That hurts. My arm is sore." Shelly stepped away.

"Don't be a baby," Sydney laughed. "You know we both wanted this."

Once they left, Jets shrugged. "I guess Shelly has a low pain threshold."

"I suppose," Olivia agreed.

"I bet you know what they got on those arms," Jets mused. "A tattoo of Juicy Fruit. Their fur baby. It's kinda cute."

"Are you and Cookie going to get tattoos of Tater Tot?" Olivia asked innocently.

"Maybe," Jets sounded noncommittal. "I'll explain later. Go ahead, ask about your hand symbol. It may lead to something."

Olivia turned to Meadow.

"That's a common symbol," Meadow said. "Lots of tourists buy the wall plaques and postcards. Native Americans call it the healing hand. A while back, I researched it in the library because I was interested in its popularity.

"According to what I read, the healing hand with a spiral attracts the powerful energy of healing and protection." When Meadow used her librarian voice, even Janis listened with rapt attention.

Warming to her topic, she continued. "I learned that a person might wear the symbol if they're seeking curative power. In a more generalized understanding, the symbol brings luck, health, and fortune."

"Like a good-luck charm," Jets stated. "Or a four-leaf clover."

"Not quite like that," Meadow replied. "I'm most certain anyone from the Hopi people, for example, would object to that comparison. The symbol is considered sacred among many Native tribes."

Jets frowned. "I bet the Irish don't care if I make fun of

their four-leaf clover." A wicked smile came over her lips. "I gave Cookie a pair of boxers with a big ol' four-leaf on the front. He got lucky."

"Careful," Olivia warned. "You'll be sent back to sensitivity training for a refresher course."

"Not if you don't tell anyone," Jets reminded her.

Meadow cleared her throat. "Janis, dear. Be more respectful. You may think those things, but don't speak them. We are your friends, but there are limits."

Jets made a face and turned away, while Olivia and Meadow nodded in agreement behind her back.

"Take a look at that. Mayor Maguire is standing outside?" Jets observed.

"Bork!" Maguire stuck his head in the door. He wagged his tail in greeting. But as soon as he saw Tater Tot, he ducked back outside.

Meadow took a dog treat from the jar. "Here, Mayor," she coaxed.

Tater Tot popped to all fours. He sprinted toward Meadow, intent on receiving another treat.

Maguire pawed at the glass, refusing to come inside.

"Come on, M&M," Olivia urged. "The door's open." *I can't believe he's letting Tater Tot dominate his space. He looks like a benign elderly uncle watching his nephew play.*

"Bork," he said.

Tater Tot spun on his bottom and ran to the window. Rising up on his back paws, he let out a series of high-pitched yips. Then he turned around and ran back to Meadow, who still held the dog cookie aloft in her hand.

Meadow leaned over. "Since you're the one who follows directions, let's learn another trick. How about shaking paws." While Meadow worked with Tater Tot, Olivia wondered about Mayor Maguire.

"Why isn't M&M coming inside?" she asked Janis.

"Maybe because my Frenchie is the dominant dog. Despite his size he commands the room." Jets sounded distracted. "Look at that. The way Tater learned to shake his paw. Meadow is a genius with dogs."

Tater Tot chomped down his treat and then sprinted toward the window again. Up on his rear legs, paws on the glass, he barked vigorously at Maguire.

The mayor ducked his head.

"Tater Tot one, Maguire zero," Janis said in a proud voice. "Maybe there's a new mayor in town."

"Very interesting," Meadow remarked. "Ever since Maguire was a puppy, he'd do nearly anything for a treat." Meadow came around the counter. She walked closer to the window. Picking up the Frenchie in her arms, she handed him to Janis.

Jets hugged her dog. "Obviously Tater Tot is willing to take on dogs twice his size. It doesn't take a canine whisperer to figure that out. That big dog is terrified of my sweet little potato-poo." Jets buried her nose in Tater's neck, her baby-talk voice muffled by his skin.

Olivia smiled at the mayor, who faced the window again. He wagged his tail. "I don't think the mayor wants to mess with your silly dog. He's staying outside. I guess he doesn't want any trouble."

"Tater Tot rules," Jets said with pride. "He's quite the protector. And now he's taking over the town and all the dog bones and shops. Wait until I tell Cookie."

She gathered her leash and hooked it to Tater Tot's collar before putting him down. "Why don't you meet me this afternoon? We can pick up the investigation then. Thyme Out at one o'clock. Our usual table." Tater Tot strutted ahead.

Olivia watched as Mayor Maguire backed up, giving Janis

and the Frenchie a wide berth. It wasn't until they disappeared from view that Maguire finally entered the shop.

He bumped Olivia's knee with his nose and then turned to Meadow. "Bork," he said.

"Sit, Mayor," Meadow commanded, and he immediately obeyed.

She tossed two treats in the air, which he caught.

"See you later," Olivia told Meadow.

Mayor Maguire stayed in the shop as Olivia made her way out the door toward and down the stairs. She continued to wonder about Maguire's change of behavior. He'd stayed outside the shop, letting Tater Tot have his way.

Maybe he has something else on his mind, something more important than grabbing that cookie from Meadow's hand...

CHAPTER THIRTEEN

Michael and Olivia sat on the back patio of Thyme Out. They'd ordered a carafe of iced coffee, which arrived with two mason jars. Michael filled both to the top. "This is the blend I concocted for the Woofstock festival," he explained. "See what you think."

Olivia took a sip. "Very earthy. Hints of the forest. Can't quite name the taste. What do you call this one?"

"Nothing original. I call it Woofstock Blend. I did some research and tastings. You know coffee isn't my thing, especially black like you drink it. But Cookie approved this particular combination. Now people at Thyme Out can immerse their taste buds in global coffee culture."

"Really." Olivia smiled. "And here I thought it was just another cup of joe."

"Are you mocking me?" he teased.

"Yup," she replied. "But feel free to top off my mug with another hit of that global tasty whatever." She lifted her mason jar.

After he poured, he leaned closer. "How are things going with the investigation? I forgot to ask."

"Not sure," Olivia said. "Maybe Janis can fill us in. She's supposed to be here soon."

"I've got muffins for you." Cookie Kravitz stood next to their table holding a basket. He wore a crisp white apron over his blue denim shirt. When he smiled, his penetrating blue eyes lit up. "Warm from the oven." He handed the basket to Olivia.

She lifted the napkin to take a sniff. "I smell strawberry and...thyme."

"That's my seasonal late-spring bake," he said. "May I sit down?"

"Of course." Michael pulled out a chair.

The men began to talk, giving Olivia a chance to observe Michael's face. *He's more rested. Finishing up the house has done him some good.*

"Look at you two, gossiping like a couple of church ladies." Janis stood beside the table.

"Mike and I are just figuring out last-minute details for our booth at the Woofstock festival," Cookie explained.

"I forgot to ask." Michael leaned over the table toward Olivia. "Will you have time to help out? Maybe just a couple of hours."

"I don't know, why not," Olivia said.

"I do," Jets barked. "You're gonna be helping me with my investigation, not pitching overpriced baked goods and dog treats to stoned tourists."

She turned to Cookie. "I presume you'll have an assortment available for purchase?"

"Small, medium, and large." He winked. "All with peanut butter, Tater Tot's favorite."

"Speaking of our fur baby..." Jets reached into her pocket. She passed her cell phone to Michael. "Here he is. I'll introduce you later. Don't scroll left or right unless you want to get an eyeful." She winked seductively at Cookie, who chuckled his response.

"Cute dog." Michael handed back the phone.

"You'd better think so. Because Cooks and I..." Janis looked over at her partner for confirmation. "Once these Woofstock hippies leave town, we want you two to be Tater Tot's godparents. There will be a ceremony, followed up by a big party. The whole town's invited."

Olivia bit the side of her cheek. Michael's expression nearly made her laugh aloud. Fortunately, he ducked his head to stifle a laugh, then coughed behind his hand to cover his smile.

"Of course we'll have to talk this over," he said seriously, deliberately avoiding Olivia's eyes. "And talk to our attorney to make sure we have enough assets to make such a serious commitment. That's what godparents do, right? Hand over gifts and a college fund."

"We'd be honored," Olivia interjected. She didn't want another lecture from Janis. "Just tell us the day and time."

Once they'd finished the basket of muffins, Janis began to talk shop. "As friends of Arlo, I want to include you in my investigation. Like unofficial deputies. We've eliminated Cayenne as a suspect. I know who did it. I just need some more evidence.

"Keep your eyes open. As residents of Lily Rock, you know the sheep from the goats. If you see Eldred or Uma do anything suspicious, text me. Don't approach them. I'll take care of that when I get there."

"What do you mean sheep and goats?" Cookie interjected.

"You can tell tourists from residents. So you'll figure out if the Whitlocks are infiltrating the Lily Rock regulars or if people are coming up the hill, planning a takeover."

"Takeover..." Cookie looked interested.

"An AKC behind-the-scenes domination."

Olivia wanted to tease Janis, but the look on her face made that impossible.

"Babe, you're kidding, right? About the AKC thing?" Cookie asked.

Jets brushed aside his question. "Like I said, keep your eyes on the Whitlocks. And send me a text. I'll take care of the rest." She tapped her fingers on the table.

"There's another reason I want to talk to you."

She glared at Cookie. "Stop delivering dog treats to that uppity Frenchie Connection Inn. Just flat-out refuse. Make up an excuse if you have to. They don't deserve to use your popular product to promote their exclusive brand."

Next she stared at Olivia. "You remain on constabulary standby. I need you to come with me after we're done here. I'm going back to The Frenchie Connection to do a little surveillance."

Jets wasn't finished. "And I want you..." she said, pointing to Michael. "Actually I'm not sure what I want you to do. Now that you've finished the big Olivia castle construction, you could be useful." She looked up as if considering. "Oh, I know. Make a note of everyone who buys coffee or dog treats at your festival table. Tell people it's for your newsletter or something. That you offer discounts. That way I'll have a list of people for follow-up. One of them has to be part of the Whitlocks' plan to take over Lily Rock."

"I do have some time." Michael rested his arms on the table. "I'm feeling really good right now; my punch list for the construction has gone from over a hundred to-dos to less than ten. I've paid my guys and given them ten days off. But I want to hang with Olivia. I've neglected her for the past couple of months."

"You can play with Olivia later," Jets said. "Just get those names."

CHAPTER FOURTEEN

Jets parked her truck across the road from The Frenchie Connection Inn. She turned to Olivia. "Let's just see who goes in and out." She rolled down the windows and pushed her driver's seat back.

"You need me for this?" Olivia asked. "I do have a life, you know."

"You'll be the first to know when I don't need you, how's that."

Olivia was worried. More about Janis than the actual investigation. *If I'm not here to rein her in, she'll arrest one of those Whitlocks without enough evidence. They'll raise a stink and most likely sue the town. People like that love to litigate.*

But instead of pushing back, Olivia said didn't say a word. *If Cay were here, I'd ask her what to do. She'd know right away.*

Jets sat up. "Look there. A delivery truck pulled up. Let's sneak through the grove, walk around back, and have a look. I wonder if they're trafficking stolen goods. I wouldn't put it past those smug..." Jets opened her door and jumped out, the expletive lost with the slamming of the door.

Jets ducked left then right, then made strides into the

woods. When she ducked behind a redwood, she called out, "Over here, Nancy Drew."

One man rolled a dolly down the plank, which extended from the back of a delivery truck. "No signage on the vehicle," Jets commented. "A sure clue. That's some nefarious under-takings right there in full view."

"Or they rented a truck for the delivery and will return it after they're done," Olivia commented.

"Check out that guy. He looks like a crook. The hoodie pulled down over his eyes, the jeans waistband clinging across his butt. He's definitely going incognito," Jets said.

"Or he's chilly. It's a bit cold out here. Not summer yet," Olivia offered.

"There's Whitlock!" Jets hissed. "Look at him giving that delivery guy a big hug and a slap on the back. Old buddies... I bet they're in on this together. Whitlock hired the hoodie guy to make his deliveries."

"I bet deliveries for dogs are a lucrative business. They must make millions on tips," Olivia replied sarcastically.

"Stick with me, Nancy Drew, I'm going in." Jets popped out from behind the tree and took off running.

"Stop. Police!" Janis hurtled straight toward the men and the truck, waving her badge in the air.

Eldred Whitlock's mouth hung open. The other man stared in disbelief. Olivia hustled to catch up.

Jets stopped abruptly, Olivia nearly colliding into her back.

"Hoodie guy is the dog trainer. George what's his name," she hissed in Jets's ear.

"Quigley," Jets agreed.

He ignored them and pushed his dolly back up the ramp of the delivery truck.

"Stop unloading those boxes. Stop means freeze," Jets commanded.

Quigley dropped his hands from the cart.

"What's the meaning of this, Officer?" Whitlock interjected. "My employee is finishing up his usual morning business. No one called for the police."

Janis slipped her badge back into her pocket, then she rested her hands on her hips. "Is that so," she snapped. "Your usual delivery, you say. What would that be then? Laundered cash, illegal drugs, maybe a weapon or two?"

Olivia felt the blood drain from her face. *She's going all in. What a wild accusation. Too many police dramas, not enough rom-coms.*

Whitlock shook his head. "Nothing like that, Officer. You tell her, Quigley."

"Shipments of dog beds, for one." Quigley lowered his hoodie. "Mr. Whitlock orders dozens to sell to inn customers. Plus we have leashes. People buy those too, sometimes as gifts. And we also have specialized dog bowls for Frenchies."

The tone of his voice suggested that he wasn't taking Janis seriously.

"Why don't you show me some of your fancy goods," Jets said. "Just open up a box or two. I may want to buy something for Tater Tot. You never know. Unless you have rules about selling to mongrels."

To Olivia's surprise, Quigley did not object. He removed a box cutter from his pocket to slit open the cardboard of the closest container. Stuffed Frenchies in bold oranges, blues, and reds spilled out. "We have an entire French bulldog collection," Eldred explained. "Do you want to purchase one for your..." He turned to cough in his hand. "Dog?"

"Let me see that." Jets snagged a toy from the box and held it up for inspection.

"Pretty cute," Olivia said.

The stuffed Frenchie wore a deep-purple sweater pulled over imitation gray fur.

"Dog-safe," Whitlock said promptly. "No squeakers for the pets to choke on. Made in China of the highest quality products. Not from hazardous toxins."

Jets's eyes narrowed. "So not American made, Mr. Whitlock. That surprises me. I won't bother to dignify the nontoxic remark. We both know that's not true."

Whitlock shrugged. "I don't make those decisions. Quigley is in charge. He consults with my wife and they run the merchandising."

"I'd never give Tater a toy without a squeaker," Jets admonished. "That's the fun part, watching him tear out the stuffing then chew the plastic.

"You're kind of a no-fun operation, aren't you?" she continued. "Protecting your investment with little thought to the Fifth's happiness. Like the way you breed dogs in a lab. Also not fun. And how you won't let them pick their own playmates. Now that's just cruel."

Janis dropped the toy back into the box. "What do you have there?" She pointed to another container.

"Quigley, show her what's in the box," Eldred insisted.

"Like I said, specialized Frenchie dog beds." Quigley reached for the box cutter. "Do you want to see those too?"

"Maybe not," Jets admitted. "I do want to see Eldred's office though. You say you're a breeder, and this here is your trainer." She nodded in Quigley's direction. "So you must have a place where you do business."

"We share an office," Whitlock explained. "I talk to other breeders and Quigley handles the contracts and most of the finances."

Jets turned to Quigley. "You don't have any stake in The

Frenchie Connection partnership, do you, other than as a hired employee?"

Quigley gave a curt nod. "That's right. I'm not a stockholder or anything fancy. Just an employee with a lot of responsibility. I have been for nearly a decade." He turned toward Eldred. "Isn't that right, Mr. Whitlock?"

The use of "mister" caught Olivia's attention. But before she could focus on the implication, Jets changed her tactic.

"How about this. Let's pretend I want to buy an AKC-registered Frenchie. Since Tater Tot is only pet quality and I had to have him neutered."

"I don't make the rules," Whitlock insisted. "Those are AKC breed standards, remember."

Jets's mouth twitched. "Like I was saying, how would I go about purchasing one of those AKC beauties and how much would it cost me, all said and done?"

Whitlock's fake smile dropped to a ready scowl.

Quigley didn't wait for Whitlock. He answered immediately. "I've got all the details on my computer. I'll bring up the prices for you and send them via text."

"We have a website," Whitlock added. "Quigley got some tech guy to play with our algorithms, and now our company is the first to show up when anyone searches on Google.

"We don't need to sit in my office. Just go home and type in French bulldog breeders. You'll find my name at the top. I'm very well known. Featherington the Fifth has his own Facebook page. He's sired several champions, don't forget. Maybe we can cut you a deal on the next litter." He looked to Quigley for confirmation.

"Who's the number one mama in the cue for Featherington the Fifth's donation?" Jets asked brightly.

"That depends. Three bitches are pregnant right now. Once they give birth I'll be given the pick of each litter. I can sell one of those puppies to you. It will be midsummer by then."

"My computer's down. How about we go in your office and you can show me the website," Jets said, a glint in her eye.

"If you insist," he muttered. "Finish up with the boxes, would you, George? I'll escort Officer Jets and catch up with you later."

Quigley frowned and then gripped the dolly with both hands. He rolled it up the ramp, disappearing into the truck.

"George is just your employee. I thought maybe you were partners," Olivia said.

"My employee only," Whitlock insisted. "What's your name again? Are you a cop?"

"She's a consultant, and her name is Olivia Greer," Jets answered before Olivia could speak. "Let's see that office now. So that I can get more information about a puppy. On the one hand, I may want two AKC-certified Frenchies. On the other hand, I don't have to keep two. I can give one away at the next Paws and Pines raffle. I'm certain someone in Lily Rock is interested in becoming a breeder."

Whitlock kept his composure. "I suppose I can't refuse," he finally admitted.

Whitlock's office appeared organized and efficient. A large mahogany desk was the main focus of the room. Another small desk shoved into a corner occupied the same wall as the door.

Behind the main desk was a swivel chair. On the wall behind the chair was a credenza, which held more Frenchie Connection merchandise. A series of candles along with a basket containing matches. All displayed The Frenchie Connection logo.

Hung above the merchandise were three expensively framed individual portraits. Each showed a nearly identical-looking French bulldog along with two less interesting humans. All eyes—dogs' and humans'—stared toward the camera.

The men dressed formally in white shirts, neckties, and dark suits. In front of them stood the dog, body weight evenly distributed on four sturdy legs.

Wide canine faces and bright eyes looked engaging and nearly human. But it was their identically shaped bat ears that added a certain endearing and comic relief.

Upon closer inspection she saw that George Quigley stood at attention, hands at his sides, while Eldred Whitlock cradled the best in show trophy in one arm.

Olivia turned from the portraits to take in the rest of the room.

A floor-to-ceiling curtain covered the entire wall. She suspected it had been hung to conceal something, but she wasn't sure what. The wall on the opposite side held one large poster advertising the AKC museum in New York City.

Her gaze returned to the three dog portraits. She read each plaque. Featherington the Third. Featherington the Fourth. Featherington the Fifth. All honored with the title best in show, along with the year.

Cookie-cutter images.

"Please have a seat. Here's my business card with my contact information. Of course we expect a deposit before we begin the background checks." Whitlock sounded smooth and businesslike.

"Background checks!" Jets exclaimed. "I'm buying a dog, not adopting a baby."

"Purchasing an AKC dog at The Frenchie Connection Kennel is a lengthy process," Eldred explained. "We have to make certain you have the right environment for the puppy. A fenced yard, for example. And we also have to make a home visit to see if your current pet will be a suitable sibling. That takes weeks."

Janis tried to object, but he kept talking. "And then there is the financial background check. We want to make sure you'll pay up before delivery. There's the cost of the breeding, the expense of the caesarian delivery, and care of the dam. And then the vet bills afterward. Frenchies can have issues after the C-section. We want to nip those in the bud as soon as we can."

When he paused to take a breath, Olivia got her question in. "Are C-sections typical? Isn't the cost lower if they're delivered naturally?"

"Heads are too big," he stated matter-of-factly. "Featherington the Fifth is known for his unusually large head, so all of his puppies require assisted birth. But for your information, most accredited breeders deliver Frenchies by C-section. Even the less famous ones."

Whitlock reached into a drawer. He used a thin-bladed letter opener to unseal a manila envelope. "I usually send these to all of my clients. Information packets that answer the most often asked questions." He pulled out a glossy brochure. "But I can save the postage. Here you go."

Jets glanced over the brochure. She mumbled and then grunted. "Write down the cost of one AKC Frenchie male on another piece of paper. And then one AKC Frenchie female. I want to show my partner before we make a decision."

Like a man making a deal, he scribbled on a small paper and slid it across the desk face down. "I can cut you a deal. As a private citizen," he explained.

Jets held the brochure in one hand and the paper in another. "I will look at your website and have an answer for you today." She stood up. "Do you happen to have a stapler by chance? I want to attach the paper to the corner. Can't be too careful."

Whitlock shrugged. "I'll ask my wife. She has one at the front desk."

As soon as he left, Janis took a tissue from the box on the desk. Then she leaned forward and snatched the letter opener. "Check this out." She held it in the air, under Olivia's nose, then leaned back and took a closer look. "Long and thin. Eight inches. Rapier-like. This would make a real nice weapon. Easy to carry up your sleeve and then *wham*. Shoved into a vulnerable armpit. Slick. And deadly."

Olivia blinked.

Janis slid the blade into the inner pocket of her blazer just as Whitlock returned.

"Here you go." He handed over the stapler. While Janis fumbled with the papers, he stood close to the door. Once finished, Jets slid the brochure and then his business card into the manila folder.

"Have a nice day," Jets told him on the way out the door.

CHAPTER FIFTEEN

Back at the constabulary Jets dropped the letter opener into an evidence bag. "I don't see any blood with the naked eye, but trust me, it will be contaminated. Forensics will find Eldred's or Uma's DNA once they have a closer look." She dropped the plastic bag onto her desk with a thump.

"Don't forget you stole the evidence without a warrant," Olivia reminded.

"I'm gonna get one of those Whitlocks to confess. This investigation isn't going to court. I won't need a warrant for the weapon. You're my secret weapon."

Olivia instantly realized why Janis was acting so cavalier with her evidence. "I'm not a sideshow," she sniffed. "What if I can't get a confession this time?"

"I disagree. Your innocent little tell-me-your-feelings routine is the greatest show on Earth. You've helped out in the past. I'll admit that.

"Remember my old assistant a while back? Spilled her guts at one of your pub gigs. You're a one-woman show. People can't wait to tell you stuff." Jets picked up her cell to make a call.

"Brad, I've got something for the lab. Come and get it. Scratch that. Pick up some lunch for us, the usual at the diner. When you bring the food, you can take the evidence.

"Where's Tater by the way? My baby is not a nuisance. So you're too busy. Well then how about Paws and Pines. He'll have to hang out with the other mongrels."

Janis smiled as she put the phone on the desk.

"Did you see Eldred's face? He knows I'm on to him, the way he looked at me when we left. A confused and worried suspect is the best kind in my book. He'll make another mistake, mark my words. After that, we only have to bring him to the constabulary and get the confession."

Her eyes took on a far-off expression. "I wish I could be there when Eldred realizes his weapon is gone. That would be so sweet."

About twenty minutes later, Janis leaned back in her chair right as Brad stuck his head inside the room. "Got the burgers and fries." He plopped the paper bags on the desk and picked up the evidence. "On this right away, boss."

After lunch, Olivia excused herself. "I'm going for a walk in town," she explained to Janis. "To clear my head."

She needed space to think over what she'd just heard and witnessed. Even if Janis was relying on her to get that confession, the police officer had committed an illegal act. It could jeopardize the entire case. And what if she put the wrong people behind bars? Would the real killer get away?

Doubts about Janis and herself filled her thoughts. She knew people confided in her. Her gift, if it could be called that, often showed up unexpectedly nowadays.

She used to sing and draw a confession, but at this point, she could no longer control the circumstances. Sometimes she'd be standing in line at the grocery store, minding her own business, and the person behind her would start talking. They'd tell her the most intimate of secrets right in public. Even strangers confessed.

Her mother pointed out her gift first, and then Don, her long-time boyfriend, claimed that she had no boundaries. That was when she'd grown self-conscious. "People look hypnotized when you sing," he'd complained, making it sound like a bad thing. "And you should tell them to back off before they even start blabbing. What's wrong with you?"

Even though she never welcomed other people oversharing, Don made her feel responsible and guilty. "Stop embarrassing me!" he'd shout. And then use her behavior as an excuse for him to keep drinking.

So she'd stopped performing to keep the peace. And she stopped having friends over after that. It wasn't until she broke up with Don and later moved to Lily Rock that she finally opened up and made friends.

Her thoughts returned to Cayenne.

She usually helps me when I'm like this. Clarifies my thinking. She reframes when I'm in the weeds. What am I going to do without her?

Slowing her strides, she found herself standing in front of The Frenchie Connection dog park. The crime scene tape wafted in the breeze. It had failed to keep people away. Two people played with their Frenchie off leash, tossing a frisbee back and forth.

Another dog was recognizable. Featherington the Fifth sniffed at the dirt. George Quigley leaned against the fence, scrolling on his phone. Olivia waved. "Hi, Featherington," she called.

Quigley recognized her, pocketed his phone, and walked closer. "Fancy meeting you here."

"How often do you exercise Featherington?" She made her voice sound casual.

"Sometimes six times a day. When I'm busy, maybe three. I also bring other people's dogs who are staying at the inn. The tips are a good side hustle and make me some cash. I'm happy to do it." He smiled. Then he frowned. He called over to the dog. "What are you sniffing now?"

The dog lifted his chin but then dropped his nose to the ground.

"That guy loves to sniff," Quigley admitted. "But it's not healthy. The dirt gets into his lungs and then I have to take him to the vet. He has digestive and breathing issues."

"Not uncommon for a Frenchie," Olivia replied.

"I know. I'm happy I don't pay the vet. But keeping that stud in good health is my job, so hold on a minute. I don't want another lecture." George turned back toward the dog. "Get over here, Featherington!" he yelled.

The dog lifted his head again. This time he trotted in the opposite direction, until he spun around for a squat.

"'Time for his poop," Quigley called over his shoulder. "Then I can take him back to the inn." Once he deposited the bag in the trash, he leaned against the fence again, seemingly in no hurry. "So was Arlo a friend of yours?" he asked.

"He was. A friend to all of us in Lily Rock," Olivia said softly. "We'll miss him greatly."

Quigley nodded. "I get that."

She could tell he wanted her to say more, but she knew that would only establish a connection between them. Her face tightened. *I could pump George for more information because he's vulnerable...*

"I'm sorry for your loss." George sounded sincere. "I hope you find out who stabbed Arlo. We worked together on a couple of projects. You know, legal stuff."

She couldn't help herself. His jaw had softened, an indication that he wanted to say more. "Legal stuff?" she prodded gently.

"Mr. Whitlock requires everyone who wants a purebred AKC Frenchie to sign legal papers. That ensures he gets paid, which lately has been in the form of the pick of a litter—the best bitch. Sometimes he wants money instead, when he doesn't need another female. Arlo wrote up both kinds of legal contracts."

Puzzled, Olivia summarized, "So Arlo was Eldred's attorney."

"Whitlock's old attorney retired. So I researched and found Arlo's name from an advertisement online. When I realized he lived right here in Lily Rock, I reached out. A nice guy." Quigley smiled. "I can see why he was so popular in town."

Olivia felt confused. *So Arlo was a practicing attorney...* He'd gone to law school, that she remembered from years past. But as far as she knew he'd not passed the bar exam.

"He was one of a kind," Olivia said. She didn't want to tell Quigley her concerns about Arlo's qualifications.

Quigley leaned closer. "Rumor has it you're helping out on the case. The cop calls you a consultant. Are you close to an arrest?"

Olivia knew she needed to draw a quick line. "Janis won't divulge anything about an ongoing investigation. She may be a small-town cop, but she's big city trained."

Quigley looked disappointed.

"I'd better get going." She pointed across the dog park. "Looks like Featherington is ready for another pick up."

. . .

Olivia crossed the street, wondering if anything Quigley told her was worth repeating to Janis. She stepped onto the board-walk in front of the Village Hardware store. *The last time I saw Arlo was here. He was in a big hurry to leave. I wish we'd been able to talk.* She swallowed hard to push back any more tears.

Standing near the paint section, she closed her eyes to picture that last time. *He was facing the counter, paying in cash. He dropped the money in front of the cashier and turned around abruptly. He held something in his hand. What was that...*

She inhaled as the image came. *A can of WD-40. Like the one Arlo bought the last time she saw him.*

She remembered he'd only mumbled, "Can't talk now, Olivia." He'd rushed past her and out the door to the street before she could call his name.

I wonder what he needed the WD-40 for...

Olivia opened her eyes. She saw a can of the familiar spray on the shelf under the paint samples. She read the label on the back. *Was Arlo fixing a squeak in a door?* Then she read the fine print with a list of common uses of the product. Cleaning tools, lubricating wheels or drawers, removing paint.

Okay, WD-40 has more uses than I thought. That doesn't make it important or relevant to his death. She replaced the can on the shelf and then glanced at the paint chip display again.

I don't suppose WD-40 is a good enough clue. If I tell Janis she'll just laugh at me. Plus I didn't find any evidence under the sink at his cabin. Maybe he was buying it for someone else.

She stopped to lift a paint chip from the rack. *I wonder if Michael would give this color a stamp of approval.*

Up until now, she hadn't wanted to interfere with Michael's vision when it came to any decision about their house. She'd agreed with his concept. But now that she was living there, she wondered if it was her turn to have an idea or two.

Taking the sample strip with her, she stopped at the counter. An employee wearing an orange builder's apron greeted her. "Need any help? You're Olivia Greer, right? The musician."

"That's me," she said.

"I've got tickets for Sweet Four O'Clock tomorrow night. I heard your gig was moved to the amphitheater. Now that Arlo's passed—"

"I'd like a sample of this color," she cut him off, holding up the paint chip. She didn't want to chance breaking down while talking about Arlo.

He took the chip from her hand. "I hear you play autoharp and that you're good. 'Magic' was the word, actually. Some guy came in here and told me I shouldn't miss the show."

"I do play autoharp." She managed a slight smile. "My sister is the star. She's a fiddle player. We cover old-timey tunes mostly. A few other songs if we're in the mood."

"I'll be there," he assured her, turning to set up the paint mixer. A few minutes later he handed her the sample container, with the swipe of gray-green on the top. "Here you go."

She nodded her approval. "I was wondering, were you here to help Arlo a few weeks ago? He bought a can of WD-40. I was standing in line right behind him. It was the last time I saw him." Her voice cracked with emotion.

"We're all doing that, you know." He handed her a tissue from the box on the counter. "We're remembering the last time we saw or talked to Arlo. It's really a tragedy, losing him that way.

"I do recollect selling him that can of WD. He didn't want

119

a bag; he seemed in a big hurry. He rushed out as I was helping the next customer." His eyes teared up.

"Do you know what he wanted it for? Maybe he mentioned it guy to guy," she asked hopefully.

"Something about ants," he said. "I offered to get him some environmentally safe insect spray, but he insisted that WD-40 would do the trick." He shrugged. "Ya never know with customers. They have their tried-and-true ways of doing things. So I didn't argue. I just sold him the can."

CHAPTER SIXTEEN

Olivia left the hardware store with the paint sample jar in her left hand. She leaned against the building to make a phone call.

"Lily Rock Library," came Meadow's cheery voice, "How can I help?"

"Hi, Meadow. I need to confirm something. Was our Sweet Four O'Clock gig moved to the amphitheater? Someone just told me, but I haven't heard."

"Oh Olivia, dear. I am so sorry. Yes, the town council approved changing the venue to the amphitheater right after hearing about Arlo's death. It was such a quick meeting on Zoom. I intended to call you, but I've been swamped here at the counter."

Olivia felt a niggling suspicion. "Am I to assume you're the one in charge of Woofstock now that Arlo—"

"That's correct, dear. I still need to sort out the booth locations. People continue to squabble about the placement and which booth attracts better traffic." Olivia heard Meadow's exhaustion in the tone of her voice.

"I'm really close to the library," Olivia said. "How about I drop in and bring a little something from Thyme Out? It sounds like you could use a break. We can chat more about Woofstock and Arlo."

"That would be lovely." Meadow clicked off the phone.

Olivia arrived with a bag of two warm chocolate chip muffins. But Meadow wasn't alone at the desk. Uma Whitlock stood across the counter. Olivia could tell by the librarian's face that the conversation wasn't going well.

"Hello, Mrs. Whitlock," Olivia interrupted.

Uma blinked. "Do I know—"

"I'm Olivia Greer. I met you yesterday at the inn. I was with Janis Jets."

She nodded curtly. "I remember now. The consultant. Excuse me, I am speaking to the librarian."

"No, excuse me." Olivia refused to be dismissed. "Meadow and I have a scheduled appointment."

She caught the look of relief in Meadow's eye.

"Come on, dear," Olivia said, deliberately echoing the librarian's tone of voice. Walking behind the counter, she took Meadow by the arm.

"Wait just a minute," Uma called after them.

"Can't stop now," Olivia answered. "We have very important town council business to attend to. Try reading a book while you wait."

Olivia closed the door to the office as Meadow slumped into her chair. "Thank you so much. I was trying to tell that woman it was too late to sign up for another merchandise table, but she wouldn't take no for an answer. She had the nerve to tell me she paid taxes in Lily Rock and deserved special consideration."

Olivia sat across the desk. She opened the bag and lifted

out the two oversized muffins. "Still warm," she said. "And here's a napkin."

The women munched in silence.

"So you probably want to know why Uma's here and more about her last-minute additional table request," Meadow said. "T-shirts, if you can believe it. On top of the bottles, mugs, dog beds, stuffed toys, now she wants one special table for shirts. She showed me photos and a few samples." Meadow frowned. "Some have questionable taste."

"Oh really? Do say more." Olivia was intrigued.

"I'm not sure I can speak them aloud," Meadow admitted.

"Be brave. Give me at least one example." Like most residents in Lily Rock, Olivia enjoyed teasing Meadow about her old-fashioned sensibilities.

"There are some cute sayings. Two paired shirts in a set, one for the human and one for the Frenchie. You know, like "Big sister" and "Little sister", printed across the front. Those were red, white, and blue. Very patriotic.

"Another set in pink and white reminded me of Janis and Tater Tot. They would be a wonderful gift for the christening."

Olivia's eyebrows flew up. "Is that what she's calling the party? A christening!"

"I think I heard her say as much," Meadow agreed. "Anyway, of the two tees, the human one said 'rule maker'; the dog's shirt said 'rule breaker.' They'd look so cute in those." She smiled.

"Okay, so I get the cute bit, but what about the questionable ones?" Olivia encouraged.

"This is embarrassing." Meadow shuddered. "One tee, just for the dog, said 'ball-less and flawless.'"

"Tater Tot is neutered," Olivia reminded objectively.

"And another said..." Meadow blushed. "'Who let the farts out.'"

Olivia laughed. "I guess Frenchies are known for their digestion issues, which result in some pretty potent gaseous events."

"When Janis brought Tater into the library," Meadow sniffed, "I did catch a whiff."

"He could clear a crowded room," Olivia giggled. "But don't say anything to Janis. She'll take offense."

"She's besotted with that dog. Rather surprising," Meadow agreed.

To the point of insanity, Olivia thought. But she didn't want to burden Meadow with the realization that the Lily Rock cop wasn't the objective police presence she'd been in the past.

"So are you going to do it—let Uma have a last-minute extra table at Woofstock?" Olivia could see that Meadow was already feeling less stressed. Her face looked less haggard for one, and her eyes had brightened.

"What could I do? If I refused, I had the feeling she'd be showing up at the town council screaming bloody blue murder.

"Don't forget she could make up derogatory shirts about any of us. You know, 'ban books,' 'the library smells like a fart' kind of things."

Olivia smirked.

Meadow frowned. "I don't approve of the word 'fart.' Inappropriate language, something I find personally distasteful." She tried to look sour, but then burst into a loud chuckle.

Olivia dabbed at her eyes with her napkin. Laughing with Meadow made her feel so much better. It had been a difficult two days since the discovery of Arlo's body. But now she had a glimmer that life could go on, even in the midst of the grief.

. . .

After dinner Olivia brought out her paint sample. "What do you think?" she asked Michael in a tentative voice. "I know everything has been freshly painted and that we haven't lived here long enough to redo the colors. But I thought this shade would be a nice contrast to all the white.

Michael shrugged. She could tell by the set of his chin that he had trouble with her suggestion. *He did run everything past me from the beginning and now he's disappointed.*

His mouth relaxed into a slight smile as he took the sample from her. "You can paint the room bright pink for all I care." He raised his eyebrow.

"But this is your project," she protested. "The entire house is your vision. You don't want me to come in here and start painting over your masterpiece."

"I care about the colors," Michael said. "But as soon as we moved in, I signed off. This is *our* house. Ours, not mine. I've done my thing here, had the chance of a lifetime to create. But it's time I let go. Frankly, I'm already looking for another project.

"I figured you'd be changing things once we'd been here awhile. So I had my painting guys use painter's white—just plain old white. Saved some money. You can redo the whole house in this." He waved the sample. "What do they call it, Serenity Now Gray?"

"Coastal Mist," Olivia corrected him. "I know we don't live on the coast, but it's so calming."

"I like that idea. No use in anyone being overly agitated when taking clothes out of the dryer. Bring it on, whatever it's called. I can order with my discount and have it here tomorrow."

She took the jar from his hand. "I'll figure out how many gallons we'll need."

"You don't have to do that." He grabbed the sample back. "I have a team to take care of those kinds of details. Plus the guys need work. And you have other things to do.

"Practicing your set for Woofstock, for instance. No one else can sing and play the autoharp like you. Now that's unique. I'll have my painters start next week."

Olivia was surprised. *This was all so easy. He's not one bit offended.*

He watched her with a puzzled expression. "Don't forget I am a full-service boyfriend aka partner aka whatever you want to call me, so long as we're together."

CHAPTER SEVENTEEN

Early Saturday morning Olivia held her phone to her ear. "Sage, honey, do you have a minute?"

"What's up?" Sage asked. "I'm sorry I haven't been in touch. I assume you're working with Janis on Arlo's murder. What a shock that has been."

"I was there. I saw his body," Olivia admitted.

"That had to be hard." Sage's voice softened. In that moment she sounded a lot like Meadow.

"It's hard," Olivia admitted. "But I called you for another reason. I found out by happenstance that our gig has been moved to the amphitheater." Olivia explained how she'd heard at the hardware store and then confirmed with Meadow, ending with, "Last minute, don't you think?"

"Can't be helped. Plus there are logistics. Without Arlo, we have no microphones." Sage paused. "Can we get the sound engineer from down the hill to handle the space? So last minute."

"We can ask. He might have had a cancellation."

"I'll make the call. You're busy playing Nancy Drew."

"I guess." Olivia felt the sadness return. And behind that was the voice of helplessness.

"Not going well?" Sage asked.

"Janis isn't herself."

"What do you mean?"

"Have you met Tater Tot?"

"Tater who?"

"The dog, a Frenchie. Cookie bought him from a breeder. Janis is obsessed." Olivia told Sage about Janis's angry reaction at The Frenchie Connection Inn. And then, because they hadn't spoken in days, she told her about Meadow and the shirts.

"Oh my goodness. Mom hates talking about farts. It's as if she never passed wind herself." Sage giggled. *Laughter helps*, Olivia thought. *I still feel sad, but not helpless.*

She had one more question. "How's our Star? Has she done anything interesting today?"

"She's sitting up and getting a tooth. Now I call that multi-tasking," Sage said with pride.

"How about I drop by after Woofstock is over and take her to Paws and Pines? She loved seeing the dogs last time."

"Good idea." Sage sounded pleased.

"Speaking of the shelter, I was talking to Janis the other day. She mentioned boarding a Shetland there. I had no idea. Name is Sparkles."

"Sparkles does board at Paws and Pines. She's been there since... Let me see. The Christmas before you arrived, when two of my students ran a gift-wrapping station in front of the library.

"Anyway, Sparkles ended up with Janis, and the pony is her soul mate. Crabby as all get out. All snort and whinny but no bite."

"The pony or Janis?" Olivia chuckled.

"Both. But Sparkles is kind of a special case. Before you came, she was owned by a clown." Sage cleared her throat. "That's another story. Why do you ask?"

"I was thinking Star might ride Sparkles, you know, eventually, when you think the time is right."

"I'd rather put her on a horse twice the size. You don't know Sparkles," warned Sage. "I'll have to introduce you. She's a handful. Breaks down the wall of her stall every month or so. She bucks and bolts. Star would have to be a very experienced rider, and by the time that happens, she'll be full grown and too heavy for a pony."

"The pony does sound like Janis."

"It's like they found each other. Of course Janis rarely sees her. Paws and Pines does most of the work. In fact, we use Sparkles to train interns. She's just feisty enough they drop any sentimental notions they have about ponies really fast."

Olivia smiled. "So Sparkles isn't a My Little Pony kind of personality. Is that what you're saying?"

"She hasn't bitten anyone. At least not yet. Gotta go. Catch you later, sis."

"Testing one, two, three," Olivia said into the microphone. The stage and sound equipment had been set up for the Woofstock closing concert. This would be their last rehearsal before Sunday evening.

Dee Dee, the bass player, smiled. She balanced the instrument on the end pin, her bow in the opposite hand, fingers sliding and tapping absentmindedly up and down the neck of the instrument.

Cornelius, the new percussionist, tossed a stick in the air. He caught it and then tossed the other stick, looking like a child who was bored and trying to entertain himself. But

Olivia knew that wasn't true. He was anything but bored. He just kept his hands busy until the time was right.

Technicians milled around the amphitheater, plugging in cables and testing connections as Sage played a perfectly tuned open A string.

Someone from the sound booth yelled. "Try it again, would ya? I'll mix the treble a bit more."

"Testing one, two, three," Olivia repeated into the microphone.

"Got it." He gave a thumbs-up, allowing her to return to her stool.

Sage held the fiddle underneath her chin. She moved her bow across each string, checking the pitch one more time. Olivia felt confident since she'd already tuned the autoharp backstage. Since she had so many more strings, it took longer.

Olivia called out, "Did you get the music to that song I told you about?"

"I did. Played it last night. So beautiful. I don't remember when I first heard it, but it was on a movie soundtrack."

Sage faced the front of the stage and began to play the chorus to the new song. The words came to Olivia immediately. She felt a shiver up her spine, and she began to sing.

After their rehearsal, a loud voice overrode the music. "Try the mic again. I adjusted the bass," he insisted.

She placed her autoharp under her stool and stood to stretch her arms over her head. "That went well," she said for the mic to pick up.

Dee Dee spoke up. "I think we should close on the new song. Let Olivia take it and then walk off stage. If the crowd wants more, we can return with an oldie but goodie."

Sage and Cornelius nodded agreement.

The sound engineer stepped close to the stage. "Okay,

everyone. That's it for now. See you Sunday for a last-minute check, then we're on at five."

"Olivia." Janis Jets gestured from the back exit. "I need to talk," the cop insisted.

"Here we go." Olivia nodded to the other band members.

"Thought I'd find you here," Janis mumbled. "I've got some information for you; I did some background checking into those Whitlock people."

"They're still your number one suspects?"

"Oh, they did it," Jets said with authority. "Why don't we take a minute and sit in the park, and I'll tell you what I know. That way I can keep an eye out for the tourists and the dogs. What a mess. I already had to cite three idiots for reckless abandonment."

"They left their children without supervision?" Olivia was shocked.

"No, their dogs. I was told that no one used a leash at the original Woodstock. And the purpose of Woofstock is to embrace that vibe. I can't wait for this so-called festival to be over."

Janis kept talking. "And your boy Maguire isn't exactly behaving. He's been hiding in the library. I thought this kind of thing would be his big moment. He should be at a table trading paw shakes for dog treats like he does at Christmas. Anyway, hurry up."

"No place to sit." Jets looked out at the overflowing Lily Rock park, a scowl on her face.

When she took a step, she nearly tripped over a Saint Bernard. She righted herself in time to avoid a fall.

The owner clasped the dog by the collar. "Sit down, Pumpkin," she commanded, giving Jets an apologetic nod.

"Just look at that, would you!" Jet pointed to a few feet away to an Airedale. He jumped four feet in the air to retrieve a frisbee. "No leash," muttered Jets.

"Someone's leaving over there." Olivia pointed to a woman who stood from a bench holding her cocker spaniel.

"You grab the seat," Jets ordered. "I have to have a word with that guy." Olivia watched as she made her way toward a miniature poodle who danced on hind legs without a leash or collar.

Olivia sighed as she sat. "It's taken," she told a man with a miniature white poodle. When he moved away, she shoved her autoharp underneath the bench to be out of the direct sun.

A red ball flew at her, and she ducked. It whizzed past her ear, followed by a short bark. *That was close.* A black Labrador pushed off on powerful back legs and caught the ball midair.

"Bring it here, Rufus," his owner called.

Olivia blinked as she rubbed her ear. She spotted something, and her heart fluttered. She blinked again, not believing what she saw.

A man holding a brindle-colored Frenchie stood partially hidden behind a giant redwood. *Is that...* Her heart thudded in her chest. Abandoning the bench, she pushed past a dog owner with two matching German Shorthaired Pointers who grabbed her seat.

That's Arlo. Olivia felt convinced. *He's hiding behind that tree. He's alive.*

Scrambling over the three-foot-tall rail fence, she broke into a run. She called out, "Arlo! It's me."

The man looked over. He turned and ran, disappearing into the crowd.

She stopped to catch her breath. Disappointment and

grief overwhelmed her, making it hard to breathe. She leaned against the redwood trunk for support.

For one moment, she'd convinced herself that Arlo was still alive. That it was all a mistake. That he'd come back. But now she knew the man wasn't Arlo. He was a figment of her imagination.

She made her way around the circumference of the giant redwood. One glance to the ground revealed no footprints.

Hands held against her face, she fought back tears. She wanted to argue. "It was him. And he had a brindle Frenchie. The dog looked at me as if he knew me. Those big dark eyes."

But no. She shook her head. Not Arlo but grief. *That's just me in denial.*

Janis Jets found her behind the tree.

She held Olivia's autoharp. "You left something." She handed it back.

Olivia took the instrument without speaking.

"What time's the concert on Sunday?" Janis asked.

"Five o'clock," Olivia said quietly.

"We have a lot of work to do before that. Why don't you leave your..." Jets pointed to the autoharp. "...instrument in my office for safekeeping. Better than under a public bench. I need to pick up my book of warrants. Left them in the desk."

"Okay." Olivia wiped away the remaining tears with her finger.

"You have something better to do?" Jets asked.

"Not really." She tucked the instrument under her arm.

"I need to tell you something." Olivia sat on a bench. She wanted to share about Arlo, how she'd seen him. How it wasn't him. How she felt. But Janis wasn't listening.

"Later, Nancy Drew. Take a look at this mess." Jets

nodded toward the park. Since they'd returned from the constabulary, the park looked even more crowded. Not just with dogs and owners. Two couples had set up camp with tents and cook stoves. They joked back and forth, pounding in stakes.

One woman wore a full blue skirt with a wide ruffle at the hem. A white peasant top exposed her shoulders. Another woman in a flowery maxi dress chatted with her as she unfolded a portable picnic table. She opened a tote.

They both stood back to admire the table with the daisy-patterned cloth.

"Check her out," Jets said. "So many flowers. The outfit and the table."

The camp attracted other women. One wandered closer. She was dressed in a sun bonnet, like an actor in a *Little House on the Prairie* episode. Done talking, the women joined hands.

"Tell me this isn't happening," Jets growled.

With their hands still joined, they circled around, reminding Olivia of young girls on a school playground.

"Those women think our park is a campground," Jets muttered. "Look at that!" She pointed to the other side, behind the redwoods. A woman created a clothesline with a rope between two trees.

How long do they think Woofstock is gonna last?" Jets said. "Mark my words. This is a disaster and it's not nearly over. Look, two more people hauling their camping gear."

Olivia realized that the festival and crowds of people only added to Janis's irritable mood. She could feel the cop's control slipping through her fingers. Jets even looked rattled, her eyes narrowed, darting from one person to the next.

I won't try to tell her about seeing Arlo, she decided. *I need to help soothe her nerves.* "I'm sure everyone will be gone by Sunday afternoon. This is just a temporary thing."

"I don't have enough backup to deal with this," Janis stated. "Mark my words. There will be alcohol and drugs, fights could break out. Is there an overdose tent?"

She looked behind herself and then to Olivia. "I remember the real *Woodstock*, I mean the film. I wasn't there in person. Not old enough... But they had an overdose tent. Maybe we need one of those."

Jets's voice rattled on in a most uncharacteristic tone.

Olivia tapped her arm. "This isn't Woodstock," she insisted. "This is a bunch of young wealthy people putting on costumes and taking their brand-new camping gear out for the first time. I'd call this glamping."

Jets stared at Olivia. Then she chuckled. "You're probably right. I'm making too big of a deal of this. It's only for a weekend. But..." She looked toward a circle of tents, "If I turn my back. I know these people will be getting naked and rolling in the mud."

"There isn't any mud," Olivia said calmly. "Just peace, love, rock and roll, man. "Check out those people. They look like they're posing for an Instagram photo."

Jets's eyes looked bleary. Then she coughed. "Okay, so maybe these folks have mixed their fashion sense metaphors. Early settlers with a dash of Yasgur's farm. I appreciate your perspective. But take a whiff. We might have more in common with the original Woodstock after all."

Olivia sniffed. "It's bad," she held her nose. "The dog poop."

"Just the tip of the pile," Jets said. "I warned the council. I knew this would happen eventually. Once people heard about our town, coming up for things like Woofstock. Then new businesses like The Frenchie Connection.

"Up until now we've been a small town. We pay a lot of attention to new businesses, making people apply and fill out the paperwork. I suppose we've neglected the other types of permits. Most of our community events get planned and executed by word of mouth. We'd just invite who we run into. You know, 'We're having a thing. Bring a casserole. See you at the park.'

"Look at this crowd. It's an invasion. Even if everyone packs up to go home on Sunday, they'll leave a lot of trash." Her voice grew raspy with irritation.

Olivia gave her a minute. Then she said, "You sound so pessimistic. Don't forget Lily Rock will make lots of money with the additional tourist trade. Small businesses will flourish. Every B&B, inn, and hotel will be booked to capacity, and we might get a name for ourselves."

Janis choked on her retort. Head turned away, she took a deep breath. "Since when have you become the town's spokesperson," Jets mumbled. "Like I said, take another sniff."

"I think they're grilling." Olivia deliberately changed the subject. "Look, an orderly line. That's civilized." She pointed toward a crowd across the park. They'd lined up in front of the community toilets. Dogs waited while humans chatted.

She sniffed again, hiding her nose in her elbow. She turned to Jets. "There's no plan for picking up the poop."

"That's right, girl detective. I already told the town council the poop is on them."

CHAPTER EIGHTEEN

"What?" Jets spoke into her cell. "You don't say. Tell him I'm busy." She clicked off and turned to Olivia. "Seems like Eldred Whitlock wants to talk to me. Brad told him I'd be available on Monday, but he wasn't taking no for an answer. Insists that I come right over to The Frenchie Connection Inn without delay.

"And then I got another message. Cooks called. He asked me to pick up all of the bags of frozen muffins and cookies at Thyme Out. He and Mike have been slammed with tourists."

"But what about the poop?" Olivia asked. "Are you really going to leave it to the town council?"

"I'll deal with that later. What about my number one suspect calling me to come over? I bet I got under his skin and he's scrambling." Jets smiled. "What a jerk. He played right into my hands. Now he'll start over explaining and then you'll catch him in that confession."

"You don't even know what he wanted," Olivia insisted. "He's a jerk, but that doesn't make him a murderer."

"Eldred wouldn't tell Brad on the phone. Said he needed to talk and that it was of the utmost importance. Something about a crime. According to my assistant he's afraid that his entire livelihood is in jeopardy."

Jets slapped both hands on her knees and stood. "Why don't we grab those baked goods from Thyme Out and then mosey on over to The Frenchie Connection Inn. I don't want him to think I'm in any hurry. But this may be the break in the case that I've been looking for."

"I suppose another muffin never hurts." Olivia patted her stomach. Before they could step away from the bench, two people scurried to take their place.

"He has a previous record," Jets informed Olivia on their walk.

"We still talking about Eldred Whitlock?" Olivia could barely keep up.

"I did some research. Eldred is an online gambler and got himself into a bit of trouble. The feds arrested him back in the early 2000s. He spent some time in minimum security for the crime. Looks like ol' Eldred isn't as well bred as he'd have us believe."

They reached Thyme Out just as a familiar couple stepped from the doorway. Sydney and Shelton held a paper bag each. "Fancy meeting you here," Shelly said. "We just got the last of the most delicious chocolate chip muffins with toasted pecans. To die for." His faced glowed with the victory.

Sydney Ayers smiled fondly at his husband. "He loves a warm muffin. After you, ladies." He held the door open.

Olivia felt him stare as she walked past. Instead of following Janis to the counter, she turned around. "Something on your mind?"

Sydney blushed. "As a matter of fact, there is something. Could we talk for a moment?"

"Be right back," she told Janis.

Sydney held the door as she slipped past. He pulled her

aside and then called out to his husband. "Hey sweetie, why don't you take that table inside and I'll be right with you. I have a question to ask the constabulary consultant."

His reference made Olivia feel self-conscious. *That's the first time I've been called that by a stranger.* Once Shelton was out of earshot, she asked, "What's on your mind?"

"I didn't want to say anything when we were checking in the other day," he began, "but I'm not here in Lily Rock just for a getaway. I'm here on a sensitive assignment for *It's a Dog's World.* And I'm thinking my assignment may be connected to your investigation. The death of Arlo Carson."

Olivia leaned closer, pretending she hadn't overheard his relation to the website at The Frenchie Connection Inn. "I'm listening."

"For the past year my publication has been hearing rumors about Eldred Whitlock and his French bulldog breeding operation. He's been inspected by the AKC on two occasions that we know of. Passed with flying colors, or so they say. But we think there's a bigger story that's not been revealed. At least as of yet."

"What does that mean exactly?"

"We think Whitlock may have paid off the previous inspectors."

Olivia registered surprise. "But I thought the AKC was on the up and up. An accredited organization."

"Even a group like the AKC has donors who call the shots," he explained. "When you peel back the cover of their organization, you find out lots of things."

"Like what kind of things?"

"Like unscrupulous breeding practices for one. The breeding of Frenchies is a tedious and specific practice, I can tell ya that." He sniffed in distaste.

"I've heard," she told him.

"But that's not all. There's a financial piece that *Dog's World* is even more interested in. That includes how Eldred ships specimens. The contracts he makes with other breeders. And how much he charges for each attempt at fertilization."

"I think you should share your concerns with Officer Jets," Olivia concluded. "She'll want to hear from you."

"I could do that, but you're much easier to talk to. That one"—he pointed to Janis just as she exited the bakery—"has too many opinions."

Janis Jets held a cardboard box in both arms. Plastic freezer bags spilled over the top. "Let's get going. Before these get stale."

"Mr. Ayers has something to tell you," Olivia said.

"Maybe later. I have to deliver the baked goods."

"And visit The Frenchie Connection Inn," she insisted.

"That too." Jets glared.

Olivia turned to Sydney. "There's been a complaint by Eldred Whitlock."

The reporter's eyes lit up. "That's really interesting. May I come along?"

"Not on your life," Jets snapped.

He leaned closer to Olivia. "Why don't you call me afterwards. I'd love to hear about Whitlock's complaint."

Jets sat in a chair across from Eldred Whitlock. Olivia sat next to her.

"Featherington the Fifth is missing," Eldred began in a loud voice.

Olivia blinked. The volume of his voice made her want to give him a good Meadow-the-librarian shush.

"He was abducted at the dog park. That idiot Quigley got

distracted. He turned his back. Any my prize stud is nowhere to be found.

"According to him, he only turned his back for a second to deposit the poop in the can. Then when he turned back around, Featherington the Fifth had vanished. I can't believe that idiot is still on my payroll."

Eldred stood up and shoved his chair so hard, it crashed into the credenza. The matchbooks fell to the floor. He bent over to pick them up and then walked around the desk. He paced back and forth, mumbling under his breath.

"Don't you have insurance on your famous stud?" Jets asked. "Maybe it's time to get someone off the bench. Another Featherington from the rookies. You've got a male queued up, don't you? I bet you'll have Frenchie females lining up for the opportunity with a younger stud."

"That's not how it works," Eldred fumed. "By the time I explain about a replacement with Featherington the Sixth, interested people with females will have already moved on. No one wants to be put off, and a missing dog may ruin my reputation. My entire livelihood down the drain because Quigley tossed a bag of dog poop." He ran his hands through his hair.

"You have no idea," he continued to rant. "It takes months of planning and legal paperwork to arrange a breeding contract. Assuming that goes smoothly, the insemination process could take weeks. The female doesn't always get pregnant the first time. And then we wait for the next heat. And then after that, if she's pregnant, there's the vet appointments and the long wait until delivery."

"Not as long as a human's wait," Olivia reasoned.

"Sixty-three days, give or take. Watching the dam to see if she stays in peak health. Then the C-section. That's a nail-biter."

Whitlock paused. "I don't have to keep explaining. You have a job to do. I expect the fullest cooperation from the Lily Rock constabulary. You have to find Featherington the Fifth as soon as possible. Otherwise I'll sue the police department for damages; if I have to cancel contracts and renegotiate, it will cost me a fortune."

"You sound kinda desperate," Jets stated sarcastically. "I think you're overreacting. So tell me, Eldred. Are there other financial problems I should know about?"

"I don't want to lose this business." Eldred groaned. He didn't take Jets's bait.

"You're kinda obsessive over your Frenchies. Maybe that's because they're a meal ticket, not a hobby," Jets suggested.

At the word "obsessive," Olivia could barely contain herself. *Like Janis is any different with her fur baby.*

"You need to calm down," Jets told Eldred. "Look at this from the dog's point of view. Maybe Featherington the Fifth got tired of being your meal ticket. This place may be too posh for his taste. So he took off and joined the Woofstock event out of boredom. I bet you'll find him mingling with the mongrels, having the time of his life."

Eldred's face turned red. "What is that supposed to mean? Associating with the festival aside, it's your job to find my Frenchie. I'm reporting a theft and it better be your top priority."

He began to mumble under his breath. "How dare you insinuate that my dog would run away. He has the very best of accommodations. He eats fresh food and is exercised and—"

"Blah, blah, blah," Jets scoffed. "I've heard all that before. And it doesn't matter much to me one way or another. I was just trying to pull your chain. Looks like it worked. Anyway, let me get this straight. You weren't at the dog park when he disappeared."

"No, I was not."

"Just your employee taking care of the dog." Jets stared him down.

"That is correct."

"Then why aren't I talking to him instead of you? He's the eyewitness to the disappearance."

"I called Quigley. He's helping Uma. The T-shirt table is taking up at lot of time now that the festival is officially open. He said he'd come right over to talk to you as soon as he's done."

Eldred raised both hands in exasperation. "Isn't there something you can do in the meantime? File a report, for instance. Call in the canine rescue. Alert other cops to help in a search. I'll offer a reward. Ten thousand dollars for his return." Eldred dropped his arms, walked to the other side of his desk, and pulled out a checkbook.

"I thought you were in dire financial circumstances. Where's the reward money coming from?" Jets asked.

"My wife," he commented in a low voice. "She can help me out if necessary."

Jets sat with her hands on her knees. She'd not reached for her tablet to take notes.

"I have news for you, Whitlock. The Woofstock festival is my highest priority this weekend. I'll require a few more days to tidy up the mess those wanna-be hippies will inevitably leave. And maybe then I'll look for the missing Featherington the Fifth. End of next week would be the earliest." She stood and tapped his desk with her knuckles.

"What you can do to further things along is send me Quigley. Assuming I have a minute, I'll get more details from him. But I suggest you keep busy. You seem really nervous. Maybe play a little online poker. I hear you're pretty good at that."

"How did you know..." he sputtered.

"We small-town cops have our ways," she assured him. "Did a little research since the last time we spoke. Gotta go now. But if and when your mutt shows up, let me know. I bet he'll have Woofstock cotton candy on his face and a big smile."

Janis grinned, enjoying her own joke. "I'm pretty sure a good-looking poodle would be right up his alley. Imagine how adorable the puppies will be." She signaled to Olivia with a quick nod that it was time to go.

CHAPTER NINETEEN

On the drive back to town, Olivia spoke first. "So what do you think? A mob of Frenchie thieves grabbed Featherington? Will they ask for a ransom? Or maybe wait for Whitlock to post the reward and then collect. That would be my bet."

"On the one hand, I hope the mutt is safe," Jets said. "I'd hate to have something bad happen to any dog." She merged into the main highway traffic. "But on the other hand, I don't have time to chase after an overpriced stud. The town is awash in tourists and dog poop." Jets made a face. "Like I've been saying, when the Old Rockers were planning this crazy festival, no one bothered to consult me. I'm beginning to wonder if I've lost control."

Maybe I can help. Olivia pulled out her phone. "I heard about this small business. Let me see if they're online." She began to scroll. "Here it is. A company that picks up dog waste. They take it back to their location and compost it. After some kind of process, the poop can be reused as soil amendment. Very posh and eco. Really costly."

"What's the name of the company?" Jets asked.

"Doody Calls." Olivia grinned. "I have it right here. They

have a twenty-four-hour hotline and will make themselves available on late notice. Oh, and get this! The team arrives in hazmat suits."

"Might ruin the reenactment vibe." Jets smirked. "I'm liking the sound of Doody Calls. I'll tell Brad to get on this. Thanks, Olivia.

"Wait a minute. I have another idea. Just to show the town council they can't do this again without talking to me, I'm going to have the Doody Calls bill sent right to the town council treasurer. It serves them right, dumping this on my plate. Get it? Dumping." Jets smiled at herself in the rearview mirror.

As the silence grew, Olivia decided to try again. "So I have something else I want to share."

Jets snapped. "I hate it when people say, 'I have something else.' I even hate the word 'share.' It goes right up there with 'we need to talk.' Nothing good comes from those kinds of conversations."

Because someone else's opinion may disagree with yours, Olivia thought. She instantly regretted her judgment. And then she knew for certain that she'd made a mistake. *Janis isn't Cayenne.*

I miss Cayenne, and I'm trying to find someone to fill her place. Cay would have understood about seeing someone who wasn't actually there. She'd have been intrigued and asked me thoughtful questions. She'd have pulled some truth from the experience. But that was Cay. She didn't see the difference between this world and the next one like most people. She lived her life looking for meaning. Do I make up an excuse or just tell Janis and get this over with?

Jets finally looked over. "Okay, tell me. I hate silent treatments. Don't have to get your panties in a bunch."

Regret lay heavy on Olivia's heart. *But now that I've*

started, the best way forward is to just tell the truth. "Before you arrived this morning, I saw something or someone in the park who looked just like Arlo. He held a brindle-colored Frenchie in his arms. And he smiled at me. And the dog stared at me with soulful eyes. When I came closer, they both disappeared."

Jets issued another side glance. "So you think you actually saw Arlo. You know he's dead, right? We both viewed the blood and his body."

"It was Arlo. I tried go after him, but he vanished. And then I realized I might have imagined the whole thing. But now that Featherington the Fifth is missing, I wondered if there was something to it. Maybe it was Arlo trying to warn me."

Olivia's voice trembled. "It's only been a few days since he passed. Could he, you know, be hanging around? One of those restless spirits, like on that old show *The Ghost Whisperer?*"

Jets shook her head. She looked exasperated. "I readily admit you have a slightly unusual gift. Kinda spooky at times. But now you're telling me that you see dead people. Are you really saying you're some kind of ghost whisperer who helps out stuck souls until they walk into the light? Just so you know, that's not real police work."

Olivia didn't expect Janis to believe her. But she knew the appearance of Arlo, real or not, meant something. Without Cayenne, she had no opportunity to explain and bounce ideas around.

Cookie Kravitz's name flashed on Janis's cell phone screen. "Oh hi, sweetie," she said before it had a chance to ring.

She's avoiding this conversation, Olivia realized. *I've made a big mistake telling her.*

"You okay?" Cookie's voice, along with a crowd in the

background, came through the speaker. "I left a message but didn't hear from you. I was wondering if you'd stop by Thyme Out and bring me the frozen cookies and muffins. We're gonna need them."

"I got the message," Janis drawled. "Baked goods already defrosting in the back seat."

"I owe you." Cookie chuckled his relief.

"I'm driving with Olivia. We're heading to town. Should be there shortly."

"Don't hang up," he said excitedly. "You're going to love the Woofstock crowd. It reminds me of a Renaissance Faire. People here are dressed like fancy hippies. Lots of tie-dye. One woman set up a table to sew braided fringe on people's bell-bottom jeans. Men and women with long hair and leather hats. A few afros. Patchwork skirts and peasant tops. Quite the scene." He sounded breathless. "We ran out of everything. It's only Friday. I'll be baking tonight."

"Great, honey. Olivia and I will be right over." She rolled her eyes. "By the way," she continued, "would you keep an eye out for any Frenchies that stop by your table? Especially fancy ones. A brindle male has gone missing."

"Come on, they're all pretty fancy," Cookie chuckled.

"Tater Tot is not a dog I'd call fancy," Janis argued. "He's one of a kind. A sturdy example of masculinity, just like his human father."

"Is he with you? Tater, buddy, it's me, your dad." Cookie lapsed into baby talk.

Janis interjected, "He's with Brad. I don't want him to be sniffing butts with any of these out-of-town mutts. He might pick up a bad habit or a stuffy nose.

"Like I said, keep your eye out. We've had a dognapping incident and I want to stay on top of it. I'll see you shortly." She clicked the phone off.

"So you really are concerned about Featherington the Fifth," Olivia said.

"Like I said, I don't want any harm coming to the overbred mutt."

Janis pulled the truck into her reserved parking space. She reached for her cell to make a call as Olivia stepped onto the pavement. The door slammed behind her. To her surprise, Meadow was waiting.

"There's a dog poop problem in the park," she announced. "I don't know what to do. The town council doesn't know what to do. There's not enough of us available to pick up after them. Arlo would have been our go-to organizer. But now..." Her eyes filled with tears.

"We've got a plan." Jets walked around the truck. "Just talked to my assistant. Doody Calls is on the way."

CHAPTER TWENTY

Janis dumped the box on the table in front of Cookie. "Here you go. I cleaned out the freezer. I hope you have enough."

Cookie lifted the bags from the box, inspecting each one over his sunglasses. "We'll make lots of money with these. Thanks, babe."

Michael leaned over to greet Olivia with a kiss. "We're very popular," he told her proudly. "Already ran out of cookies, dog treats, and can't brew the coffee fast enough."

"I heard." She turned to look at the setup. A collection of retail goods and foodstuffs had been arranged on tables. Vendors stood behind tables, chatting with customers about their wares.

Straw had been strewn on the ground to keep down the dust. Her eyes stopped on Uma Whitlock. She stood behind stacks of shirts, folded and organized by color.

Olivia expected to see George Quigley. But it was Shelton Ayers who chatted with Uma. She giggled and touched his arm. He leaned over to whisper in her ear.

She turned back to Michael. "Uma's doing a good business."

"She stopped by earlier to speak with Cookie," Michael mumbled. "Uma is concerned that Thyme Out no longer delivers dog treats to The Frenchie Connection Inn. Apparently the treats were a huge hit with her customers. People are complaining."

Cookie interrupted. "I made no excuse. I tried to explain how the inn's exclusivity rules didn't fit in Lily Rock, that we make it a point to welcome everyone. She got upset and argued. But then she got around our boycott. She pulled out her credit card and Venmo and bought us out. I couldn't say no without making it a big deal."

"You tried," Michael said. "That Uma's a tough nut."

Jets looked up from her phone and scowled. "Like I was telling Olivia, this Woofstock thing has me worried. Nothing good will come from inviting a bunch of tourists to town. I have a lot on my mind right now, so if you'll excuse me." She didn't offer a goodbye.

Cookie frowned. "Arlo's death is eating away at her. She knows who killed him." He lowered his sunglasses to look Olivia in the eye. "It's a good thing you're helping her out. She's not her usual self. We've been up nights with Tater Tot. He's had some breathing issues." Cookie pointed to his nose.

"That's difficult," Olivia agreed.

Before she could say more, Michael spoke. "Can you handle the traffic? I'd like to walk around with Olivia and check out the competition. Unless you need me here."

"No problem. I don't suppose Janis'll be back for a while." Cookie opened a plastic storage bag to remove the bakery-made dog cookies. Michael came from around the table to take Olivia's hand.

"Let's leave now," he whispered in her ear. "Before he changes his mind."

"I want to look at Uma's booth," she announced. With a yank on his hand, she dragged him away.

Stacks of red, navy blue, and white T-shirts gave the table a patriotic vibe. "Let's get Cookie and Janis a gift for Tater Tot," Olivia said.

Michael's brow wrinkled. "What for?"

"As a welcome to your forever home kind of thing."

"I see. I suppose that's a good idea." He glanced past the table. "Where is Uma anyway..."

"Over there." Olivia pointed. Closer to the woods, way behind the table, Uma and Shelly sat side by side in folding chairs. They were deep in conversation.

"Those two are cozy," Michael commented right as Uma reached her index finger to lightly touch Shelly's cheek.

"I guess they're friends," Olivia commented. She picked up a shirt. "Check this one out." The front spelled Security in bold black letters. Michael chuckled.

"Perfect. Unless you want those." He pointed at two shirts, one for a dog and the other for a human, both in red with black print. The large one read "Where I Go, Trouble Follows." The small one only had one word: "Trouble."

"Not this time. Maybe for Christmas." Olivia smiled. She thumbed through the stack for more.

"May I help you?" Uma stood behind the table and pointed to the yellow shirt in Olivia's hand. "All my shirts are wash and wear, a blend of cotton and polyester." Her voice sounded smooth and confident. "No returns or refunds." Uma pointed to the notice at the corner of her table.

"I'm buying a shirt for my friend's dog. He's a Frenchie. Do you think a medium is too big?" Olivia asked.

"Depends on the Frenchie," Uma said in a helpful tone. "The females run smaller. My husband's dog—he's a male—wears a medium. Of course I prewash in hot water first, to make sure it will still fit after you launder. How much does your friend's dog weigh?"

Olivia met Uma's friendly gaze but didn't respond. *She's kind of nice when she isn't running her inn.* Then she turned to Michael. "You're good at sizing things up. How much do you think Tater Tot weighs?"

"I only saw him briefly. I'd say twenty pounds, give or take," he instantly replied. "Tater is still a puppy."

"Then I'd go with the medium," Uma advised.

Olivia handed over the shirt as Michael reached for his wallet.

Once Uma finished the transaction, she turned to Michael. "You're Cookie's business partner, right?"

"Cookie and I have a side gig. I'm Michael Bellemare. We live up the hill from your inn. We're neighbors."

"Oh." Uma's eyes grew wide. "I've heard about you. The famous architect." She offered her hand for a shake. "Can I get you anything else? We have a festival T-shirt for pets if you want to have a look. A lovely tie-dye."

Finished with their browsing, Olivia and Michael sat in the park sipping lemonade.

"Janis has a right to be concerned. I've never seen the center of town so chaotic," he observed. Just inches away, two women played catch with a frisbee while their golden retriever ran from one to the other, barking incessantly.

"Meadow and Janis are beside themselves." Olivia took a sip from her straw. "What did you think of Uma?"

"She seems nice enough. Did you tell me she's one of Janis's suspects? I don't see her knifing somebody in the armpit. Feels a bit off to me."

"I agree," Olivia admitted. "Janis is focusing on Uma's

husband right now. She stole what she thinks is the murder weapon from his desk. And she's doing a deep background check into his past. I'm not sure she has any warrants to make her search legal. And she's not following up with the search at Arlo's cabin. I thought she'd do that right away but apparently not.

"I'm concerned she's setting up Eldred. And if that doesn't work she'll turn to Uma and do the same."

"She can't get a conviction with sloppy police work," Michael said.

"She thinks I'm her answer. That I'll get the confession so she won't need the evidence." Olivia shuddered.

Michael ducked as a frisbee flew over his head. The golden retriever chased after it, barking excitedly.

Two other dogs, a German shepherd and a Rottweiler mix, joined him. All three barked at a bush where the frisbee landed. "No one's enforcing the leash policy," Michael shouted over the barking.

"Janis is busy," Olivia reminded him.

One of the women arrived to retrieve the frisbee. A quick jerk of the wrist and it flew back into the park toward her friend. The dogs right behind.

Michael began to chuckle. "Remind me to skip the town council meeting when they sort out this weekend and start placing the blame on each other."

"They'll blame Arlo," Olivia realized. "Since he's not here to defend himself."

"Wouldn't surprise me," he agreed. "But what are you going to do with Janis? That's a problem. Do you think you can get a confession? That's a lot of pressure to put on a volunteer."

"I want to help," she insisted. "But I've tried to reason with her and she just doesn't listen. Plus there's the journalist." When Michael looked curious, she filled him in.

"Interesting," Michael admitted. "So how did you end the conversation with Ayers?"

"We got cut off when Janis came back with Cookie's baked goods."

"What was your take on Eldred Whitlock?" Michael asked. "Does he seem like the murdering type?"

"Whitlock has an alibi. So he's not even a real suspect," Olivia insisted.

"But Janis found a possible murder weapon on his desk in his office," Michael reminded her.

"But she stole the weapon. Even if they found blood evidence, it wasn't legally obtained. And anyone could have left the letter opener just to implicate Eldred. He doesn't seem like a man who has many friends."

"I guess that's possible," he responded thoughtfully. "I can see that now."

Olivia reached into her pocket. "I have Ayers's business card right here. Maybe I'll give him a call and tell him about Featherington the Fifth being missing. Act like I'm helping with his article."

Michael took the card to read. "What if I come with you, you know, as the consultant to the consultant." He winked.

"I'd like that," she agreed. "By the way, you've been really helpful listening to me with all of this. I know you're not a fan of me working on police business, so thank you. Usually I go over my suspicions with Janis, but she's emotionally unavailable right now."

"Janis is now a mother. Her priorities have shifted." Michael smiled.

Olivia rolled her eyes.

CHAPTER TWENTY-ONE

Sydney Ayers agreed to meet Olivia in front of The Frenchie Connection Inn. "This would be a good time," he'd told her. "Uma's at her Woofstock table and Eldred's out searching for Featherington the Fifth. I can show you around the breeding lab."

Michael parked in front of the inn. He stood at the entrance outside, shielding his eyes from the sun. "Nice structure," he commented. "Made to look mountain-rustic. I've seen this in Colorado and Wyoming."

Sydney Ayers came through the door, his glance stopping on Michael.

"This is my partner, Michael Bellemare," Olivia explained. "I invited him along."

"I see." He looked Michael up and down. "Another French bulldog lover," he commented dryly.

"Not me," Michael admitted. "I'm a tagalong."

"Okay then. Follow me. I want you to see this. Then you'll know why I'm—I mean my editor—is so concerned. Breeders get used to what they do behind closed doors. But to the average person, it seems odd. Not that you're average." He took another look at Michael. "But you're inexperienced with the dog world. That's what I meant to say. That's why I want your take."

They followed Ayers through the lobby, down the hall toward Eldred Whitlock's office. "Close that door, would you?" Ayers instructed.

"Looks like a normal business office," Michael commented.

"Of course this looks normal. But you need to see what's behind curtain number one." Ayers pushed aside the full-length curtain Olivia had previously wondered about to reveal a door and a large plate-glass window. The window reminded Olivia of a hospital nursery, where visitors would stand and point at newborns, holding balloons and wearing smiles.

She looked through the glass and asked, "Is it a nursery or a veterinarian's office?" There were upper and lower cabinets lining two walls. The banks of cabinets were separated with a stainless-steel countertop.

A stainless-steel examination table sat in the center of the room. Olivia could see no other windows or doors. *To gain access, you have to go through Eldred's office.*

Michael moved beside Olivia. "Why is this room so carefully concealed?"

"You may know already that the breeders of French bulldogs, the ethical ones, use artificial insemination," Sydney began.

Olivia felt her stomach tighten as he continued.

"I know. Most people don't want to talk about the how of high-end dog breeding, and I understand. But I think the public needs to know. The French bulldog became the most popular breed in 2022. Everyone thinks they're so adorable, but no one stops to consider how they breed the little darlings to get them purchased and into households."

"I know they cost a lot," Michael said.

"Besides the exclusivity and the markup, the breeding practices themselves cost a fortune. The room you're looking at is Featherington the Fifth's breeding room. Only for him," he said flatly. "Whitlock brings his stud to the same place every time so that he's comfortable with the surroundings. They play calming music and provide the scent of fertile females on cotton swabs, just to get the dog interested. And then Whitlock collects the specimen by using artificial plastic replicas of the female."

Olivia felt the blood rush from her head. *I don't think I want to hear anything more about this.* Ayers nodded toward her. "But it's more than that. Once the dam is pregnant, she requires constant supervision and a C-section delivery. The cost mounts up because none of this is exactly what you'd call natural. Lots of vets and paid employees."

"Plus I've heard Frenchies have a lot of health problems to begin with. Is that true?" Michael asked.

"That's putting it mildly," said Ayers. "Frenchies are prone to skin, eye, and ear infections for one. Considered one of the brachycephalic breeds, they are susceptible to respiratory distress, heat intolerance, and frequent vomiting.

"Then later in life they can have spine deformation and nerve pain," he added.

Michael ran his hand over his own lower back. "I know about that. I'm not as young as I used to be."

Olivia suppressed a grin as Sydney kept talking. "The high-volume breeders, known as puppy mills, don't stop to consider the consequences. All they care about is the cuteness factor.

"Some experts say that Frenchies are popular because they look like humans with their small nose and wide-set eyes. Even the way the dog smiles looks a bit human. And then

Frenchies have that way of vocalizing in the back of their throats, which sounds kind of human."

"Projection," Olivia interjected. "Humans project themselves onto their dog." *Just like Janis and Tater Tot.*

"That can be a serious problem," Ayers stated firmly. "And I'm going to expose Eldred Whitlock for the unscrupulous breeder he is. I want to raise public awareness, and maybe I'll even get a Pulitzer for my investigative journalism. I'm not stopping until the public knows every detail, no matter how uncomfortable."

Aware from Ayers's tone of voice that he was on a mission, Olivia took a quick glance at Michael. *He has such a great poker face. Didn't even flinch at the mention of the Pulitzer.*

"Step back," Ayers said. He slid the curtain closed, his attention now on Olivia. "You said on the phone you had something to tell me about Eldred."

"Could we get out of his office before we talk about him behind his back?" Michael said. He turned to open the door.

Once in the lobby, Ayers turned to Michael. "So what do you think?"

"I think I prefer cats," Michael said immediately.

"That's not the point." Ayers's eyes narrowed. He turned to Olivia. "What about you? You're the one who's connected to Whitlock. Isn't he your main suspect in the death of that Lily Rock resident?"

"Arlo Carson," Olivia said. "I do think Officer Jets is considering Whitlock as a person of interest. But he has an alibi, backed up by his wife. We might find out more once forensics takes control of his laptop."

Ayers frowned. "Even if he didn't kill Carson, he's still an unscrupulous breeder. And there's no excuse for that."

Michael took her by the hand before she could answer. "We have to go now. Time to feed Mayor Maguire."

Olivia looked at him quizzically. She knew that was an excuse, and she was relieved. To tell Ayers anything more might compromise the investigation. But Michael's mention of Mayor Maguire bothered her. *When did I last see him?*

"We have to go now," she hastily agreed.

Ayers nodded. "Contact me if you hear anything more about the investigation, or Whitlock for that matter."

She turned to follow Michael to the exit.

"I expected to see the mayor on our front doorstep." Michael unlocked their door.

Olivia put her purse on the kitchen counter. "He acted so strangely at Lady of the Rock, refusing to come inside when Meadow offered a cookie. I wonder if he's okay."

"Maybe he's down in the park trading paw shakes for treats. So let's relax and have a quiet dinner. If he doesn't turn up by morning, then we'll look for him."

Olivia tied an apron around her waist. She turned to pull salad vegetables from the bin in the refrigerator. Stacking the lettuce, tomatoes, and cucumber on the counter, she grabbed a cutting board and a knife and began to chop. She looked outside hoping to see the mayor.

"Nice salad." Michael had changed into a soft blue flannel shirt that hung over his jeans. "I'm going to pour a beer. You ready for some sparkling water?"

"Sure," she mumbled absentmindedly.

She put down the knife. "I'm still concerned about Maguire," she admitted.

"He may be dining with someone else this evening," Michael reasoned.

"I know he's free range. But he's pretty much picked us for his meals. He even sleeps here most nights."

"I'll get steaks ready for the grill. Let's sit outside with our drinks. It's been a long time since we've done that." She could tell he was trying to distract her from worrying.

"Sure." Olivia slid the salad bowl to the center of the island.

It had been a while since they'd made an evening about them. He'd gone upstairs to shower and put on casual clothes. *Maybe I can do the same...*

She picked up her drink. "I'll go upstairs and freshen up. Meet you out front," she told him.

The last few days, with Arlo's death and now a missing Mayor Maguire, made her antsy. *Plus Janis*, she told herself. *I've gotten myself all tied in knots.*

CHAPTER TWENTY-TWO

The following morning, Michael greeted Olivia in the kitchen with a mug of fresh coffee. "Hey, sleepyhead."

She took the mug from his hand. "I was up most of the night. Any sign of Maguire?" She turned her head to yawn.

"Not at the back door. We'll go looking right after breakfast." He dropped two pieces of sourdough into the toaster.

Olivia opened the back door to look outside. Sometimes Maguire got distracted with a squirrel. Instead of a familiar bork, a crow greeted her overhead. No sign of Mayor Maguire anywhere. No rushing past her legs to get to his food bowl. No smell of dog on the run.

"You want jam on this?" called Michael.

"Not hungry," she called back, feeling irritation rise in her gut.

He came closer to stare over her shoulder. "We can take the toast and coffee in the truck. Start right now."

She closed the door, unable to answer.

He waited for a reply, and when he didn't get one, he said, "I'll get things ready."

While Michael put the jam away and then dropped the

buttered toast slices into a plastic bag, she knew her silence must be bothering him. But she really had nothing to say. Like yesterday, when she longed for Cayenne.

Michael was a get-things-done kind of guy, but Cayenne, she liked to talk through the meaning of everything just like Olivia. *I've lost her. I've lost Arlo. And now Janis is acting weird. I need Maguire, and Michael isn't as concerned about him as me. First he wanted to have an evening together, now he wants to eat breakfast before we search; he doesn't care enough.*

She looked at the plastic bag with two slices of toast inside. *I told him I'm not hungry,* she complained to herself. *Why didn't he listen?*

Michael popped a bite of toast in his mouth and began to crunch loudly. "Ready?" he asked.

Stop chewing! her mind screamed. *I can hear your jaw popping from across the room.* She looked around. Unexpected impatience clouded her judgment. *I hate this kitchen. There's no window over the sink. Nowhere to look out at the woods. I really need some alone time.*

He stared at her, a look of confusion on his face.

And you're clueless, or just pretending to be. She sniffed.

Michael held up the bag with toast. "There's more for you," he coaxed.

"I'm not Mayor Maguire," she snapped. The look of hurt on his face didn't help. The mood had taken hold of her, pushing out any semblance of goodwill.

If he asks, "What's the matter, honey?" I'm going to scream. It should be obvious.

Olivia did not take the toast. She honored her feelings of frustration instead. Her mind picked up where it had left off. *I liked our table in the other kitchen. So cozy. And by now, friends would be dropping in for a cup of coffee. Mayor*

Maguire would be begging for bites of toast. No one will come here. It's too far away from town and way too fancy.

She reached for the plastic bag and pulled out a slice. Then she took a huge bite. *Take that*, she thought, appreciating the loud crunch. Chomping her teeth, she swallowed and smacked her lips.

Why does that feel so good? Okay, I'm going in for a second bite.

Michael waited and watched, his face drawn with concern.

By the time she'd finished the first slice of overly crispy sourdough, she was in the rhythm, eating and enjoying every minute. *Nonverbal communication works for me*, she decided, reaching for the second slice.

She tilted her head to the side to watch him as she took the last noisy bite.

"You seem to be enjoying your breakfast more than usual. Are you by any chance mad at me?"

Olivia licked her bottom lip. She savored the butter without answering.

"Are you going to tell me about what's bothering you?" She could hear the strain in his voice.

"I am not." She reached for a napkin and made a thorough job of wiping her lips and chin.

"So that's the way it's gonna be. You not telling me what's bothering you and now I have to guess. I know it has something to do with Maguire."

"Yep."

Let him think this is all about M&M.

"And the investigation."

"Yep." *Look at him trying to read my mind and getting it wrong again. I'm liking this.*

"But there's something else, isn't there..." His voice wavered.

When she didn't offer another confirmation, his bottom lip drooped.

"Want a hug?" His eyes lit up.

"Nope." She dumped most of her coffee into the kitchen sink. "I have to get my shoes." She felt his eyes on her back as she walked toward the stairs and disappeared from his view.

It wasn't until she pulled on her boots that she let her feelings out. Sobs filled her chest. *I hate this house. It's just not my home.* Once the tears stopped, her irritation lessened. She ran a cold cloth over her face and looked at herself in the mirror. *You're not yourself either, Olivia Greer. You've been pointing that finger at Janis, and now you're mad at Michael. You're angry at Arlo for dying and at Cayenne for leaving you to cope alone. You're one big mess.*

She made her way downstairs, pushing all thoughts away except Mayor Maguire's whereabouts.

Michael drove his truck onto the main street. Dogs and people already filled the boardwalk. Vehicles, stacked bumper to bumper, lined the road. The park was filled to overflowing with people and grills. "Looks like a tent city," Michael said, echoing her thoughts.

Then she realized something. "What about the redwoods?" She groaned.

Lily Rock's mission was to preserve the giant redwoods and keep them safe. Arlo was the one to spearhead the conservation program. He worked for months, pitching in with labor, gathering a volunteer workforce. And now all of his planning and effort was gone, as tourists trampled the redwood roots, constructing campgrounds in their shade. "The Old Rockers will be furious," Olivia said.

Michael inched forward in traffic. He hit the palm of his hand against the steering wheel with exasperation. "Ouch," he moaned.

Normally Olivia would ask about the pain, but she wasn't in the mood. Instead she looked back at the park, flaming her irritation. People mingled in small groups, chatting with each other. A man dumped his cold coffee over the trunk of a redwood.

"I wonder where Janis is," Olivia fumed. "Isn't she supposed to be warning people about the dogs and the trees, issuing some citations and tickets?"

A chorus of barking came on cue. A pack of dogs ran through the crowd from person to person. They stopped when offered food and then moved on. None wore a leash. One Labrador circled a Chihuahua. He lowered his nose to sniff the small dog's tail. The Labrador backed off, but only after his advances were met with a series of high-pitched yips. The Lab wagged his tail, but the Chihuahua wasn't interested.

The smell and smoke from outdoor grills made Olivia cough. *Visitors have no idea about the fire danger in Lily Rock.* "Janis is going to have to shut this down," Olivia told Michael. "There's a risk of fire."

"I agree." Michael accelerated to close the gap behind the car ahead, then he slammed on his brakes and muttered, "Tourists." He turned to Olivia. "Look at those outdoor grills."

Three kettle-shaped barbecues lined one side of the park. People milled around, eating and talking. "I smell sausage." Her stomach growled.

"I'm surprised the fire department hasn't shown up. Open fires are strictly prohibited." Michael slammed a foot on the brake again. Olivia's neck jutted forward then back.

"Ouch." She rubbed the back of her neck.

"Sorry about that," he mumbled. "That BMW guy is a terrible driver." He raised his palm to slam on his horn but then stopped midair. "What the..." He pointed toward the park.

Olivia began to chuckle. "Well look at that," she said. They weren't the only ones to notice. Vehicles came to a complete standstill. Drivers and passengers looked toward the center of town. The pack of dogs froze. People who stood by the outdoor grills stopped talking. One woman held her breakfast burrito midair as if afraid to take the next bite.

Three figures elbowed their way through the crowd, dressed in identical hazmat suits and masks that shielded their head and face.

"Looks like we've been invaded by Stormtroopers," Michael said.

Olivia watched with fascination as a flick of one of the workers' wrists slid a mound of dog waste onto the dustpan.

"They're not Stormtroopers," she explained, "they're Doody Calls. A company Janis hired. They pick up dog waste, compost it back at the plant, and make it useable for consumers to sprinkle on their plants."

Michael sighed. "Looks like we've been Lily Rocked."

CHAPTER TWENTY-THREE

Each Doody employee held a rake in one hand and a dustpan in the other. "That guy's really fast," Olivia noted. With another flick of the wrist, the rake deposited a pile of poop into the pan.

Michael chuckled. "I've heard of them. They charge a fortune to pick up dog poop. The space suit and the ordinary household tools—that's quite a sight."

Olivia stuck her head out the open window for a closer view. "At least the dogs have gotten quiet." She pulled her head back.

The sight of the unexpected shifted her mood. She no longer felt annoyed with herself or Michael. Until a nagging voice inside her head gave one last push. *Don't give in. You still have that house problem.*

She recoiled back into a cloak of resentment.

"We still don't have a place to park," Michael commented.

She crossed her arms over her chest, refusing to speak.

"There's a space." Michael executed a U-turn in the middle of the road. Accelerating past another car, he slipped into the spot. A horn honked disapproval. The man in the waiting car shook his fist.

"I'm a resident," Michael insisted. "I get special privileges." He raised his hand to lift his middle finger, then looked at her to find a scowl on her face. "Don't be so judgy." He dropped his hand, staring ahead.

Michael opened the door. "Let's find Maguire," he muttered.

Olivia and Michael stood outside the fence at The Frenchie Connection Dog Park. "I know those two." She pointed. "One is Juicy Fruit. He belongs to Shelly and Sydney. And the other dog..." She paused. "He looks a lot like Featherington the Fifth. Maybe they found him. Come on, let's ask George Quigley."

The trainer looked up as they approached. "If you don't have a Frenchie, you're not allowed in this park. It's private. Did you read the sign?"

Olivia ignored him. "We need to talk."

George blinked. "Hello, cop assistant." He glanced at Michael. "You don't have a dog," he warned.

"I'm Michael Bellemare, Olivia's boyfriend. We haven't met."

"You need a dog no matter who you are," George warned.

"We're looking for Mayor Maguire," Olivia curtly replied.

"Haven't seen him." Quigley shrugged.

"This morning or recently?" Michael asked.

"Not since Woofstock kicked off."

Olivia frowned. She took a glance over her shoulder. "Isn't that Featherington the Fifth?"

"Nope," Quigley said. "That's Featherington the Sixth, Whitlock's other male stud. They look nearly identical."

"Littermates?" she asked.

"None of your business," he said.

Michael leaned forward. "Will he, you know, be bred with Juicy Fruit? That's the name of the other dog, right?"

"It's possible." Quigley nodded. "My employer has very detailed plans for his stock. He doesn't consult me."

Olivia watched as Featherington nipped at the female's hind quarters. She ignored his advance by trotting away.

"Is this a getting-to-know-you kind of thing?" Michael asked. "First date at the dog park. Looks like she isn't interested." He pointed to Juicy Fruit on the other side of the grass.

"I suppose you might think that," Quigley answered. "The female's owners paid for a Lone Ranger package, which includes extra walks by yours truly." Now Juicy Fruit occupied herself by rolling in the dirt, her sturdy legs poking up in the air.

That's how I feel. In a bad mood and I don't want to play, Olivia thought. *If only I could roll over and ignore the rest of the world.* She reached to rub the soreness at the back of her neck.

She stopped rubbing and asked another question. "I thought Whitlock's dogs were all bred in vitro. The samples are collected in a lab."

Quigley glared. "Since when are you so interested in the sex lives of French bulldogs? Part of your research for the cops?"

I must have hit a nerve.

"Doesn't Juicy Fruit belong to the Ayerses? I saw them check in on Friday." Olivia didn't back down.

"Yeah, that's why I'm with her. Once I'm done here, I'll take her back for a massage along with a bath. The whole grooming package."

The lives of the rich and famous.

Michael held up his phone. "Are you sure you haven't seen Mayor Maguire? Here's his photo." The lock screen showed M&M with a red, white, and blue ribbon holding a gold medal around his neck. It was the photo posted all over town, announcing him as the mayor.

"You actually *call* him the mayor?" Quigley muttered. "You people are worse than breeders. Giving a dog a title with special privileges."

"Our only official politician," Michael insisted.

Quigley rolled his eyes dramatically, meant to be seen.

Michael adopted a calm voice. "Maybe you're not familiar with our little town. But just to be clear, Mayor Maguire is psychic."

Quigley groaned. "You small-town people are the worst. Bunch of sissies letting your favorite son wander around as if the town is safe and no harm can come to him."

"We're not the only ones looking for a dog. What about you? As the official dog trainer of Featherington the Fifth, shouldn't you be scouring the backstreets instead of hanging out here?"

"Featherington isn't far. He always shows up eventually." Quigley pulled out his cell phone, and his thumb moved about on the screen. "Nice chatting with you, but I've gotta check on my boss. I track his location and his texts so I know if he's close. As long as I stay one step ahead of Mr. Micromanager, I can avoid conflict. You know what I mean." He looked toward Olivia for a sign of approval. When she let her perplexity show on her face, he nervously added, "You know what I mean. I'm sure you do the same thing with each other."

Before Olivia could deny his impression, Michael reached out his hand to take the phone from Quigley. "Show me that. I know they make tracker apps for parents with children. But tracking your boss..."

171

Quigley pushed his hand away. "I know how to take care of myself. And if Whitlock squawks about being tracked, I'll delete the app. It's not as if he's tech savvy—he won't go to any extra trouble to check what I'm doing. I know him pretty well."

It was Michael's turn to roll his eyes.

Olivia walked away with Michael close behind. "I don't like that guy," he said.

"Me neither," she agreed.

Michael headed toward the exit, sounding more irritated with each step. "Instead of paying attention to the job he's been hired for, he's avoiding his boss. I've had employees like that. Hours wasted on avoiding work. As soon as they see me drive up, they pick up a hammer just to act busy."

Olivia ignored his complaints. "I think we should try to find Maguire at Lady of the Rock next. That's where I last saw him. Maybe we'll have more luck there."

"Sure," Michael commented. "But let's walk. I don't want to give up my parking space."

CHAPTER TWENTY-FOUR

Meadow stood behind Lady of the Rock's counter, her arms folded over her chest. Instead of her usual smile, she wore the scowl of a disgruntled employee. Gone were the gracious welcome and the familiar use of "dear."

"Remind me to veto Woofstock for any future events," she huffed. "It's been a nightmare. Hold on." She sprinted out from behind the counter to confront a customer coming through the entrance. The bell rang overhead as he and his dog stepped into the shop.

"Put that dog outside. There's a canine occupancy limit." Meadow sounded commanding and more overwrought than Olivia could remember.

She leaned closer to Michael. "Occupancy limit? Since when?"

After the man and the dog were escorted outside, Meadow returned.

"I know what you're both thinking," she said, "That I'm spending too much time at my extra job. But people called out from the shop because of Woofstock. I had to rearrange my hours at the library plus make up rules for this unprecedented weekend. It's not as if the tourists know the difference. I don't care if they give Lady of the Rock a bad Yelp review. This is just too much. Once they're gone, I'll go back to my usual days and we can learn from our mistakes and return to normal."

Everyone's in a foul mood today. Me, Michael, and now Meadow.

Instead of sympathizing with Meadow, she changed the subject. "We're looking for Mayor Maguire. Has he been back since that standoff with Tater Tot?"

"Now that you mention it, no. I haven't seen the mayor. But I've not exactly been looking either." She blinked. "Did you happen to notice if the Doody Calls people arrived on your way through town?"

"They're here," Michael said. Normally he'd be laughing about the hazmat-wearing people romping through the park. But now he looked irritated.

Meadow must have heard his tone. She took a minute to look at one then the other. "I hope you find the mayor, dear. But I have to pay attention to the shoppers. Have a nice day," she dismissed them both.

Michael waited for Olivia outside Lady of the Rock. "What's the matter with you today?" he asked. "Even Meadow noticed."

Olivia felt a surge of anger. "What's the matter with *you?* Having a temper tantrum over parking," she retorted.

He shrugged. "Your bad mood is all my fault, is that what you're saying? This is a new side of you I haven't seen before."

"You're not exactly my favorite either." She looked down to avoid his gaze.

He gestured toward the stairway with his head. "Come on. Let's see if Maguire is at the constabulary."

. . .

"I haven't seen the mayor," Brad said. "I hope he's hiding from all the tourists. I wish I could."

"Is Officer Jets in the back?" Olivia asked.

Brad let out an exasperated sigh. "The boss isn't here. She isn't keeping her regular hours. That's what I keep telling people. Not a clue where she's gone. And now I have to explain to everyone who calls and listen to them go on and on. You should hear the complaints."

His voice shifted to a professional tone. "Too many people overcrowding the streets. Dog poop everywhere. Who's giving out citations to those disobeying the leash ordinance? Have you seen the outdoor fires in public areas? Plus there are tents pitched in the park. And people are hopping over the protective guardrails to unsettle the giant sequoias.

"This behavior is equivalent to sequoia assassination. An environmental nightmare." Brad coughed into his hand. "You name it, someone has called it in, and I have to fill out a report." He pointed to his computer and a stack of papers on his desk. "And that's just this morning." He hid his face in his arms.

A series of yips made him look up.

"Is that Tater Tot?" Olivia asked.

Brad stood abruptly. "That's him. Been barking all morning. Cookie brought him over. Since when is dog sitting in my job description? Watch the front for me, would you? I'm gonna check on the mutt."

Brad huffed away, taking his bad mood with him.

Olivia turned to Michael. "You'd think Janis would be out there issuing citations. And what's up with everyone's bad mood? First me, then you, now Meadow and Brad. Janis is crabby every day without this."

"On the one hand..." Jets boldly stepped through the doorway, entering the conversation as if she'd been there all along.

"I resent that you think I'm always in a bad mood. That's my poker face persona you're referring to. It's a professional ruse to keep people guessing. No one knows what I'm thinking. Plus I'm really quite congenial when not on the clock."

She smiled brightly. Michael's face flushed as he opened his mouth to interrupt. She dismissed him by holding up her palm.

"I haven't gotten to the other hand. You know better than to interrupt." This time her forced grin made Olivia fidget.

"On the other hand," Janis began, "I don't like the idea that you two are standing in my constabulary like you don't have anything better to do. Go outside. Enjoy the sunshine and the wafting scent of dog poop that's settled over the entire downtown. Embrace your inner hippy why don't you. Put on some tie-dye so that you can take off some tie-dye and dance naked. Leave me to my job."

Olivia shrugged.

"We're looking for Mayor Maguire. Any idea where he might have gone to?" Michael asked anyway.

"What now? We have two missing dogs. I don't suppose he and Featherington the Fifth have become a crime-solving duo like Batman and Robin. Maybe they're tracking down Arlo's killer. I bet they're in the middle of that park palooza, begging for treats. Another Lily Rock legend in the making."

Jets stared them down. "I might help you find the dogs if I weren't attending to other important matters. Like Arlo's murderer. That's a high priority, don't you think? Or have you forgotten already? Get outta here, you two. I don't need to be worrying about the town's loveable labradoodle. He'll turn up. He always does."

. . .

Having been dismissed by Jets, Michael and Olivia stood outside. "The library's closed," Olivia noted. "It's usually open on Saturday."

Michael scratched his head. "Lily Rock has been turned upside down with this festival. Meadow can't be in two places at once."

He leaned against the side of the building. She joined him. When he slid closer, she moved away to avoid contact.

"Come on," he moaned. "Tell me what's going on. Then we can make up and find Maguire. What do you say?"

Olivia felt cornered. To her surprise, she wasn't ready to give up her anger. Suddenly things that usually didn't bother her loomed as character flaws. *He doesn't always listen for an answer, even when he asks me a question. Plus he built me a house, a castle, like I'm chattel and I belong to him.*

Before she could stop herself, the truth came out in one awkward announcement. "I hate our new house."

"You what?" His mouth hung open in surprise.

Once she started, she didn't know how to stop. "I feel uncomfortable living in so much open space. It's like a gigantic barn. There's no way I can make a home there.

"I miss where we used to live. You yanked me from my home with Sage and Star just for your privacy. I was fine with my family.

"I know you included me on all the decisions. I know." She stepped away, creating distance from his shocked expression.

Michael took a big sigh. "Are you done?" His shoulders drooped.

She looked past the crowded street toward the park. *Where are you, M&M? I need a hug.*

"That's disappointing," he finally said. "I have to admit."

"I'm disappointed too," she defended herself. "You were so enthusiastic with the design and the construction. I thought we were doing everything just right. Making all the choices. You considered my opinions. But after a while I stopped listening. I just agreed with you. I had other things on my mind, and now I feel like I'm stuck. In a barn. Not my home."

A long-haired beagle tugged on his leash. The dog wore a helmet shaped like a medieval gladiator. He had a "Woofstock Forever" tie-dye scarf wrapped around his neck. "Peace out," a man said as he picked up the dog. He shot them a smile. "Don't forget. Love means you never have to say you're sorry." He nodded and walked away.

Michael grimaced. "We can't talk here," he said, "too many people."

Olivia's cheeks flushed with embarrassment.

"Come on," Michael encouraged. "We don't need to share our grievances in public. I'll give up my parking space. We can go home."

George Quigley waited for them across the street. "I took Featherington the Sixth and Juicy Fruit back to the inn. Whitlock's busy interviewing a new potential breeder. Do you want help searching for your mayor? I have some time."

Olivia was surprised. She had not expected Quigley to care about Maguire, let alone offer to help find him.

"That would be great. We've already checked the Fort. He's not at Lady of the Rock or anywhere close by," she said.

"We stopped by the constabulary. No sign of him there. And the library's closed," Michael added.

"Those are Mayor Maguire's usual places to hang out," Olivia explained.

"What happened with your boss? Did he show up at the dog park?"

"I avoided him." Quigley tapped his phone. "Love this app. Keeps me away from that micromanager."

"What about his spouse?" Olivia asked. "Do you have an app on her?"

"Uma's more easygoing than Eldred. She keeps to her side of the partnership, basically running the merchandising and guest check-in. All the slick advertising of The Frenchie Connection is on her. Plus I only answer to Eldred."

He looked to Michael. "That Jets woman doesn't do her job. She's refused to look for Featherington the Fifth. And I called the constabulary and the kid in charge told me she's not available."

"Janis Jets is an excellent cop," Michael said. "She's been good for this town, solving all kinds of crimes. She's a one-woman police force."

This speech from Michael came as a surprise to Olivia. *I don't think I've ever heard him defend Janis so vociferously before. Usually he's complaining that she's endangering me. Apparently he respects her work.*

She felt anger stir in her gut. *Because I'm his princess, that's why. Because he wants to find me all safe and cozy in his castle when he gets home. He doesn't want to find me missing or in danger while tracking down murder suspects.*

"How about this." Olivia swallowed her indignation. "Why don't the three of us stop talking about Janis Jets and start looking for Maguire. He loves the dog treats at Thyme Out. Let's begin there."

She felt the full force of her disgruntlement as she spoke to Michael. "We can walk to the bakery. You'll love that. Because you won't have to give up your sacred parking space."

CHAPTER TWENTY-FIVE

A line trailed around the block outside of Thyme Out. Olivia stepped in front of two people to look inside the front window. She could barely see Cookie, there were so many people standing elbow to elbow, waiting to place their orders.

When he looked toward the window, he nodded. He'd taken off his usual apron, and his shirt was untucked. Turning back to the next customer, he gripped the counter with impatience.

She turned to Michael. "If he's working the counter, who's selling coffee and treats at the Woofstock table?"

"I have no idea," Michael admitted. "But this place is a madhouse. I don't see an empty table, at least in the cafe. There may be one out back."

"We don't have to stand in line," she reasoned. "I'm feeling really anxious about Maguire. How about I check the back patio while you stay here? I'll text you if I see him. Maybe you and George can show people his photo and ask around while I'm gone."

"Got it." Michael opened his phone with the smiling Maguire on the screen. "Meet you back here."

Quigley's phone pinged. He read his text. "Actually, I have to go now. I missed what you were saying. There's a back patio?"

Olivia explained, "There's a shortcut by the back alley over there. I'm going to look for Maguire."

"Maybe I'll catch up later. I've gotta go."

Some help he is.

The entrance to the alley had been entirely blocked by an overgrown bougainvillea. Not just the spectacular array of flowers but the branches posed an obstacle. Olivia knew they held sharp thorns and without clippers, she'd have to slip past very carefully.

Lifting one large branch, she ducked under, only to come face-to-face with another. Her cheek began to sting. Her finger touched oozing blood. *Not serious*, she concluded.

She pulled the next branch aside and then the next.

The sweet scent of star jasmine filled her nostrils. She held another branch and ducked underneath. Red-orange flowers and thorn-filled branches surrounded her, making it impossible to see.

Alerted to the sound of footsteps, she turned. No one pushed aside a branch and the footsteps stopped. *No one's going to follow me here. Unless Michael changed his mind.*

She shoved aside the last heavy branch to stand in the clearing. A quick examination of her arms showed scratches but not broken skin. She raised her chin to better hear voices coming from the other side of the wall. *There must be a lot of people on Thyme Out's back patio.*

Outside the back entrance, she confirmed her suspicion. People crowded around bistro-sized tables. Some had brought camp chairs due to the limited seating.

A basset hound stood on four stubby legs. He lifted his

head with a quick succession of barks, then waited for someone to pay attention.

The people at the table paid no attention. The dog tried again. This time with a long low bay that sent a shiver up Olivia's spine. When it died out, she felt her back stiffen.

Is someone behind me?

Stepping to the side, she looked back to where she'd come from. When no one appeared, she shrugged. *I'm just edgy,* she concluded. *Time to take a closer look at the patio.*

Filled with various breeds, only one labradoodle stood in the corner. But his fur wasn't as dark as Maguire's. He smiled with his tongue hanging out the side of his mouth. Her heart tugged. *Where are you, buddy?* Even more discouraged, she turned back making her way down the path to the front of the cafe.

With a low-voiced bay, the basset called again. His heartfelt cry made the hair on her neck stand up. *Is he trying to warn me?*

Her mind raced. She came to a standstill. Worst-case scenarios filled her thoughts. *Maybe Maguire's lost. He could have taken off or been hit by a car. He could have been picked up by someone on the main road and taken who knows where.* She felt her gut clench.

Footsteps trod against the solid dirt path. Before Olivia could spin around, a sharp blow at the back of her head knocked her forward. And then everything went blank. Slumping to the ground, her head began to spin.

She shielded her head with her hands and waited for a further assault. When none came, she heard footsteps again, this time running away. Try as she might, she couldn't open her eyes to identify her attacker.

She reached a finger to her scalp. Wetness accompanied

the tangy smell of blood. Her hand dropped to the dirt. That was the last thing she remembered before passing out.

"Olivia," a voice called. She lifted her head to answer but quickly dropped it back. *I know that voice. But not now*, she concluded. *I need to sleep.*

She woke again as someone lifted her torso with strong arms. Her eyes refused to open. They dragged her across the dirt. "Put me down," she mumbled.

"I've got you," the voice said.

She recognized Michael's voice. With one more yank, he propped her back against the fence. "Come on, talk to me, Olivia," he coaxed. He held her head gently between his hands.

"I'm too dizzy," she explained.

"Open your eyes and keep talking," he insisted. She felt him touch her head.

"Ouch." She winced. Her eyes fluttered open. "There's blood. Somebody hit me from behind."

Michael's face looked grave. "Eyes open now. I need to call Dr. Martinez."

She inched her knees closer to her chest, still overcome with dizziness. "Just give me a minute. I think I'm okay."

"You're not okay." He showed her the blood on his finger for proof.

"I'm good enough to get home. He wouldn't be able to get to me with the crowds. And I don't need an ambulance. Call him once I'm home." Exhausted from explaining, she closed her eyes.

"Lean forward." Michael's fingers gently explored her scalp. "I think the bleeding has stopped. We can take this slowly. At least get you out of this overgrown jungle."

Olivia's eyes fluttered open. "Hi," she said softly. Her lids felt impossibly heavy, so she closed her eyes again.

He bent closer. With an expert hand, he lifted one eyelid. "Maybe a concussion," he assessed. "Keep talking."

"It hurts too much with my eyes open. Plus I feel dizzy." She held out both of her hands. "Help me to my feet."

He half pulled and half lifted her to a standing position. He placed one hand on each shoulder to give her support. "Steady there," he cautioned.

"I think I might throw up. Don't look." When he didn't release her shoulders, she swallowed.

"What about Maguire?" Michael asked.

She sensed he was trying to keep her distracted and talking.

"No Maguire. What did you find out?" she asked.

"I showed his photo to everyone in line. No one has seen him. Not surprising. With so many dogs in town, he's just one more labradoodle."

She thought about the dog on the Thyme Out patio. "He stands out. He's unique and the mayor," Olivia objected.

"To us he's one of a kind," Michael admitted. "Ready for another step, or do you want me to carry you fireman-style? I can do that. Been trained, you know." He made an effort to sound lighthearted, but she wasn't fooled.

As he held her shoulder, she took one step forward. She waited for the dizziness to stop before taking another step. Michael dropped his hands but stood close by.

"Hey, did you see who did this to me?" she asked.

Michael's hands returned to her shoulders. "I saw the back of someone shoving their way through the bougainvillea.. They wore jeans and a Woofstock shirt. Like everyone else in Lily Rock."

"Don't beat yourself up. I might have been there for hours if you hadn't found me."

"You didn't text, so I got worried." His voice sounded gruff. "I found you face down in the dirt. It terrified me." He pointed a few feet away.

Her eyes searched the area, stopping at a nearby brick. "Could that be the weapon?" she asked. "It would fit in someone's hand. Big enough to do damage."

"Can you stand by yourself?" he asked.

She tried to nod, but that made the throb in her head hurt more. "If I don't move my head, I can stand while you look." He released his grip.

She called after him. "Don't touch the rock. Janis will send it down the hill to the lab for prints." His back to her, he kneeled to have a closer look.

"There's something lodged underneath," he called back.

"Nudge it with your foot," Olivia suggested.

"A paper. Forget Janis. I'm taking a look."

He stood. "It's a matchbook. Don't see many of those nowadays." He turned it over. "A label on the front. The Frenchie Connection."

Michael held it gingerly between his thumb and forefinger. "I see scribbling on the inside. I'll bring it for you to read." He came closer, and she took the matchbook from his hand.

"'Stop looking'," she read aloud. "Is that for me? A warning? But I've only been looking for Maguire and Featherington the Fifth." Then it dawned on her. "And Arlo's killer. Do you suppose that's who left this for me and who hit me over the head?" Sighing, she concluded, "This isn't a job for an amateur detective."

"Is that how you see yourself?" Michael sounded surprised.

"Isn't that who I am? Janis calls me Nancy Drew every chance she gets."

Olivia forced her eyes to stay open. She kept talking despite the pounding in her head. "I seem to be playing a role in everyone else's drama. I'm your girlfriend living in a castle. I'm a disposable amateur detective. I'm a part-time musician whose band no longer performs."

Michael reached for Olivia and pulled her into his warm embrace. He ducked his head and spoke in her ear. "You are the most persistent woman I've ever met. You don't give up. Knocked on the head, blood on your hands—you can't be stopped. You are the main character in your own story, Olivia. The rest of us, we're revolving around you, trying to capture some of that magic."

Despite her throbbing head, his words had an effect. She felt her mood lift. Her earlier rant, the intensity of the feelings, no longer mattered. She could see more clearly, even with her eyes closed. As if she'd fallen and then, by some miracle, been put back, only this time on higher ground.

He buried his face in her neck, no longer sounding angry. "Don't worry. I'll build us another house. I'm good at it. This time you can tell me what you want. Just as long as we're together."

She gripped his back, tightening her fingers on the flannel of his shirt.

"Let's get you home and call Luis Martinez," he added.

She mumbled, unwilling to lift her head from his chest. "Call Janis first. She needs to be informed. One death and now an assault. It's time for our constable to get back to work."

CHAPTER TWENTY-SIX

Janis Jets sat on the edge of the oversized sofa. She patted Olivia's hand, then adjusted the ice bag on her head. Olivia kept her eyes closed.

She felt Jets lean her back against the cushion. "Geez this place is enormous. How do you find your other half? He could stand in a corner and be invisible for days."

Jets's assessment, though unwelcome, was strikingly true.

"Do you mind if I stretch my legs?" Olivia bumped her knee against Janis. *She's sitting on top of me. Way too close.*

"No problem. I'll take a hike to that chair over there on the other side of the room and be back by tomorrow. Then we can talk. What was he thinking..." Olivia knew the *he* was Michael. But now she was prepared to defend herself.

I hope she lets up sometime soon. I have enough trouble adjusting to my new surroundings. I don't require another complaining voice either. I have an overactive one inside my own head.

Olivia opened one eye. Jets had shoved one oversized occasional chair closer. Olivia quickly closed her eye with a shudder.

"Are you ignoring me?" Jets asked. "I can't understand why you'd do that. I'm visiting a sick person, which I never do."

Olivia chuckled. "I do admit that I've been thinking the same thing about this place for days. I'm convinced Michael built a house for a family of ten. Like McDonald's. He super-sized. I don't need that big of a burger, and I know I don't need this big of a house." She adjusted her own ice bag, eyes now wide open.

"The damsel in distress castle isn't working for you, huh? I hope you told the big lug. He thinks he's an expert. Just because of those awards. Male superiority. It doesn't help that he's so good-looking. High on his own imaginary horse, racing through town in tight jeans. Handsome to a fault. Speaking of faults..."

Olivia held back a laugh. *Is she talking about herself or Michael? Sometimes it's hard to tell.*

Jets continued to muse. "I suppose he didn't do it on purpose, treat you like a queen. To give him some credit, you're more than just a client. Even experts can make a mistake."

"He never built a house for his ex-wife," Olivia mused.

"Enough about your boyfriend. It's kind of a shock that Michael Bellemare isn't perfect. I can't wait to tell Cookie."

In the past, when anyone suggested that Michael wasn't perfect, Olivia was the first to his defense. But not this time. Janis had a point.

"I don't think Michael ever asked for me to put him in perfect jail. I did that all on my own. I wonder why..."

When Jets just sniffed, Olivia nestled her back against the cushions. She spoke with eyes closed. "Dr. Martinez said I'm going to be fine. In case you wondered." She reached a finger to touch the bandage on her head for confirmation. "He told me to stay awake for another hour or so just to be safe."

"A house call from the doctor. You got some of his special treatment." Jets sounded envious. "He's a great-looking guy. Maybe I'll get bonked on the head next time. I could use a little of his expertise. Get myself a fancy bandage and a few weeks off of work. Now we're talking.

"Open those eyes," Jets warned. "You can't go to sleep. We're closing in on this investigation and I need your help."

Olivia waved her hand in the air. "Go away." Sleep nestled in her brain, causing a yawn. But before she could let go, a nagging thought popped up.

"We tried to find you at the constabulary, before the assault. Brad said you've been missing. We need help searching for Maguire."

"I was avoiding the town council, if you must know."

Olivia opened one eye. "What do you mean?"

"They made this Woofstock mess and they need to clean it up."

"But you're the Lily Rock constable. Don't you need to help?"

"That's the thing, Nancy Drew. I'm not a helper. I'm in charge. The sooner the local Lily Rock residents realize the limitations of my involvement in their stupid ideas the better. Doody Calls is a great example. They'll have to pay the bill. Not just say, 'Good ol' Janis. We can always depend on her.' I'm not in the business of cleaning up after every one of their bad ideas." Jets let out a loud breath of exasperation.

"Don't you worry," she continued. "I'll be available as soon as the Old Rockers wake up. And then I'll do something really important. I'll point in the direction of change. Maybe suggest some more effective policies. But not yet."

"So you disappeared on purpose."

"That's right. I'm waiting. Look at me being all patient." A smile crossed Jets's lips.

"What about Arlo's murder?"

"I have more forensic information. Everything points to Whitlock and his pretty-in-pink wife. I heard back from the lab about the stiletto. Talk about overkill. It doesn't take a six-inch blade to open a letter. I knew that was the weapon right away. And sure enough, they discovered Arlo's blood. Right where the blade connects to the wooden handle."

"But your evidence won't hold up in court without a warrant."

"I told you how we're handling that. You are my secret weapon. You'll get one of them to confess."

Olivia objected. "Did you forget that they both have an alibi?"

"Like I said before, a wife is not a reliable alibi. I'll have a quick chat with Mrs. Whitlock. By the time I'm done, she'll throw her hubby right under the bus. And then he'll follow suit. I'll get one or both of them either way. This isn't my first rodeo, don't forget."

The longer Jets talked, the sleepier Olivia felt. Her head fell farther back into the pillow. Blah, blah, blah were the only words her brain registered.

"You should be paying attention." Jets spoke sharply. "I think Whitlock was the guy who assaulted you. He must be getting nervous that we're onto him now. He wants you to give up looking for Arlo's killer. I've already sent the brick and the matchbook to forensics. Bellemare contaminated the evidence with his big thumbprint on the front of the matchbook."

"You can find of those matchbooks at the inn," Olivia reminded her. "My assailant doesn't have to be a Whitlock. Anyone could have written a note and hidden it under a rock."

"I already sent Brad to pick up a few more from The Frenchie Connection lobby. I'm planning to superimpose the ominous message onto a fresh matchbook cover without Belle-mare's big thumb. That will give me plenty of evidence."

Olivia sat up straight. Her head wildly throbbing. "You're going to plant evidence just to convict one of the Whitlocks!"

"Just stop," Jets drawled. "It happens all the time. I know who did it and I'm going to bring them to justice if it's the last thing I do.

"Stay in your lane," Jets insisted. "You'll get the confession. I'll use the evidence to make them squirm. It's almost time to invite them both to constabulary and then double down."

Olivia lay back her head, which felt like a watermelon ready to explode.

"I told Mike I'd keep you awake for an hour, and my time's up. Sweet dreams, princess." She felt Jets's awkward pat on her hand right as Michael's voice spoke from across the room.

"Time for you to leave, Officer Jets," he announced.

As the two chatted by the front door, Olivia's thoughts turned to the missing Mayor Maguire. He appeared behind her eyelids. Dark eyes pleaded with her the way they did when he really wanted a dog cookie.

I'll find you, buddy. Right after I take a little nap.

CHAPTER TWENTY-SEVEN

"Stop looking at me," she cautioned. "I'm okay. No headache this morning. Just some soreness." She touched her head to press on the bandage. "I'm going to wear a hat," she concluded.

Michael quirked an eyebrow. "How about you just stay home while I continue the search for Mayor Maguire. In fact, I think you should call Sage and cancel the Sweet Four O'Clock gig. It could be dangerous."

"Not on your life." Olivia thumped her empty mug on the nearby table. The sound of water trickling made her look toward the bridge. *The last time I saw Cayenne.*

She dragged her thoughts in a different direction. "That bonk on my head gave me an idea. I think I know where we might find Maguire."

"Where's that?"

"Do you want to come with me?" she asked.

"You want me, not Janis?" He looked rather pleased, smiling over the top of his mug.

"I don't want Janis because she's become unreliable. You should have heard her yesterday, doubling down on the Whitlocks. She's closed her mind to all the other potential suspects, including George Quigley."

"Does she know something we don't?"

"Maybe she does. But that's no excuse. She's going to plant a fresh matchbook into evidence since yours was contaminated."

"Her mind *is* closed." Michael shook his head. "Okay, I'm in. Where are we going next?"

Half an hour later, they stood at the entrance of the chapel. Michael reached to touch Olivia's elbow. "Don't forget, no sudden movements."

"No Cayenne." Olivia cast her eyes toward the labyrinth. "It was wishful thinking that I'd find her walking the labyrinth like I used to."

"She hasn't contacted you since the last time?" he asked.

"Not even a text. Nothing." Olivia sighed. Her chin jerked up at the sound of a sharp bark coming from around the corner. "Did you hear that?"

Michael nodded. "Sounds like..."

She explained, "I saw Maguire in my mind right before I fell asleep last night. He looked at me with those big dark eyes." She cleared her throat. "He stared at me like he does when he begs for a treat. But it wasn't until I woke up this morning that I realized he's calling for me. Come on, it's just a short walk around the chapel."

"Which way do we go?"

"I forgot that you've never been to their house." Her heart began to race at the sound of another distinctive, "Bork!"

"Did you hear that!" She picked up her pace.

"Take it easy," he called after her. "Don't forget your head."

She called over her shoulder, "It's the mayor," right before Arlo's cabin came into view.

And there he sat. Mayor Maguire. On his back haunches, his tongue hanging out.

"Maguire!" she called.

"Bork." He stood to all fours, his jaw dropping in a smile, his tail wagging.

Olivia ran up the two steps and dropped to her knees. With both arms wrapped around his neck, she buried her face in his fur. "I missed you." Tears came to her eyes.

Michael came alongside to pat Olivia's back. He bent down. "Hey, buddy. You had us worried." He ruffled Maguire's ears.

Back on her feet, Olivia scolded, "We were worried sick, M&M."

Maguire jumped on all fours and turned a circle. Then he trotted to the front door, which he shoved open with his nose.

Olivia explained, "When Janis and I came over that first day, someone had broken in." She used her hip to widen the gap.

Inside the mudroom another sound erupted. "Yip, yip, yip."

Maguire trotted toward the living room. "Bork," he called out, as if to say, "I'm coming."

"Smells like dog in here." Michael rubbed his nose.

"And I think I know why." Olivia followed Maguire.

A wire dog kennel stood at the far end of the room in front of the fireplace. Featherington the Fifth ran from one side to the other. *Bam!* The Frenchie hit his body against the wire, only to run to the opposite side. He threw his weight again, with even more force.

"It's okay, Featherington." Olivia used her most soothing voice. "We'll let you out."

She reached to unclasp the lock. The Frenchie rushed past, straight toward Mayor Maguire. Featherington lowered his front end in a gesture of doggie recognition.

Maguire looked imperious when Featherington stood to all fours. The shorter dog reached his face up to sniff Maguire's chin. "Yip," he called again.

"Is that Featherington the Fifth?" Michael asked.

"In the flesh," Olivia confirmed. "Let me find a leash. Then I can take him outside. Keep your eye on both of them."

She found the leash right underneath a stack of legal-looking documents on the dining room table. Once secured, Featherington took off running toward the door before Olivia could grasp the other end of the leash. He skidded to a halt in the mudroom and then lifted his leg.

"Stop that." She opened the door wider to let him out.

Featherington stopped at the edge of the porch. He sat down and looked back at Olivia.

"Don't be such a scaredy cat," she coaxed. "You can walk down the steps by yourself." When he refused to budge, she half dragged him by the collar. Finally he sniffed at a mock orange hedge next to the cabin. After several more sniffs, he lifted his leg.

"Do you want to investigate the cabin before we leave?" Michael called from the porch. "I saw some legal documents next to Arlo's old computer."

Olivia tugged on the leash. "Be right there."

In the mudroom, she unclipped Featherington. Maguire stood at the end of the hall to watch. Then he ducked and growled, ready to play.

She found Michael at the dining table. "Whoever kidnapped Featherington must have known the cabin was deserted," he reasoned. "They probably came back every few hours to take him out and feed him."

"Most likely. Did you get a look at those papers?"

"They're legal documents," he concluded. Taking the one from the top of the pile, he continued to read to himself.

Olivia opened the laptop, only to be confronted with a locked screen. She closed it again. "I don't have his password. Plus I'm surprised this hasn't been recovered as evidence. I guess Janis never followed up with forensics."

Michael handed her a document. "This is a legal contract. Arlo's logo is at the top of the form. We'd have to find a billing statement somewhere to prove that he wrote it up. Look, it's signed by Eldred Whitlock. He's asking for the pick of a litter as his payment."

"He wanted a dog, not money?" Olivia asked, remembering Sydney's claims about the same topic.

"I guess so. Right here it states all the details. How The Frenchie Connection will send the sample. How they will continue to monitor the fertilization process in real time. There's a Zoom link. And then Whitlock expects frequent updates during the pregnancy. There are spaces for the exact dates.

"They listed every appointment time and the shots the puppy will get and at what age. All of it signed by Whitlock and witnessed by Quigley."

Olivia took a closer look. "'Arlo Carson, Attorney at Law, Consultant Litigation Support Specialist.' When I first came to Lily Rock, Arlo offered to represent me. That time when Janis thought I was the number one suspect to Marla's death."

"That's right." Michael smiled. "Seems like so long ago. I also asked Arlo to help with that letter Marla left for you. That was before we'd actually met. He told me then he was an attorney."

"But don't forget." She shook the paper. "Arlo went to law school, but he never went into practice. He'd say he was a lawyer, but when it came down to it, he exaggerated. I don't think he passed the bar exam."

"Arlo played fast and loose with the facts," Michael admitted. "Like that time he opened his weed shop without getting a permit from the town council. He tended to make his move first and ask for forgiveness later."

"So are you thinking what I'm thinking?" Olivia asked. "That Arlo told Whitlock he was an attorney, even though he wasn't?"

"I think Arlo got paid by Whitlock to write up these contracts," Michael stated firmly. "That we know for a fact."

"I think so too." Olivia glanced at the closed laptop. "I bet we'd find invoices right there."

A low growl came from the living room. Maguire stood to all fours. He shoved Featherington with his paw, apparently finished with playing.

The Frenchie rolled over, his four paws in the air. Maguire didn't bother to sniff his belly. He walked away, bounded over, and reared back to place his front paws on Michael.

"Maguire might be hungry," he laughed. "Get down." He pushed the dog back to all fours.

The mayor turned to Olivia and lowered his back haunches in a perfect sit, looking up with pleading eyes.

"My turn, huh? I'm the soft touch." She leaned to scratch behind his ear. She made her way to the kitchen, aware that the odor still lingered. She called out to Michael. "Let's stop by our place to feed the dogs before we deliver Featherington back to his owner."

"I'll look around for kibble. Maybe we can feed them some dry food instead." He reached inside the pantry and returned with a half-opened bag.

"Bork," Maguire approved. He lifted his front paws to the counter, his eyes on the bag.

"Yip." Featherington scrambled past Michael to stand next to Maguire's back feet.

"I'll look for dog bowls," Michael laughed and left the room.

He returned holding two metal containers aloft. "There's a problem. Ants." He slapped at his hand.

He rinsed the bowls at the sink. "Some ants in the mudroom and over here on the window sill," he observed aloud. Placing the bowls on a dish towel, he glanced underneath the sink. "Nothing here to spray them with."

Olivia felt a prickle up her neck. "Is there by any chance a can of WD-40?"

Michael looked again and reached into the cabinet, removing a familiar blue and gold spray can. "Right here." He fiddled with the red top, securing the narrow tube.

"Try to spray that on the window sill," she said. "My mom used to use WD-40 for all kinds of weird things. The guy at the hardware store told me Arlo killed ants with the stuff."

Michael adjusted the tube and then directed it toward the corner of the window sill. He sprayed. The familiar smell of chemical and butterscotch assaulted Olivia's nose. "Got 'em," he announced. "I never used WD-40 to kill insects." He turned away from the sink. "I'll spray the mudroom too."

"Don't do that," Olivia warned. "It may be bad for the dogs." She turned to Featherington. "Especially Mr. Sniffy with the flat nose. Frenchies already have breathing issues, and a snort of WD-40 might make him sick."

Michael gave the window sill one more squirt before returning the can under the sink.

Olivia reached for Featherington's collar, clipping the leash to the ring. Maguire waited in the mudroom.

"Do I take these papers and the laptop with me?" Michael called from the dining area.

Olivia hesitated. "Technically speaking, they're evidence. Janis would be furious."

"I'll leave them right where we found them."

Olivia didn't remember until they left, because of all the ant drama, they never did feed the dogs.

CHAPTER TWENTY-EIGHT

In the car, Olivia took one more glance over her shoulder. Pine tree branches swayed in the breeze, bits of yellow pollen floated through the air. Two people walked the labyrinth, neither one familiar.

A warm breath against her neck interrupted her thoughts. Maguire peered over the back seat. He lifted his nose to sniff the bandage on her scalp.

"I got into some trouble," she explained. "You probably smell the blood."

He sat back on the seat, his eyes downcast.

"I know, buddy. Sometimes I don't see what's right behind me."

Michael turned to look at her and then back at the road. His jaw tightened.

"Let's top by the house. I'll leave Maguire his dinner. Then we'll take Featherington home," she suggested.

He nodded his head reaching across to rest his hand on her knee.

. . .

It was Michael who carried Feathering the Fifth in his arms as they made their way toward The Frenchie Connection entrance.

The dog lay passive in his embrace, his chin drooping over Michael's forearm. Once inside, he put the dog down on all fours. Featherington hid behind Olivia's legs.

She clipped on his lead to drag him toward the front, right as Uma Whitlock greeted them. "Checking in?" she asked without looking up.

"We found Featherington the Fifth." Olivia felt the dog flop on top of her feet. Then he rolled to the side with his legs sticking straight out. *He's playing dead.*

Uma seemed mildly interested. "Eldred's stud. You found him."

"He's down here." Olivia pointed to the floor. Uma leaned over the counter to have a better look.

"I'll let Eldred know." Uma picked up a phone and pressed a button. "Your dog has returned. He's right here. The police consultant brought him in." She paused. "You'll have to ask her." She replaced the receiver and turned to her computer.

Eldred bustled from around the corner. Featherington did not rise to greet him. "Where did you find him?" he demanded. Then he glanced at Michael. "Got someone else with you today. Not the caustic cop."

"This is my boyfriend." Olivia pulled on Featherington's lead, urging him to stand up. The dog opened one eye and growled but remained on his side.

"I'll take that." Whitlock reached for the leash. "Sit," he commanded.

The Frenchie stood and then shook from head to tail. He did not sit. Instead he glanced at Olivia with a disappointed glare.

Uma placed her hands on the counter and spoke to her husband in a firm voice. "Would you hurry along and take him away? I have work to do."

Eldred stooped to pick up Featherington, but the dog avoided his grasp with a well-executed duck and dart. Eldred tried again. The Frenchie growled at the back of his throat.

"Up you go." Eldred lifted the Frenchie into his arms. Featherington the Fifth immediately squirmed for release.

"Looks like he's happy to be home," Michael whispered to Olivia.

Eldred clamped his arms around the dog. "I want to hear more about how you found him. I'll leave him in his room and meet you in my office."

Once seated, Olivia explained about Arlo's cabin and how Featherington was trapped in a dog crate. Then she took a long breath and sat back in her chair.

"Sounds fishy to me," was the owner's only comment.

"What's behind the curtain?" Michael nodded.

"A restricted area," Eldred said dismissively. Then his expression changed. "It's not a secret," he explained. "The curtain provides privacy. We have to keep our prize stud very calm, that's why we use the same breeding room each time. After he does his duty, I collect the specimen and then send it to the female breeder via certified mail.

"I go out of my way to make the environment familiar for my stud. I play soothing music and bring scents to heighten Featherington's libido. I use plastic female Frenchie molds—"

"That's enough." Olivia's head throbbed, now having heard this information for a second time. "I don't want to hear about the details of Featherington's sex life. You know, there are animal activists who think the breeding of Frenchies and all flat-faced breeds should be shut down."

She intended to make him defensive, but instead Eldred smiled. "That's not a new issue. People are jealous. The truth is that a good owner can keep a Frenchie well and safe for years with the proper care.

"I tell people, 'If you don't want a Frenchie, you don't have to buy one.' I don't know why activists think they get an opinion. All that talk about health issues. Every breed of dog has problems. They criticize about the price of AKC dogs too. It's a free country, and I can set the price for a well-bred French bulldog who is AKC certified. That's capitalism."

Eldred continued, "I only make money because people are willing to spend. It doesn't take any arm-twisting to sell a puppy, believe you me." He pointed to the photos behind his chair. "Our dogs are adorable. You can show them if you're so inclined. I send all the proper credentials with each purchase, enabling people to register with the AKC." When Olivia didn't respond, he reached into his desk.

He held a checkbook in his hand. "You are, of course, aware of the finder's fee for Featherington. I've received several calls, but you actually *found* my dog. I'll write a check and then our business will be finished." He put his pen to the paper and signed with a flourish. "If there isn't anything else..." He held the check to Olivia.

When she didn't take it right away, he looked impatient. "Not enough. I'll add another thousand. But I want to have my vet check him over first. Stop by tomorrow."

Olivia rose from her seat. "I won't be taking your money, Mr. Whitlock. I'm a police consultant. You reported a lost pet and I found him. That's part of my job." She nodded to Michael and made her way to the door.

CHAPTER TWENTY-NINE

Olivia felt lightheaded. She took hold of Michael's arm for support.

"Let's sit over there," he suggested. "It will give you a chance to regroup. That was quite an exit." He ushered her toward the overstuffed sofa in the lobby. She gratefully lowered her body onto the cushions. He sat next to her.

Lifting her finger, she touched the bandage. "It's very tender," she admitted. "The madder I got, the more my head throbbed. I'm kinda tired." She laid her hand on his knee. "That's your first meeting with Eldred Whitlock. He's intense, don't you think?" She looked to him for confirmation.

"He's a handful," Michael admitted. "Totally obsessed with his breeding business and he thinks everyone else wants to hear the details. I get why Janis doesn't trust him."

Michael chuckled. "I'm really happy that you cut him off about the insemination."

"I felt kind of defensive for Featherington." Olivia rested her head on his shoulder. "The dog didn't ask for that kind of life. His only purpose is to produce sperm. Plus the breeders are genetically engineering a species who cannot sign a consent form."

Michael turned to look at her. "You are a true canine advocate." Keenly aware that she'd surprised him in a good way, she felt her heart warm. She listened for a moment before holding her finger to her lips. "Uma's talking," she explained.

"You don't have to have a Frenchie to stay here," Uma explained in her assertive tone. "But if your plan is to sneak your dog in your room behind my back to avoid the pet fee, there will be an extra cost! And you will be evicted with no refund."

"She's fierce about running her inn," Oliva said quietly. "And not much escapes her attention. Once she's finished, let's make our move. I can think up some excuse to engage her in conversation."

"Not without Janis," he cautioned. "You two are a team. When you take me, it's not the same."

Olivia realized he was right. But that didn't make it easier for her to hear.

Michael kept talking in a low voice. "I know I haven't been that supportive in the past with you volunteering as Janis's consultant." He pointed to the bandage on her head. "But I've been watching you in action for two days. Even when you're knocked down, you stand back up. And the way you told off Eldred, that was kind of a turn-on. Plus your control. You begin by listening. But when people cross the line, you call them out."

Olivia didn't know what to say. Feeling flabbergasted that he'd seen her so clearly required a reassessment. *Maybe I'm not invisible.* She pulled his head down to speak into his ear.

"That right there, your observations and feedback. I don't have words..." She kissed his ear. "Let's talk more later. Right now, I want to interview Uma."

. . .

Shelton Ayers stood at the counter holding Juicy Fruit in his arms. "Take some time off," he urged Uma. "We can stroll through town with Juicy. Maybe stop for a drink at the pub."

A smile played at the corner of Uma's mouth. "I would love to take that stroll with you and Juicy. Give me a few minutes and then I'll call for backup."

Olivia blinked at Michael and then reached into her pocket for a leftover dog treat. "Juicy Fruit," she called in a loud voice. "Look what I have." She waved the treat in the air. The Frenchie needed no further coaxing. She leapt from Shelton's arms, her feet skittering across the floor. Olivia held the treat in her open palm, which the dog immediately took and swallowed, leaving a trace of saliva on her palm.

Shelton came closer. "Oh, it's you." He pulled on the dog's leash. "You should ask before you give an unfamiliar dog a treat. Here, Juicy. Come with me."

Shelton scooped Juicy Fruit into his arms. "I'm waiting for Uma," he explained, sitting in a nearby armchair.

"Sorry about that," Olivia said. "But at least your dog seems well trained. Are all Frenchies so easy to teach?"

Michael gave her a side-eye.

He's wondering why I'm asking questions I know the answer to. But it helps ease people into opening up. We have to find Arlo's killer. Shelly could give up an important clue.

And to Olivia's delight, Shelton began to explain.

"Oh no, French bulldogs are notoriously stubborn. It took me months of training with Juicy to get her to come when I call. Even now, she doesn't consistently respond to my husband. Do you, sweetie?" Shelton tweaked the dog's jowl.

"Janis Jets," Olivia began," has a young Frenchie named

Tater Tot. She might need a good referral for a trainer. Anyone you'd recommend?"

Shelly's brow wrinkled. He shrugged. "I can make a list later and drop it by the constabulary."

"What about George Quigley?" Olivia thought he would be an obvious choice.

"No, I don't think so."

He doesn't want to recommend George. Interesting.

"I'm ready for that stroll." Uma Whitlock emerged wearing black leggings and a form-fitting Woofstock T-shirt.

Shelton stood up. "Nice talking to you," he said.

Uma turned to Michael instead. "I've been thinking about a new project that I'd like to run past you. When you have a moment, of course. I know you must be busy." She tittered and blinked. "Do you have a card perhaps, with your contacts?

He handed her a card from his back pocket.

Olivia didn't want to waste any more time. "So I overheard that you're going for a walk. Why don't we join you? As a matter of fact..." She turned to Michael. "We can stop at the brew pub for a drink and you two will have a chance to discuss Uma's project."

"I could show you the rest of Juicy Fruit's tricks," Shelton added with enthusiasm. "She's quite fun. And then maybe you can give her another treat."

Michael and Uma walked ahead as Olivia talked to Shelton about his dog. By the time they reached town, he'd lost all of his defensiveness. "Call me Shelly. All my friends do."

"I will, Shelly," Olivia agreed.

They stopped to cross the road. Vehicles sped past. "It's so crowded here," Shelly observed. "When I first arrived in Lily

Rock last Wednesday, there was barely any traffic." He stepped into the road, rewarded by a horn blast from an SUV.

"You see? Look at that man. So impatient." Shelton picked up Juicy Fruit, hurrying the rest of the distance.

"The Woofstock festival brought so many tourists up the hill. It caught the town council by surprise," Olivia explained, once all four stood safely on the curb.

"Small-town life, so quaint. I could never live here full time," Shelly explained.

"It's not for everyone," she admitted.

Voices drifted toward them from the brew pub's outdoor patio. "Sounds crowded this afternoon," Michael said.

Uma looked disappointed. "Will there be a place to sit?"

"Wait right here." Michael maneuvered up the stairs past two people looking at their phones.

"Here you go." The server handed out menus. "This table just opened up. I hope you don't mind sitting on the lower deck. We had to open it up for the weekend."

"They usually reserve this space just for parties," Michael explained. By the time they gave their orders, Juicy Fruit had made herself comfortable under the table.

When the waiter returned, he placed their drinks on the table and then bent over to put a metal bowl in front of Juicy Fruit. "Would you prefer tap or bottled water for the Frenchie?" he asked.

"Bottled," Shelton insisted. "Room temperature."

"Got it." The server disappeared into the crowd.

Olivia lifted her glass of sparkling water. "To new ventures and friends."

Uma raised her beer, as did Shelly and Michael.

Michael elbowed her under the table. She took his hand,

then cleared her throat and leaned toward Uma. "That first day, I was under the impression you and Shelly didn't know each other. But now it seems as if you're old friends." Not wanting to cause any defensiveness, she used a soft voice, as if observing something natural, like the weather.

Uma and Shelly turned to look at each other at the same time. Shelly hid a self-conscious grin.

"Should I tell her? She seems nice," he asked. Then he reached his arm around Uma's shoulders. "We're twin flames."

Olivia gulped. She'd not heard that expression for some time.

"Not quite, dear. But I do think of you as my very own son." Uma kissed his cheek. She plunged ahead. "Shelton was my therapist. We've been working together for a year or so. But it wasn't until he unexpectedly showed up at the inn that we met in person. What a surprise. Such a happy coincidence." She patted his hand.

"Your therapist," Michael said with surprise. "Isn't friendship precluded from the therapeutic relationship?"

"You could say that." Shelly's tone sounded cautious. "But let me explain. This was an accident. I had no idea Uma was calling me from Lily Rock. My state license requires that all my clients call from California and also verify the location they're calling from.

He leaned closer to Uma with a playful nudge. "You can imagine my surprise when I saw Uma behind the reception desk at the inn. Of course I knew immediately; the sense of peace and recognition in my heart. She's just like my mom, may she rest in peace."

"I was shocked," Uma admitted. "Dr. Ayers never mentioned anything about himself. I had no idea where he lived. He's such a professional." She added the last part sounding as if she needed to convince herself.

"I was there the day you first saw each other," Olivia inter-jected. "I sensed something was going on. But you"—she nodded to Uma"—seemed more interested in Juicy Fruit's AKC status."

"I was covering up," Uma tittered. "It's not every day that you run into your therapist in the flesh. He's so much more handsome in person." She playfully pinched his cheek.

She leaned closer to Olivia. "I am on my toes every minute behind that counter. People come at me day and night. I never know when George Quigley is going to show up. He's a pest. And he takes over if I hesitate for a minute. I think he wants to run the inn. Onerous man."

"But I'm taking care of all of that." Shelton's eyes narrowed. "Now that I'm here, I can deal with Quigley. She's been worried for months. Uma's told me everything, and believe me, he's a menace."

"So you're no longer in a therapeutic relationship." Michael looked stern.

"Oh no. As soon as I realized the problem, I called my company. So understanding. They said it happens occasion-ally, especially now that teletherapy has become the rage. They removed Uma from my client list." He looked at her fondly. "And now we can be friends."

"Friends who love Frenchies." Uma smiled, displaying two rows of small, perfectly white teeth.

Uma checked her phone. "It's only a couple of hours until the Woofstock parade. I need to get to our booth. Time to help people dress their pets." She looked at another text. "I offered all the guests staying at the inn a free embossed shirt and a tie-dyed scarf. And I gave everyone a 15 percent discount on grooming."

"Maybe you can show me Juicy's tricks another time," Olivia said.

"That would be marvelous," Shelly replied.

Michael reached for the bill. "I'll take care of this, since you're new to the neighborhood."

Uma looked pleased.

He paid the bill and they walked single file down the crowded stairway. On the sidewalk, Olivia bent down to say goodbye to Juicy Fruit.

"I hope Juicy gets a medal," Shelton said. "She's a beautiful dog and so worthy."

Olivia rose. "Are they offering prizes at the parade? I thought it was all in fun. You know, dressing up and cheering. A joyous celebration of dogs and life. There may be a participation certificate, I can see that. So Lily Rock."

"I can't believe they won't have a prize," Shelton fussed. "What's wrong with you open-minded people? If I bother to groom and dress my dog I— I mean *she* deserves a reward."

Michael used a firm voice. "We're like that in Lily Rock. A bunch of perfect snowflakes who prefer to enjoy their pets, not use them for financial gain."

"But it's fun to win," Shelly grumbled.

"And now we have to go. Olivia has to rest and then check in with the constabulary."

Once they were out of sight, Michael put his arm around her shoulders. "All that talk about dogs and outfits. Did you see Juicy Fruit's nails? Bright pink."

"Sometimes owners and dogs have matching polish," she explained. "At least in Los Angeles. It's called a pawdicure."

"Give me a break." He looked both ways and ushered her across the street.

CHAPTER THIRTY

"I've been thinking," Michael began. "Is it right for you to volunteer without compensation. You're risking your life and you have a unique skill set. The way you get people to open up. How you ask questions you have answers to, for one. It works. By the time people get talking, they can't stop.

"The way you chatted up Shelly and then Uma at the pub," he continued. "I don't know how you do it. By the end they were eating out of your hand. Telling you their entire story. I don't think either one realized how odd it sounded because you listened with such an open expression.

"No wonder Jets wants you on her team. That's the exact opposite of how she interviews people. She picks them up by the feet and shakes them upside down until everything drops out." He stopped to wait for traffic.

"You, on the other hand," he continued, "smile with genuine appreciation. You listen and don't judge. Those people just opened up, and opened up like a book." He took her hand to dart across the street.

She stopped on the boardwalk to take a breath. "That's a lot to think about." She smiled and then glanced toward the constabulary entrance. "But now I need to connect with Janis."

"How's the wound?" he asked softly.

"Not great, but I'm hanging in there," she admitted.

He opened the constabulary door, standing aside to let her go first.

"What do you want?" Jets glared as they both sat down. "Get a load of this, Bellemare. Just like old times, when we investigated together."

Michael turned to Olivia. "Before I met you, Janis and I caught a couple of bad guys. One time she assigned me the job of painting a wall to eavesdrop on her interviews."

"I haven't heard that story before," Olivia commented.

"I was at a low point for the holidays. I think she wanted my help, but she most likely wanted to distract me from my low mood. All this happened before you arrived."

"This one," Jets said, pointing at Michael, "is responsible for getting me hired. I was not going to take on a small-town job until he convinced my boss. Did it behind my back."

"Speaking of behind the back," Michael began, "Olivia told me that you're playing fast and loose with the evidence. The letter opener, for one, and now you're going to plant a matchbook. What are you up to, Officer Jets? This isn't the woman I went out on a limb for. The one I got hired as the first and only Lily Rock constable."

Jets's eyes narrowed. "So Nancy Drew spilled my plan. Don't you worry. I'm not going to bring up the evidence until we've arrested one of those Whitlocks."

"Do you *really* think Uma's a suspect?" Olivia insisted. "We just had a drink with her at the pub. She's a very nice woman."

"She looks like a 1950s housewife. Not all of them were so innocent. But I got her fingerprints on a matchbook. Stopped in and waited. No one wants a cop hanging around, so she offered me the matchbook to get rid of me. Once I got back to my desk, I wrote 'stop looking' on the inside cover. Just like the original. You're the only two who can tell the difference." She glared at Olivia then Michael.

"You didn't," Olivia objected. "That's tampering with evidence 101."

"I did, and I'd do it again." Jets shook her head. "You're not the professional here. We do what we have to do to get the guilty put behind bars."

She turned to Michael. "What did you think of Uma?"

"A bit money conscious," he said. "No one's getting past her without paying for their dog's stay."

"A bit too smooth if you ask me. She'd probably bump off her grandma under the right circumstances. Right after Woofstock I'm going to bring her in. And her husband too." Janis's eyes narrowed again. Then she changed the subject.

"By the way, now that you two have agreed to be Tater Tot's godparents, we'll be throwing him a Welcome to Lily Rock party after all of this is over."

"Party..." Olivia's head throbbed.

"That's right. Our Tater Tot is inviting a few friends to celebrate. The little rascal." Her eyes grew moist.

This is crazy, Olivia thought. *She's crying over her dog and a party.*

And then Jets's face shifted. She'd gone from tears to anger in a matter of seconds. "I think Uma's complicit," Jets snapped. "But she wasn't the one to clobber you from behind. That's all Eldred. He's a piece of work. But once I've read Uma her rights, I'll crack her open like a hard-boiled egg.

Then you'll peel off the shell and we'll get to the truth. She's lying for Eldred. The dirty scum."

Olivia couldn't believe her ears. "I don't think Uma's necessarily lying."

"I don't trust her," Jets fumed. "What else did you learn at the brew pub?"

"It was mostly chitchat," Michael chimed in. "But there's something else. We found evidence in Arlo's cabin: paperwork and his laptop."

Jets sat up straight. "I thought I told my guys to sweep the place three days ago. I suppose they might have dropped the ball. The traffic up the hill could have done it."

"You might have forgotten," Olivia suggested.

"Not on your life. It's their fault. Okay, spill, Mike. What did you find exactly?"

"We found breeding contracts written by Arlo," he said.

"But more importantly, we also found Featherington the Fifth," Olivia added.

Jets's eyebrows shot up. "Did you now? At Arlo's, you say? I may have underestimated you two."

"The dog was trapped in a kennel," Olivia explained.

Janis's eyes drifted down to her desk. "So it was a case of dognapping. Probably one of those crazy Woofstock people." She looked up. "Imagine that. Did you return the mutt to his rightful owner?"

"We did. Took him right over to The Frenchie Connection. Eldred offered us the reward," Olivia said.

"She didn't take it," Michael inserted. "She told Whitlock that as a police consultant, she wasn't able to accept a fee."

"Did she now." Jets's gaze shifted to Olivia.

"Like Michael said, we also discovered paperwork, legal contracts. It seems Whitlock expected to get a puppy as payment. Lots of stipulations about timing and health."

Jets looked surprised. "That's a new one on me."

"I thought something else was odd," Olivia hurried to add. "Featherington the Fifth didn't act one bit happy to be reunited with Eldred. He played dead in front of the desk at the inn, rather than run into his owner's arms. No love lost there."

"I can explain that," Jets said. "Dogs are for business. Featherington probably senses he's a meal ticket. Not like our Tater Tot. He's our little love bunny."

Olivia resisted rolling her eyes.

"Just so you know, Officer Jets," Michael began. Jets startled at his use of her official title. "Now that I'm thinking about it, Sydney Ayers was acting really suspicious yesterday. He's the investigative reporter."

"For *It's a Dog's World*." Janis looked skeptical.

"According to him, he's doing a deep undercover piece about French bulldog breeding practices," Michael explained. "Maybe he tangled with Arlo. It could happen."

"Nah, there's no tangling. Ayers works for a dog tabloid, not the *Enquirer*. That guy is a Frenchie lover. He didn't come up to uncover anything. He combined work with pleasure. The assignment gave him a chance to hang out with his husband and to flaunt Juicy Fruit. She's a pretty little thing. Pet quality, of course. Like Tater Tot."

Jets's eyes glazed over. "They could have made such cute puppies."

"Maybe Ayers didn't know Arlo. But what about the trainer, George Quigley?" Olivia asked.

"We also suspect him," Michael said. "We found Quigley at the dog park with another Frenchie. He told us it belonged to Whitlock. Almost identical to Featherington the Fifth, but this one's called Featherington the Sixth."

"Easy come, easy go," Jets muttered.

"There's more," Olivia continued. "Quigley has apps."

"What do you mean 'apps'?" Now Jets looked interested. "We all have apps. How are his any different?"

"Quigley has an app to locate his boss and another one to intercept his text messages." Michael frowned. "Kind of sophisticated and suspicious in my opinion."

Jets held her finger to her chin. "Apps. I admit, on the one hand, the dog trainer is sneakier than I gave him credit for. Kinda clever, keeping track of his employer that way. But on the other hand, just having those apps proves my point. Even he didn't trust Eldred. It all goes back to him."

Her eyes sparkled with victory. "Plus it's not Quigley. He told me the first day when he found the body that he'd never seen Arlo before."

Olivia's heart pounded. "But listen to this. Quigley showed up out of the blue and insisted on helping us find Mayor Maguire. Doesn't that look suspicious, as if he were trying to keep us away from Featherington the Fifth's hideout?"

Jets placed her arms on the desk. "Sounds like the act of a Good Samaritan to me."

"Not exactly," Michael said. "The way I look at it, Quigley wanted to find Featherington the Fifth first since he was the one responsible for losing the dog. Maybe his job was in jeopardy."

"Tell me more about how you found Featherington in a dog crate."

"We were looking for Mayor Maguire," Olivia explained. "We found him on Arlo's porch. Then we walked inside and Featherington started to yip. Once we saw him in the crate, we released him. I think Maguire kept his eye on Featherington until he was rescued."

"Maybe Maguire deserves the cash prize." Jets slumped

back in her chair. "Come on, you two. We've gone in circles and come back to where we started. We have a dog trainer named George Quigley who uses apps to check on his boss. He told me at the dog park the morning he found Arlo that they'd never met. I have no reason not to believe him.

"Then we have Ayers, who showed up for Woofstock on the dime of his editor. He used his work budget to take his dog and his husband on a paid vacation. Ayers ran into you two and thought he'd have a bit of fun exposing the breeding room.

"We have no evidence that he knew Arlo. He's more likely a typical tabloid journalist. Pulling back the curtain on stuff people would prefer not to see. But when they do, they can't stop looking. He's a sensationalist at heart, waiting for the moment to reveal a scandal.

"Then there's Eldred," she said with finality. "And Uma, of course. He had the murder weapon right on his desk. You were my witness, Olivia. And Uma, she lied to cover up what he did."

"Would he be stupid enough to leave the murder weapon in plain sight?" Olivia asked.

"He's stupid enough to breed AKC-certified Frenchies and exclude my Tater Tot," Jets fumed. "Don't forget, the lab identified Arlo's blood." She looked thoughtful. "Plus you got assaulted and were left with a warning written right on The Frenchie Connection matchbook. Those clues lead right back to the Whitlocks. You said Eldred was not available when Ayers gave you that tour. He probably followed you to Thyme Out and then snuck down the alley to give you that whop.

"Like I've been telling you, as soon as this festival is over, I'll bring in Eldred and Uma. Then I'll get to the bottom of Arlo's death, one way or another."

"But you still can't explain," Olivia stated flatly, "why Eldred or Uma would have wanted to kill Arlo."

"Don't you worry, Nancy Drew. That's for me to know and you to find out. Get out of here," Jets grumbled. "I need to order some deli trays for Tater Tot's party."

Olivia and Michael walked down the hall in silence. Janis Jets called out, "One more thing. Don't show up empty-handed. Bring a side dish."

CHAPTER THIRTY-ONE

Olivia collapsed on the sofa. Michael tucked a blanket up to her chin. "Janis is making me crazy," she commented, eyes closed.

He sat next to her. "Here, let me have your feet." He lifted them gently to his lap.

She opened one eye as he began to massage her right foot.

"Does this help?" he asked.

"You're magic." She closed her eye. "I don't know how a foot massage fixes a headache, but I don't need to know. Just don't stop."

Michael continued to dig his fingers into her arch. "I haven't paid close attention to Janis for quite a while now. Been preoccupied with the house. But after this afternoon, I have to give you a lot of credit. Janis has that stubborn streak, so determined that she's right, even when faced with facts to the contrary."

"Ooh, that feels good," Olivia moaned. "She's worse than usual. From tears over Tater Tot to rage at Eldred Whitlock. I can't take much more of this—the way she's made up her mind and then uses all of the facts to support her first rush to judgment."

"So it's all because of Tater Tot?" Michael sounded puzzled.

"I saw it happen right in front of my eyes. As soon as Eldred excluded her precious dog, her mind shut down. Her emotions got the better of her."

"She's fierce, defending her dog as if he were a child," Michael mused.

"Thanks to Cookie," Olivia muttered. "He bought Tater Tot for her since she didn't want to have children."

"So what are we going to do?" Michael picked up her other foot. "Do we keep up our investigation or do we let the cop handle it herself? She's the one paid to do the job." He kneaded the arch of her foot, making her groan.

"I've made it a point to keep mostly quiet, especially during our interviews with suspects. But I can't let her use me to get a confession if the person isn't guilty. That's where I draw the line."

Michael smoothed his hand over her calf. When he stopped she opened one eye. "Are you thinking..."

"I've got a lot going on in my mind," he assured her. "But the most important is to make sure you're okay. Do I need to call Sage and cancel the concert?"

Olivia sighed. "How long until the parade? That's first, before the gig."

"We've got an hour or so."

"If I can get a nap, I think I'll be fine. We planned a short set, maybe an hour at the most. It's important that we send the Woofstock people home with a song and a good impression of Lily Rock."

"The Old Rockers would like that," Michael chuckled. "But not at your expense. So how about this..."

His words quickly grew distant as her eyelids slid closed. And before she could hear his suggestion, she fell asleep.

"Testing one, two, three," Meadow McCloud's voice blared over the microphone. "Would all of the dogs and their owners line up over here. Alphabetically, please, according to breed."

"My dog is first," a man with an Afghan announced.

"What about mixed breeds?" asked a woman with a dog who looked like a mixture of Labrador and German shepherd.

Meadow looked confused. She bent down to talk to Olivia. "I never thought of that. What about mixed breeds?"

"You could separate them from the others."

"Since there are no prizes, does it matter where you are in the line? This is supposed to be fun," Michael insisted.

"You are right as usual." Meadow leaned closer to the microphone. "Forget what I just said. Line up in whatever order you want. This is a Lily Rock parade, and we don't care who's first."

"What about Mayor Maguire?" someone else shouted.

He pointed to the mayor, who waited in the passenger seat of an old Mustang convertible with streamers hanging off the back bumper. Two magnetic signs, one on the passenger side and one on the driver's side, read: "Mayor Maguire, Lily Rock's Favorite Politician." The mayor also sported his straw cowboy hat and a bright red necktie.

"He has no choice," Meadow snapped. "He leads the parade. Everyone else, just get in line."

One visitor, dressed in cutoff shorts and no shirt, had to have the last word. "We could line up the dogs according to size. And then let the tallest go first. That would be my Irish wolfhound."

"Like I said, get in line." Meadow switched off her microphone. She took a seat on the edge of the platform between Olivia and Michael. "I can't wait until Woofstock is over."

"You must be missing Arlo," Olivia said. "All of this was his vision."

"He was in charge," Meadow agreed. "And I keep thinking I see him in the crowd. Look over there. Doesn't that look just like Arlo carrying a French bulldog?" She pointed toward the park.

Olivia gulped. A tall man with a short beard ambled toward them. "That's him. I saw that same guy a day ago. He was carrying a Frenchie too, but then he vanished into thin air. At least now you see him too." Olivia blinked. "Wait a minute. I know that guy. He's not Arlo."

"That guy over there?" Michael wanted to make sure. "That's George Quigley. He's carrying one of the Featheringtons."

As Quigley came closer, Olivia realized what she'd not connected before—his similarity to Arlo. "Same height. Similar facial hair. Same thin build. He's wearing a Bob Dylan sweatshirt, but you'd have to get close to distinguish the difference. Let's face it, Arlo looked like and dressed like Quigley."

"And the baseball cap," Meadow added. "That man Quigley, he's wearing the same navy-blue baseball cap. Identical to Arlo's. Faded the same way."

Quigley and Featherington ran across the street. He hurried toward Meadow. "Are you the one in charge?"

"Yes I am, dear. How can I help?"

"I have an AKC fully certified French bulldog stud right here. His name is Featherington the Fifth. If you would, please announce to the crowd that any dog here today who is not spayed, who may be in heat, must exit this excuse for a parade and leave my dog in peace. We can't have any unwanted pregnancies, and Featherington is a highly desirable stud."

Olivia rolled her eyes at Michael.

Meadow looked stunned. The sheer audacity of the request rendered her speechless. Her mouth hung open slightly as if she couldn't quite believe what she'd heard.

She cleared her throat. "I won't do that," she stated calmly.

"Then I'll do it." Quigley snatched the microphone, the stand toppling over. Michael caught it midair. "I don't think so, Quigley." He shoved Quigley off-balance and took the microphone from his hand. "You're not in charge of this parade. You're a guest in Lily Rock. If you have grievances with our policies, I suggest you take them up at the next town council meeting."

Quigley puffed himself up. "Is that so," he growled.

Fortunately Featherington the Fifth had grown impatient. He decided to distract everyone with a whine and a sharp bark. One good yank on the leash and it tore from Quigley's grasp.

"Better get your stud," Meadow said dryly.

George ran after the dog.

Olivia breathed a sigh of relief.

"I'm so tired of representing Lily Rock," Michael said. "This weekend is taxing my patience. No more tourists." He replaced the microphone on the upright stand and then turned on the switch. He seemed to take a moment to think, then removed the mic from its stand. "Okay, this is the last announcement, so listen up. Anyone can participate in the parade. We're not changing the rules for your pet, no matter how special it is. This is a come one, come all event. No one gets special status.

"Second of all, there will be no prizes. No participation

medals. No giveaways or compensations for participating in this event. You just get to have a good time.

"And finally, we welcome visitors, but there's a limit. So pick up after yourselves and your dog. We've provided lots of free poop bags. I know most of you do yoga, so do a downward dog and pick up the poop and pretend it's exercise." He turned off the mic. Instead of replacing it on the stand, he slipped it into the pocket of his cargo shorts.

Olivia wrapped her arms around him for a hug. Once she released him, he patted his pocket. "I always wondered if cargo pockets were just a fashion statement. And now I found a use for mine. Form and function. Just like a good architectural plan. I'm not done with this, however." He pulled her in for another embrace.

Once all the hugging was over, the three of them sat back on the edge of the platform. They watched the crowd. Meadow reached over Olivia to pat Michael's shoulder. "Well done, dear. Arlo would have been proud."

Michael took charge of dinner. He made a simple green salad and then placed burgers on the grill, along with corn on the cob. All while Olivia rested on the sofa.

Hearing him hum as he worked made her smile. She felt a cold nose bump her arm. "Hello, M&M. You were quite the star at the parade." He nosed her arm again. Before she could say no, he jumped onto the sofa. Gently placing his paws on her shoulders, he edged his body on top of her, resting his head under her chin.

"Well this is a surprise." She scratched behind his ears. Holding him with both arms, she appreciated the weight and his steady breath. *Dog as weighted blanket*, she thought, relaxing her entire body into the cushions.

"What's going on?" Michael held a glass of sparkling water. "I turn my back for a minute and Maguire takes over."

She held her finger to her lips. "He's asleep." The dog's gentle snores made her smile.

Michael put the glass on the table. "That mutt deserves a lot of credit. He led us to the discovery of Featherington. He led the Lily Rock parade. And now he's taking the lead on comforting you. He really must be psychic. No more doubts."

Maguire woke up and lifted his head at the sound of his name. He turned to lick Olivia's chin and then eased himself off of her body, onto the floor to make his way to the rug in front of the fireplace. Three turns and he lay wrapped up in a ball, his head on his front paws.

"Come sit down." Olivia patted the sofa. "I'm feeling better thanks to you and M&M."

He offered her the glass. "Keep hydrating. It will help."

She took a sip. "In his own way, Maguire has been leading the investigation. He wasn't missing, he was working. Acting as Featherington's bodyguard. If it weren't for him, we wouldn't know that Janis's team never picked up the evidence."

Michael lifted her feet, laying them in his lap.

Olivia started to theorize. "We found those contracts. We know Arlo may have exaggerated his role as an attorney. What if his death has something to do with his lie? Of course we'd say his...embellishment...was Arlo being Arlo, but someone who isn't from Lily Rock might conclude they'd been swindled and gotten really angry."

"I see where you're going with this," Michael said. "So someone might have killed Arlo because he was being Arlo; he stretched the truth and got involved in a not quite illegal but not really legal scam. But this time he couldn't apologize and fix the problem. Maybe somebody killed him before he could make it right."

Olivia remembered the first time she'd seen Arlo make an apology. When he admitted in front of the entire town that he'd failed to apply for a legal new business license. She'd watched in fascination how everyone responded.

The photo on his wall commemorated the small moment, the one when everyone agreed not to punish but to forgive. *Maybe Arlo should have paid a fine,* she thought. *Maybe the consequences of lying and moving ahead without obeying the rules led to him doing it over again. He could have learned if the town had bothered to hold him accountable.*

"What are you thinking?" Michael asked.

"About a photo I saw the first time Janis and I went to Arlo's place."

He glanced across the room toward the fireplace mantel. "What happened to our photos?"

"In the garage," she said. "Still boxed up. I forgot all about them. Why do you ask?"

"I designed that mantel for photos. Lots of pictures of us and our friends. I have one of Daniel, if you remember. And you have that funny photo of your mom when you were really young. You held an autoharp."

Olivia felt her heart beat faster. "Yes, that one," she said in a quiet voice. "Did you really design the mantel deliberately for photographs?"

"I did. There's a small carved-out ledge to keep them from toppling over. My guy carved it when he made the shelf.

"Before you came, I was pretty low after my son passed, especially around his birthday. It was Christmastime, and I finally opened up to Sage. She was so understanding. Afterward I felt much better. I was able to put the anger from my sadness into perspective. I realized I couldn't change

227

anything; Daniel was still gone. But Sage and Meadow, Arlo and Cayenne—they became my family.

"In fact, it was that Christmas morning that I knew. And then the year after that, you showed up." He looked into her eyes. "Nothing's been the same since. For me. For any of us."

Olivia squirmed. She wasn't used to having Michael's full attention. "Can we talk about the investigation now?"

CHAPTER THIRTY-TWO

Olivia took some time to dress for her gig. It had been a while, so she needed to reassess her closet, shoving to the side outfits that no longer felt right. She knew she was odd in her choice of clothing. Because she didn't take to trends, nor wear something because it was readily available.

Instead, she chose her gig wear based on how it felt. Holding one of her black leather cowboy boots with the fringe, she waited. Her heart softened and she felt a ripple of energy up her spine.

Definitely those. They reminded her of how she felt just before Sage played her first note. The anticipation and jittery nerves pushing her past her usual reserve to the place of showing who she was in real time.

The rest of her outfit came from that initial decision. *What will go with my black fringe cowboy boots?* A full black flounce skirt with a white peasant top. Hair hanging over her shoulders in waves. Light foundation and some eyeliner. "I'm done," she announced to her autoharp, which waited in the corner.

"All ready?" Michael called. He looked her up and down

as she came outside. "Ready for me at least," he said appreciatively.

She looked toward the bridge, into the woods. No word from Cayenne, but she felt her presence in the pine-scented breeze and the sound of water gently flowing past rocks in the creek.

Michael wore black jeans and a button-up plaid shirt. His leather square-toed boots were fashionably scuffed at the toe. "You smell nice," she commented, reaching for his hand.

He squeezed her fingers. "I just want to make sure. Cayenne is no longer a suspect in Arlo's murder, right?"

Sometimes Michael could be so perceptive. *He must have known I was thinking about Cay.* Olivia sat down next to him. "Janis has waffled on it. I never thought she'd kill Arlo, but she did disappear. I think she has a solid alibi. That's what I know."

"I presume Jets would have said something if she were still considering her as a suspect."

Olivia did not feel convinced. "Janis is obsessively focused on Eldred and Uma. Cayenne may be off of her radar. I'm certainly not going to bring her up at this point."

"Are you always like this? Evaluating Janis's moods and working around them?"

Olivia tilted her head in surprise. "I never thought of it that way. But now that you mention it, it feels true."

Michael gave her a half smile. "So what are you singing tonight?"

"Most of our oldies but goodies," she said. "But one new cover. A Bonnie Raitt song. It's called 'Feels like Home'."

"I don't know that one," he said.

"It was on the soundtrack for an old John Travolta movie. Guess what the movie was called."

"Tell me."

"*Michael.*"

"Really? Named after me." He looked pleased.

"Let's rent it and you can see if there are similarities between you and Travolta's character," she teased.

A sharp bark came from the driveway. Tater Tot trotted across the bridge looking quite pleased with himself. "I think we have a visitor," Olivia said.

"Tater, come back," came Jets's desperate call.

The dog ignored her, making a beeline for Michael. He used both paws to scramble onto his lap.

"Geez." Michael grinned. "Hey, Tater Tot." He scratched under the Frenchie's chin.

Jets arrived breathless. "Oh good, I caught you both." She looked more tired than usual. Dark circles under her eyes were red from lack of sleep. She slumped in the closest chair. "This is nice. Like your deck at the old house." She rubbed her forehead with one hand.

Nothing about Jets's small talk caught Olivia off guard. *She has something on her mind.*

"And that bridge. It's kind of symbolic, you know," continued Jets in an uncharacteristically philosophical tone. "Like as soon as you get out of your car and step across, you leave your cares behind. Very peaceful."

She continued sounding more and more reflective, which caused Olivia to sit forward.

Jets droned on. "This house is somewhere you can be accepted. Maybe even with people who know you better than yourself. People that you can say, like for example, that you've made a mistake. People who would hear that confession and realize that you were sorry, even." Her voice got quiet at the end.

Olivia's full attention focused on Janis, she asked, "What are we talking about here?"

"Look, Nancy and Ned," Jets began. She glanced back and forth, her eyes begging for something unspoken.

"She's Nancy Drew, but who's Ned?" Michael looked puzzled.

"Don't you read? Ned is Nancy Drew's dumbass boyfriend, that's who. Ned is to Nancy like Ken is to Barbie. Kinda neutered males without a backstory. Ned looks handsome and follows Nancy around because he doesn't have a life."

Michael burst out laughing. "Nice try. You can call me Ned, but I'm not buying any of it. Now what's going on, Officer Jets? Did I hear someone will be making a confession?"

Michael handed Jets a cold beer. She sat back in her chair and took a slurp. "I haven't slept since Arlo died. So I got to thinking... Actually, after you two left yesterday, I did this test on myself. Something I use with people when an interview has stalled.

"I asked myself on a scale from one to ten, how strongly I believe that Eldred and Uma killed Arlo Carson." She took another long gulp and waited.

"Okay, I'll bite, how strongly did you feel?" Olivia asked.

"You see, I didn't have an answer right away. It was like my brain got stuck. I was so busy feeling certain. I was venting my emotions in some kind of self-righteous defense of my first judgment. I admit it took me a while. But then I realized. I was only at an eight."

"Not a ten." Olivia's voice was tentative because she was still uncertain about where Janis was going with this.

"Well that's the problem, isn't it," Jets admitted. "A cop has to be at a nine point five at least. Preferably a full-on ten before she makes an arrest. It's a waste of money and time to arrest an eight. So I finally had to admit to myself that this may be a first. That arresting someone on an eight would be contrary to my own procedure. So there was no sense in starting now."

"Who taught you to do that, the one to ten thing?" Olivia wondered whether this was Janis's personal invention or something more.

"My old captain. He told me when I was a recruit. It's a technique he figured out the hard way. He was almost scientific in his approach. He told me if people lock down on their feelings and attach an emotion, the brain is unable to consider new information.

"The only way to unlock the brain is to suggest that they might want to evaluate their experience. That's where the one to ten comes in. In the process of evaluating, the mind opens. Just a little at first. But at least there's a chance to disengage and consider the facts. Not all at once, but little by little.

"Once I put my feelings for the Tater aside, I only had to think about Arlo. I mean who would want to kill him. I know he wasn't the smartest tool in the box, but he wasn't a terrible guy.

"After that, I realized I'd ignored all the usual evidence. Not ignored exactly, but I didn't give it any weight. All that stuff about Quigley and Ayers. And I didn't follow up with forensics.

"Now we have to find Arlo's killer before it's too late. Once this festival is over, people will go home. After that it will be much harder."

"Aren't you forgetting something?" Michael reminded her. "In your confession."

"No. I've told you everything." She narrowed her eyes. "Well, there are a couple of details. Like Uma and Eldred were seen on camera at the time of death. My forensic team found them on the video setting up their T-shirt booth for the festival. The camera from outside the hardware store picked them up as well. A very clear picture."

"So they alibied each other after all," Olivia said.

"And aren't you forgetting something else?" Michael prodded.

Jets took another sip of beer. "Oh okay, Bellemare. I did come here to say...I'm sorry. I dismissed your evidence for no reason. My emotions got in the way. Fine. Now are you happy? That's my full confession and an apology." She thumped her bottle on the table.

Michael smiled. "Actually, I am. Happy. It does a man's heart good to hear a woman admit she's wrong."

Olivia raised her eyebrows. "Maybe that's enough confessing for one day. He's getting cocky."

Jets looked thoughtful. "It finally happened to me. You worked your mojo. I don't know how, but I knew I'd feel better once I told you the truth. As much as I hate to admit it."

"That's all well and good," Olivia said in a mild tone, "but you have to stop being so introspective. It's out of character. And we need to get going to catch the real killer."

"Plus I don't want Ned to think the story is about him."

CHAPTER THIRTY-THREE

The loud voices at the Lily Rock Amphitheater made it difficult to hear. Sage leaned closer to Olivia to speak into her ear. "Star's in the front row with Luis."

Olivia made a face at her niece, who sat on Luis's lap facing the stage. He gripped her around the waist as she bounced on his knees, her face aglow with excitement.

"She's so cute. Sorry I've been busy," Olivia apologized. "After this weekend I'll come by."

"We'd like that a lot." Sage nodded right as the announcer picked up the microphone. "I think that's our cue." She stepped farther onto the stage as Olivia then Cornelius and Dee Dee followed.

Over the applause, the announcer introduced the band. "And now, ladies and gentlemen, it's what you've been waiting for, Sweet Four O'Clock."

Sage stepped up to the microphone. "Hello, Lily Rock," she called out.

A loud burst of cheers erupted from the crowd.

"And hello Woofstock," she added, her voice bright with welcome. To the sound of whistles and shouts, Sage spun around, her short, ruffled skirt rising up to her thighs. "I dressed up," she told them with a cheeky grin. "What do you think?"

A dog barked, accompanied by hoots and hollers. More dogs joined in. Between the howls and the barking, Olivia could barely hear. She bent over her autoharp to listen to her strings, checking the tuning one last time.

A surge of excitement ran through the audience. Sage turned and nodded to the band, the sign to begin their opening song. But then she bent her head down as if to reconsider. The rest of Sweet Four O'clock waited.

Instead of counting them off, she turned back to the microphone. In a deep loud voice she called out, "This one's for Arlo."

Olivia felt her heart crack open as the crowd roared.

Sage lifted her fiddle to her shoulder. "One, two. One, two, three, four." She began to play. The solo sound of the violin lifted above barks and cheers as she leaned into "Will the Circle be Unbroken," a familiar old-time tune.

Cornelius joined her on drums, laying down a distinctive groove, making the way for Dee Dee's bass notes, which balanced the lighter fiddle melody. And finally Olivia lifted her autoharp across her chest, nestled in her left shoulder. Her thumb picked and her fingers flew over the strings as she began to sing, "Will the circle be unbroken by and by, Lord, by and by." Her voice brought the crowd to their feet.

Once Olivia rounded into the chorus, everyone joined in. Some sang, some waved their hands in the air.

Her jittery nerves were replaced with the tingle of pure excitement in the moment. *Welcome to Lily Rock*, she thought. *I'm finally home.*

On the last chorus she slowed the tempo as the song came to an end. She felt Arlo standing right next to her. She could see him in her mind's eye. His smile, the goofy Grateful Dead sweatshirt. The stringy ponytail that looked lame compared to his wife's luxurious black braid.

The way he'd greet and listen to her when she showed up at the pub. Standing in his usual place behind the bar. The way he poured her a sparkling water without her having to ask.

She thought of him then and she thought of him now. Her feelings brought him alive as she rounded the corner to end the song.

"In the sky, Lord. In the sky," she sang, her throat thick with emotion.

And the crowd went wild.

Olivia caught sight of Janis Jets standing stage left. Her arms were folded across her chest, a grim expression on her face.

Janis gestured and mouthed, "Get over here."

Olivia shook her head. "I've got one more song," she yelled over the crowd noise.

Jets gestured with two thumbs-down.

Determine to ignore her, Olivia bent closer to the autoharp. She plucked and listened, waiting for the right moment to make her introduction.

Jets glowered as Olivia rose from her stool.

But Olivia felt pulled. In the end, she walked over to Janis. "What do you want?"

The crowd began to jeer. "Leaving so soon?" someone called from the back.

Jets yanked her by the hand. "I need you. Got some new information about our suspect. You're not gonna believe it."

"Can this wait? I have one more song."

"I suppose, but don't take any encores."

Olivia turned back toward the stage.

Sage handed her the mic with a quizzical expression.

"I rarely speak at concerts," Olivia explained. "But this song came to me out of the blue. I was feeling kind of low, and then I remembered hearing Bonnie Raitt. She sang the Randy Newman cover.

"The band agreed to include the song in our set. But the thing is..." She looked out at the crowd. Her eyes found him, standing nearby.

"This song is dedicated to Michael. My Michael. Who, no matter where we live...is home for me." The crowd cheered as Olivia looked at Michael. He held his arms over his chest, with a huge smile on his face. She sat down on her stool and lifted her autoharp to her lap and then began to sing.

"Hurry up, Nancy Drew. Let's go before they start asking you for autographs." Janis ushered her toward the exit.

"Give me a minute." Olivia slid her instrument into the case.

Stepping toward the boardwalk, Olivia dodged an over-flowing trash can. Dog waste baggies spilled over the side. One couple had pitched their tent near the curb in the street. They sat on beach chairs with a polite dog wearing a scarf. "He's adopted," the man called out when he caught Olivia staring. "Not fancy."

Jets pushed past, mumbling under her breath. "I've got my suspects in three different rooms," she explained. When they stood in front of the constabulary, she turned to face Olivia. "It's your job to get the confession. Follow my lead."

. . .

By the time they entered the break room, Olivia felt nervous. Janis had made her role clear. She only hoped she could deliver. *This case felt different, even from the beginning.*

"Mr. and Mrs. Whitlock," Jets began. "You both know my consultant, Olivia Greer." She gestured with her head toward Olivia, who sat in the chair next to her.

Eldred wasted no time. "We came when you asked. I think you're way off course. Didn't even call my attorney because this is ridiculous. So if you're not going to charge me, I'm leaving." He looked at his wife. "You can decide for yourself."

"We just have a few details to clear up." Jets pulled out her tablet. "And Olivia will record with her cell phone, if you don't mind."

Olivia nodded and started the recording.

"Get this over with," Eldred muttered.

"So your alibi checked out," Jets began. "Both of you were folding shirts and setting up the Woofstock table at the time of death." She read a few notes on her tablet while everyone else waited. Then she looked up.

"There is the small matter of the murder weapon. I found it on your desk." Jets raised an eyebrow.

"What do you mean 'found it'?" Whitlock looked dubious.

"You sound surprised," Olivia said quickly.

"Of course I am. I admit it's my opener. Not like I had anything to hide. Do you think I'd actually be stupid enough to leave a murder weapon on top of my desk!"

Jets's eyebrow rose. "What about you?" She glared at Uma.

"It's just an old letter opener," she said with a bright voice. "We've had it for ages. I think it originally belonged to Eldred's father. When he passed, Eldred kept it to remember him by. At the time I said, 'Eldred, that's a dangerous weapon. Let's use something less alarming to open our mail.'

"But he didn't listen. He never does." Uma blinked. "I

poked myself on the hand once." She rolled the sleeve of her pink top to give Janis a better view. "So I never used it again. It stays on his desk." She rolled her sleeve back down.

Eldred rolled his eyes. "Did you find blood or fingerprints?"

"No fingerprints. It had been wiped clean. But we did find traces of the victim's blood between the blade and the handle."

Eldred looked skeptical. "Obviously somebody used my letter opener and then set it back on my desk. You're trying to imply that I had a reason to kill Arlo just to make your case." As he said the last part, he leaned over the table to speak firmly into Olivia's cell phone. "I can assure you I am innocent."

"Keep your panties on, Mr. Whitlock," Jets said. "Nobody who's guilty ever admits they are, so your bluster is getting you nowhere."

Olivia said, "You're adamant about your innocence." She paused to closely observe the man across the table.

"At least *you* can hear the plea of an innocent man." He sat back in his chair.

"But you did have a relationship with the deceased," Olivia said quietly. "Arlo Carson was your attorney. We found paperwork with your signature. Contracts concerning Featherington the Fifth and a stud fee."

"I'm not denying that I knew Arlo. Yeah, I hired him. A few months ago. Quigley stopped at the pub one day and they got to talking. Arlo chatted with him and told him he was an attorney. So I put him on retainer to write up my breeding contracts."

"What goes into a breeding contract exactly?" Jets asked.

"Specifics of how to ship specimens. The timing of the fertilization. Plus sometimes I waive my usual fee to have pick of the litter. I don't publicly breed females, but I do have a few on hand. Especially if the puppy comes from a reputable breeder with a few AKC wins.

"But I had to fire Carson," he added angrily. "Turns out he wasn't an attorney after all. He'd gone to law school and knew how to make it look good, but he didn't pass the bar."

Jets smiled. "Everyone in Lily Rock knew Arlo wasn't a real attorney. But how did you find out?"

"I sent Quigley to pick up a puppy at the airport down the hill. No one showed. When I used my contract to take them to court, they came back at me. Thumbed their noses. Told me my contract wasn't worth the paper it was written on. So I let Arlo know right away, and he admitted the truth. Fired him on the spot."

"So you were real mad at Arlo then, weren't you?" Jets said. "Mad enough to kill him."

"Ah come on, Jets. This was on me. I never vetted him because I was in too much of a hurry. I consider Arlo to be a fumble, the price of doing business. Plus I can always get another female Frenchie."

Olivia's stomach clenched. His casual reference to females, even a dog, was distasteful.

All of the energy across the table came from Eldred, penetrating Olivia's chest. She knew paying close attention was called for, despite her urge to get up and walk away. Whitlock kept explaining. "So as I said, I fired Arlo right after that. He wasn't really mad. Kind of apologetic, actually."

"What about you?" Jets turned to Uma. "Did you know Arlo?"

"Not really. I stay out of Eldred's breeding business. And he stays away from mine, the business of running the inn."

Jets glowered. "Well you see, Uma, that's a contradiction right there. If he insists that your inn only cater to AKC Frenchies, then he is in your business now, isn't he."

Uma's face drew a blank. "I suppose that's true. I really meant that Eldred and I don't mingle our financial dealings. We do influence each other. We're husband and wife after all."

While Jets wrote notes, Olivia gingerly picked up the conversation. She directed her attention back to Eldred. "I noticed when we returned Featherington the Fifth, you didn't seem that surprised."

"I already figured out what had happened. It was only a matter of time before he was returned. Featherington wasn't stolen by some rando.

"George Quigley was responsible. He's been standoffish ever since I fired Arlo. George is no longer satisfied working for me. I can tell that he and Arlo were in cahoots to start up their own business. George assumed I wouldn't miss the Fifth so long as I had the Sixth ready for action. So he took him and hid him, waiting to see if I noticed."

"Don't be ridiculous." Uma gave him a disdainful side glance. "You're so skeptical of everyone." The sound of contempt in her voice unnerved Olivia.

Jets cleared her throat. "Eldred, you are still my number one suspect. I suggest you find a real attorney because I'm this close"—she held up her thumb and forefinger—"to arresting you.

"The murder weapon was found on your desk. You fired Arlo Carson for lying to you and leaving you legally vulnerable. That's motive. Probably premeditated. I can see a guy like you, used to being in charge, exacting revenge. And I think you're in the right time frame despite your wife's alibi.

"At first I thought we had video footage of both of you setting up the merchandise table. I jumped to conclusions that was proof of your innocence. But then I reconsidered.

"It would only take ten minutes to leave Uma alone to fold

her shirts, run to the dog park, and stab Arlo in the armpit. Then a quick jog back to fold some more tees. And Uma here"—Jets looked across the table—"probably didn't miss you."

Uma looked thoughtful. "I suppose that's realistic. I don't keep track of Eldred every time he walks away."

"So am I to understand you're revising your statement? That Eldred may not have been with you the entire time?" Jets looked hopeful.

Uma nodded. "I think I will revise the statement. I can't be sure he was there the entire time and I don't want to be held accountable for his whereabouts."

Jets turned to Olivia. "Like I told you before. Spouse alibis are easy to break. Just like that." She snapped her fingers.

Eldred slumped in his chair.

"Do I need to put my revised statement in writing right now?" Uma asked.

Jets placed her tablet on the table and stood. "I have other interviews. Don't leave town. I'll be in touch."

Olivia followed her out the door.

CHAPTER THIRTY-FOUR

The Whitlocks exited the constabulary through the back door.

"Okay, so you heard them," Jets said. "What's your take?"

Olivia spoke slowly. "I think Eldred's telling the truth. Firing Arlo wasn't that big of a deal. Dogs and breeding are a means to an end for him. It's all about the bottom line. I don't think he'd risk being arrested for killing Arlo."

"Eldred is a cold-hearted business man, I'll give you that," Jets reasoned. "And I think Uma may not care if she's setting him up for jail time."

"It's as if she's beyond caring," Olivia observed.

"But I can check the boxes. Motive. Means. Opportunity. That may not get me a conviction in court, but a confession will." Jets made her expectation clear.

Olivia gulped. *So this all comes down to me, her volunteer consultant.*

"Do you need a drink or something before the next interview?" Janis asked.

"I'm fine. Who's next?"

"I've got Shelly and Sydney in room number one. After you."

The couple sat behind the interview table, staring ahead.

Jets sat down, pulling out a chair for Olivia. She explained about the recording and turned to Sydney first. "So you're doing an expose for *It's a Dog's World* about Frenchie breeding practices?"

"That's correct," Sydney confirmed. "By the way, this won't be the first time the police have pulled me in for an interview. It goes with the territory of being an investigative reporter. I have all the resources of my magazine behind me. If I'm falsely charged, they will provide bail and an excellent attorney for my defense."

"Well isn't that convenient," Jets said. "So you're calling yourself an investigative reporter. Very fancy. That's like saying the grocery store magazine at the checkout counter is worthy of the Pulitzer. Give me a break.

"So you think you're the guy to pull back the curtain on dog breeding practices and then tell the world?" Jets's tone was condescending.

"There are many reasons not to breed Frenchies. Health concerns, for one." His eyes blazed. "You probably have no idea, but breeders work with their DNA to get them to look more attractive to humans. The wide set of the eyes, their broad faces with the round chins. People want to see themselves in their dog."

"I have a Frenchie," Jets commented. "He's adorable—his sweet expression, how his eyes light up when he sees me." Jets's face softened. "He doesn't look like me," she insisted. "More like my partner. Tater Tot has the same smile and excited expression as Cookie.

"You don't have to tell me about the health issues. We've been to the vet several times already. If you consider the snoring, belching, and farting, Tater Tot is a regular machine. And his breathing gets labored in the heat. Maybe breeders could experiment with his DNA to make all that go away."

Sydney frowned. "It's because of the flat face. That's why they have breathing and digestive issues."

Jets opened her tablet. "Back to my murder investigation. What I want to know is what your relationship was to Arlo Carson."

"We talked a few times." He sounded noncommittal.

Olivia felt the hair rise on her neck. She leaned forward. "Could you tell us more about your relationship?"

"I guess it's not a secret. Actually Carson contacted me a month before Woofstock. He knew something hinky was going on with the inn. When my editor mentioned the Woofstock festival right in Lily Rock, I jumped at the chance.

"I interviewed Carson right away for my article. He was a really interesting guy. He said I could also quote him—just not mention his name. Arlo was really transparent about his feelings. I liked the guy. Especially when he explained that he'd broken up with his wife and felt lonely. I guess he empathized with the dog because he seemed lonely too.

"So abducting the dog seemed a good way to free him, just to give him a better home. It turned out Arlo needed Featherington to ease his loneliness. Plus he took great care of the dog.

"Took him to his place and fed him ordinary dog food. He let him run around the house, sit on the furniture, sleep with him in his bed. Arlo even arranged a playdate. He invited that dog mayor of yours to come over to keep Featherington the Fifth company while he was at work."

Olivia remembered how Maguire acted earlier, standing

outside Lady of the Rock. He observed from afar rather than taking over. He even let the smaller dog take his treat.

Maybe Maguire figures he's some kind of Frenchie guardian or something.

"But it wasn't for long. Arlo had to bring the dog back," Ayers said. "It was Arlo's opinion that Whitlock didn't miss Featherington at all."

"Why did he return Featherington?" Olivia asked.

"Things were going fine until Arlo used WD-40 to kill some ants at his cabin. He hated the smell of the usual ant and roach spray, but he liked the smell of WD-40. He sprayed one morning and left for work.

"Featherington decided to sniff around. No one was there to stop him. By the time Arlo got home, Featherington was wheezing and coughing and gasping for breath. Arlo rushed him to the vet. Once the dog recovered, he returned him to Whitlock."

"And Whitlock never said a word about Featherington, that he was missing?" Olivia asked.

"Not a word. At least that was Arlo's impression."

Jets cleared her throat. "So what you're implying is that you had no reason to kill Arlo. To you, he was an informant."

"That's right," Sydney said. "Plus I was driving up the hill to Lily Rock at the time of death. You can check my GPS. You don't even need a warrant. Have at it." He looked at his husband for confirmation.

I nearly forgot about Shelly. He's been so quiet.

"What about you?" Jets followed up. "I hear you've gotten pretty chummy with Uma Whitlock."

Before he could speak, Jets did a double take. "Do I know you from somewhere?"

"I've never met you before," Shelly said in an annoyed

tone. "I didn't know anyone in Lily Rock before this weekend. I didn't know Arlo Carson," he sniffed.

"Except for Uma. According to my assistant, you knew her before," Jets reminded him.

"But that was an accident. I already explained to your consultant. In telemedicine sometimes we bump into a client. It's just the way of things."

Olivia felt the hair on her arm rise. *Telemedicine has changed a lot of our practices with doctors and therapists. But I don't think running into clients is necessarily more prevalent.*

"I told her that Uma and I realized the problem as soon as we recognized each other. I am no longer her therapist." He smiled. "I'm a friend now."

"But very good friends. Or so it seems." Jets sent Olivia a quick glance.

Olivia spoke slowly. "Your relationship with Uma is quite special."

"Yes, it is," he said promptly. "Uma and I are twin flames. And she's filled a void in my life since my mother died." He looked away, his eyes shiny with tears. "Mom and I were so close and I miss her dreadfully."

Jets looked skeptical. "What's a twin flame?"

"Two people who share the same soul," Shelly explained.

More like his surrogate mother, Olivia thought.

Jets finished taking notes on her tablet. "I've got all the information I need. At least for now. You can both go home. We'll have a look at Sydney's GPS. I'll call your editor to confirm the rest of your story."

"We plan to head home after Woofstock," Shelton stated firmly.

"And I have some loose ends to tie up before I can go," Sydney added.

Jets interrupted. "So you're staying an extra day. Then I'll download that GPS info right now. That should solidify your alibis and I'll be able to wrap up my investigation." She glared at them both. "But nobody's off the hook quite yet."

"Couples are complicated," Olivia said once the door was closed. "The Whitlocks are full of contempt. And the Ayerses. Something's amiss."

Jets looked thoughtful. "And I know Shelton from somewhere. I didn't really do a background check on either of them. But I have some time."

"Any more interviews?" asked Olivia.

"We've got Quigley. He was the first one to find Arlo's body. You and Michael think he's a prime suspect. So I'd better have a chat."

Quigley sat behind the interview table. "I found Carson dead, I didn't make him dead," he insisted.

"That's what you told me the first time, George," Jets stated calmly. "But here's what I really want to know. Why did you whack Olivia over the head in an alley?"

Olivia felt her eyes grow wide. *Janis never told me she suspected George.*

He started to protest. "That wasn't me."

Jets leaned in. "Really, that's what you're going with? Come on, I'm not new at this job. I've got you hands down."

Quigley squirmed, looking away from Olivia. When Janis didn't speak, he turned back. "Okay, it was me. But how did you know?"

Jets smirked. "It was a guess. I wasn't completely sure until now. But you can't take it back. We've got a recording." She pointed to Olivia's cell phone. "Why did you hit my worthy assistant over the head, George?" Jets's voice resumed a serious tone.

Olivia touched the bump on her scalp. "Still hurts," she admitted. "What have I ever done to you?" She glared at George.

"I needed some time," he explained. "I didn't want you and your boyfriend to discover Featherington the Fifth before I could move him. I wanted the reward. Sorry about your head." He looked slightly remorseful.

"Save your apologies for later," Jets interjected. "You admit to taking Featherington the Fifth?"

"It was the second time," he said. "I convinced Arlo to take him originally. But he did that stupid WD-40 thing. A dead dog was not the goal, so we returned him to Eldred. Obviously I couldn't trust Arlo to keep him safe.

"But once Arlo was out of the picture, I figured I'd try again. I cleaned up the all the WD-40 residue and then left Featherington in the empty cabin. This time in a crate, not wandering around."

"Did you break into the cabin by chance?" Jets asked.

"I never had a key in the first place. I used my shoulder to shove the door open. Then I left the dog. Everything went okay, but then I got nervous. Because of that other dog, Mayor Mc-what's-it. He kept hanging around. When Olivia and Michael told me they were looking for him, I knew I had to do something. That's when I delayed her in the alley. But she and her boyfriend got there first in the end." Quigley's look of disappointment made Olivia want to laugh.

"You seem pretty familiar with Arlo's cabin. At least enough to break in," Jets said.

"I'd meet him up there now and then. It was the perfect place to hide a dog. No one would think of looking there, behind a church."

Jets paused. *She's planning what to say next,* Olivia realized.

"You let Arlo take the fall for that botched puppy handover, didn't you? That's despicable, Quigley."

Olivia felt Jets's disdain like a stab wound to the heart.

Quigley made more excuses, his voice rambling as he explained. "Arlo wasn't that interested in breeding Frenchies anyway. He got fired instead of me. But it's not what you think. I wanted to get my own breeding business started. You know, like Eldred.

"I needed in influx of cash to get things off the ground. A male and a female could make that happen. Plus Eldred wasn't going to miss that puppy. Like I said, I didn't kill Arlo. I have no hard feelings about him fumbling the dog napping. Oh sure he caused trouble because he misrepresented himself as a qualified attorney.

"That one time I let Eldred think the deal fell through because of Arlo. But I got a free female Frenchie in the bargain. I took her down the hill to stay with my cousin. She's all safe and sound."

Jets's eyes lit up. "I bet you were riding high on that plan."

"It seemed perfect," Quigley admitted.

"But what about the puppy?" Olivia asked. "What happened to her?"

"I sold her in less than twenty-four hours. Of course I told Eldred she never showed up. That I got a good buyer online."

"It doesn't take a genius to see that you're a ruthless and calculating businessman," Jets said harshly. "That you'd do anything to get going with your own breeding practice. That makes you capable of murder or at the very least of being an accessory, in my book.

"I bet Arlo was on to you. Maybe he refused to keep cooperating or maybe he threatened to tell me. So you knifed him in the dog park and then waited for him to be found. Once he was out of the way, you could start up again."

"That's not true!" Quigley exclaimed. "I admit that I've wanted to better myself for a few years. Establish my own breeding business. Arlo was going to help, but then he backed out. That's no reason to kill him.

"I didn't kill Arlo, but I know who did. It's right here on my app." He held up his cell phone for Janis to see.

Janis took the cell in one hand. "What do we have here, George?" she asked.

"I track my boss. That way I know where he can be found. Then I stay out of his way. But I can also read his texts. You can see there." He leaned over the desk to point at his screen. "Every text for the past six months. Go ahead and read," he insisted.

Jets scrolled. "Most of these are between him and Uma. Partner kind of squabbling."

"Keep scrolling," he demanded.

Jets bit her bottom lip. "So Eldred thinks Uma is having an affair." She looked up at George for confirmation.

"That's right. With me, as it turns out."

"She denied it of course," Jets said.

"Because we're not," he said adamantly.

"At first he takes her word for it," Jets summarized. "But here I can see that he hired a private firm to investigate." Jets continued to read the texts. Her eyes grew wide. "No way!" she exclaimed.

She dropped the phone on the desk as if it were hot. "You can leave now, George. I'll be in touch."

He reached across the desk to retrieve his phone right as Janis slapped at his hand. "I'm keeping your phone as evidence. By tomorrow I'll have some answers. Until then, don't leave town."

CHAPTER THIRTY-FIVE

Once George Quigley left the constabulary, Olivia breathed a sigh of relief. "It's getting late," she reminded Janis. "Can we pick this up tomorrow? I'm exhausted." She rubbed the bandage on her head.

"Pipe down, Nancy Drew. I've got an important lead right here. I can't believe it came from that Quigley character, but here you go." She finished typing her report to turn her computer around for Olivia to read.

Olivia held her breath as she read each word, feeling more and more surprised. "I don't believe it. I remember hearing about this case several years ago."

"Eight years, to be exact. The first year into her sentence, she got sick. Cancer. It took her quick, only two months later." Janis looked pale. "I never saw this coming. I got it so wrong. All because I was focused on the Whitlocks. Once I get an arrest warrant you can meet me at the truck. Oh, and take an aspirin for that head."

. . .

"Come on," Jets shouted. "They've driven halfway down the hill."

Olivia buckled her seat belt.

Jets turned left on Main Street only to slam on the brakes. Leaning out the window, she yelled, "Get that dog out of my way!" With a flick of her wrist, the police siren blared.

People stopped to look, and the dog's owner picked it up and ran out of the street. The car ahead let her pass. Olivia braced her hands on both sides of the passenger seat as Janis drove through a crosswalk without stopping. On the main road out of town, she took the first curve at breakneck speed.

A truck with a fifth wheel blocked the road. "Out of my way," Jets roared, as if the driver could hear. She reached for her microphone. "Move over. Right now." She put the microphone down, still muttering. The truck kept driving. It wasn't until he reached the next pullout that he slowed down and moved to the side of the road.

Jets's foot slammed on the brakes to avoid a collision. Olivia gripped her seat harder. Janis pushed her foot to the accelerator as she drove past.

Around the next stretch of road, Olivia saw blinking lights.

"Cops from down the hill," Jets explained. Her foot landed on the brake as tires screeched. Olivia felt her stomach lurch, bile in the back of her throat.

A Honda SUV held a driver, a passenger, and a cream-colored Frenchie. Excited yips came from the rolled-down window.

The driver hunched over the steering wheel, while the passenger looked straight ahead. "Got 'em." Jets pulled the emergency brake. "Stay here," she told Olivia.

As Janis approached the vehicle, Olivia pulled out her cell phone to text Michael.

I'm with Janis.

Coming home soon?

She's making an arrest.

Does that mean no?

Not no. Just not yet.

Can you tell me who killed Arlo?

She clicked the phone off.

Olivia watched as a tall uniformed officer yanked the SUV driver from behind the wheel. Janis stepped forward, yanking his arms behind his back. Once the cuffs were secured, she marched him toward the police car. With a hand on the top of his head, she shoved him into the back seat of the police car. As soon as the door closed, Janis returned to the truck.

Hands on her hips, she waited for Olivia to open the passenger window.

"What's going on?" Olivia asked.

"I handled this investigation all wrong. I'm really going to need that confession now. This time it's more crucial than ever."

Olivia soothed her upset stomach with a sip of peppermint tea. On the other side of the break room table, Jets filled out paperwork, scratching at the sheets with her pen.

"I'm doing this old-school," Jets commented. "In case you wondered. I don't want any loopholes. But now comes the hard part." She placed her tablet on top of the stack of papers.

"We arrested him for obstructing justice. But that isn't what I'm going for. I need a confession if I want to make the murder charge stick. Are you up for it? Can you work your special mojo and make this happen?"

Olivia glanced uneasily around the break room. Nothing about this case felt like any of the others. Janis had never been so direct, asking for a confession. Before, they just seemed to happen.

"I'm ready." She put her mug down. Her words conveyed a confidence she did not feel. But she wasn't going to tell Janis.

The door to the break room opened. Shelton Ayers walked slowly forward. Brad settled him into the chair on the opposite side of the table. He removed the handcuffs.

"We're recording this interview," Jets reminded him.

Shelly was no longer magazine cover worthy. His hair unkempt, his mouth downturned, his eyes issuing a blank stare.

"Okay, my first question," Jets began. "What about staying put didn't you understand?"

Shelton looked away.

"I arrested you for obstruction of justice."

He looked down at his hands.

Jets's body tensed.

"Come on, Shelton, we did the background check. You don't have to pretend any longer. Look right here." Janis opened up her tablet to show him the webpage she'd previously shown Olivia.

"Your full name, before you married, was Shelton John Muller. See, here's your picture. Snapped right after the not guilty verdict." She shoved the tablet closer. When he refused to look, Jets glanced at Olivia, her jaw tight with anger.

Janis's irritation wasn't helping her case. Her hard attitude was understandable but not useful with this suspect. He wasn't going to speak to her so long as she tried to bully him into talking.

Olivia gave her head a slight shake, hoping Janis would take direction and back off, though she braced herself for a verbal rebuke. But Janis surprised her by taking a deep breath and leaning back in the chair.

"May I see the article?" Olivia reached for the tablet.

Shelton shrugged.

Olivia smiled gently. "I want to know you better."

He looked away.

"Oh, I see," Olivia commented. "Your mother went to prison. That must have been so difficult for you, after what the two of you had been through."

Shelton spoke hauntingly, without eye contact. "My stepfather abused us both, but her especially. She loved me so much and tried to protect me, but he wouldn't stop." He turned to face her. His eyes lost that dazed expression as he blinked back tears.

"Once I'd had enough, I just waited and took my time. He came home drunk and I killed him. A kitchen knife." Shelton spoke in a matter-of-fact voice. "Mom took the blame. And she went to prison."

"And then your mother passed away. Was it cancer? My mom died of cancer."

"You too?" He wiped his eyes. "She forgave me right before she died. She never blamed me, but I still feel guilty. Her sacrifice and love. How could I repay that?"

"And that's why you felt so strongly about..." Olivia left the sentence open again.

"I love Uma," he answered. "At first I felt sorry for her. Our initial appointment, it only took minutes for us to bond. Twin flames are like that, once they find each other.

"I told some small lies about the timing." He smiled at

Olivia. "You understand, don't you? How small lies are necessary."

Olivia gazed at him as if he were a child who'd lost his way, not a grown man who'd committed murder. When Shelton didn't keep talking, she asked, "Were Quigley and Uma in a relationship?"

"No, not that!" he insisted. "Quigley dominated Uma and pushed her around behind Eldred's back. He showed up when she stood behind the desk. He'd look over her shoulder at the computer.

"One time she caught him using her password to check out her bank balances. And then he'd stop by their house unexpectedly, when she was alone. He'd push his way in, asking impertinent questions.

"Uma asked for help, but Eldred was too busy. There was no one she could depend on," he said sadly.

"So Quigley must have reminded you of your stepfather," Olivia said.

"He bullied her." Shelton hung his head. "You're right. Uma did remind me of Mother. But not like you think. I felt loved and seen again when I was talking to her. It was so wonderful to be treated like a son. To be confided in and fussed over. She sent me Juicy Fruit for my birthday.

"I didn't tell Sydney right away. He wouldn't have understood." He leaned over the table. "You've got to understand. Juicy Fruit is my life. A gift from my mom." His face turned pale.

Olivia wondered if he realized what he'd just said. That Uma was his mother. She waited for him to register how he'd inadvertently given away an important insight into his behavior.

It took a minute before his face fell. "I don't mean my mom. I meant Uma."

Jets had remained quiet as Olivia asked the questions. But now she fidgeted in her chair.

"There were texts between George and Eldred. Nasty ones from Eldred accusing George of having an affair with his wife."

Shelton smiled. "Uma and I had a good laugh about that. Eldred had no idea about me. He was home one time when George showed up unexpectedly. Then he jumped to conclusions that she was having an affair. The truth is that Uma thinks her husband is a sorry excuse for a man. Of course Eldred didn't know her like I do." Shelton nervously shifted in his chair.

Olivia took a leap, making the next question count. "When did you and Uma come up with the plan?"

Shelton didn't flinch. He'd come to the point in the interview where he wanted to explain his behavior.

"It was for the best. George Quigley needed to go," Shelton stated flatly. "I took a bus and then an Uber to Lily Rock the day before Sydney. Not the time I told you. I met with Uma before my husband showed up. She gave me the letter opener.

"I'd never met Quigley face-to-face, but Uma described him so carefully. I asked for a photo but she nixed the idea. Said the photo would be traceable and that it was important to protect us both. So I was on the lookout for a tall man in his fifties with thin hair, a short beard, and a worn baseball cap.

"She said he looked like Shaggy from Scooby Doo. She even told me how I could always find him at the dog park early in the morning.

"I showed up at that time the next day. Sure enough George was there. What a loathsome man." Shelton shuddered. "I had Uma's letter opener tucked inside my jacket. I walked right over to the bench, introduced myself, and offered to shake. When George raised his hand to take mine, I jabbed the blade right under his armpit."

"Did he mention his name as he raised his hand?" Olivia asked quietly.

"He tried, but I'd already stabbed him." Shelton looked to the right, his face slightly flushed.

"Did you realize then that you'd killed the wrong man?" Olivia's jaw tightened.

Shelton gulped. "When I got back to The Frenchie Connection, I left the weapon on Eldred's desk."

"When did you realize you'd made a mistake? That you hadn't killed George Quigley but a complete stranger?" Olivia asked again, this time with a firm voice.

"So unfortunate," Shelton sighed. "That man you call Arlo looked just like George. Uma's description might have been either man. I didn't mean to hurt him." He held his fist over his mouth. "I feared for Uma's safety," he insisted. "I wouldn't have killed anyone otherwise. Arlo was at the wrong place at the wrong time. I can't be blamed."

Jets intervened. "I have everything I need to arrest you for the premeditated murder of the wrong man. Mr. Shelton Muller Ayers, you have the right to remain silent."

CHAPTER THIRTY-SIX

Janis Jets stood on the front doorstep holding a pink cardboard bakery box. "Good morning," she announced. Maguire followed the pink box with his nose in the air as Olivia smiled.

Jets placed the box on the counter. "I smell fresh paint." She looked around the kitchen.

"We're just finishing up our first painting project." Olivia peeked inside the box. "Lemon thyme muffins. My favorite."

"Is there any baked good that is not your favorite?" mumbled Jets.

"I do love everything your boyfriend bakes," Olivia said agreeably.

Jets sat on a stool as Olivia pulled out napkins and small plates.

"My boyfriend is very excited that you agreed to be Tater Tot's godparents."

Michael arrived from the back door. "Coffee with that?"

Jets reached for a plate and answered, "Yep, I'd love coffee. But I came early because I thought you'd like an update on the arrest of Shelton Ayers."

"Have a muffin first," Olivia offered.

Jets reached into the box. "So the confession is rock solid. I don't think anyone will be able to poke holes in it. The recording caught his whole story. Once you were done with the questioning, I couldn't shut him up, even after you left.

"I followed up with Uma, who did admit she'd bad-mouthed Quigley to Shelton. She never liked the trainer and she was letting off steam. But she denies having anything to do with plotting his death."

"You believe her?" Michael asked.

"She's one of those women who finds herself in situations with men and then cries help and then stands back wondering how it got so complicated. I think I can nail her as an accessory. Especially since she handed Shelton the murder weapon to kill Eldred with.

"But Shelton. He's done. He admits to killing his stepfather and to letting his mother take the blame. The guilt made him more sensitive to Uma's complaining." Jets took a bite of her muffin. "Twin flame nonsense aside, he's the guy."

"But what about Quigley? He assaulted me." Olivia touched her scalp.

"Up to you," Jets said. "You want to fill out the paperwork and file a complaint, I'll arrest him."

"He's a jerk," Olivia mumbled. "I just don't know if it's worth it."

"You have time to reconsider," Jets said. She spun on her stool to glance toward the living room. "I see some photos on the mantel and lots of throw pillows. Still unpacking?"

"Olivia is making this place feel like home." Michael patted her back.

"It's taken me a bit of time," Olivia admitted.

Jets rolled her eyes. "I heard the song and your dedication. Michael is your home. Kinda sappy if you ask me."

"No more muffins for you," Michael chided. "She dedicated the last song to me. It was perfect. I am home, isn't that right." He quirked his eyebrow at Olivia.

"There's something in your eyes," Olivia quoted the first line.

"And your coffee." Janis held up her empty mug.

After Michael refilled everyone's mug, Janis cleared her throat. "There's something else. I got this approved." She shoved a paper toward Olivia.

"What's this?" Olivia asked.

"It's official. I've been given permission to offer you an official position at the constabulary." After a moment, she added, "As a paid consultant. No more volunteering."

Olivia replied at once. "I say yes." She turned to Michael.

"I admit I'm uneasy when you put yourself at risk. But after the past few days hanging around with you, I realized this is your thing. You're very good at getting people to admit what they won't admit to themselves. It's a gift. And I'm just happy Janis is finally paying you for the work."

Jets took a bite of muffin and began to chew slowly. She swallowed. "So on the one hand, now that you receive pay, you're not an amateur detective any more. I'll miss calling you Nancy Drew. But on the other hand, things are looking up.

"Now I'll have one more person at the constabulary to get me coffee. Speaking of which, I need another refill."

She held her mug aloft with a huge grin.

EPILOGUE

Olivia stood at the entrance of the labyrinth. She closed her eyes to focus on her breath. She opened her eyes to take the first step. A rush of emotion made her chest feel warm. With each intentional step, her heart expanded. Her hands, lying open by her sides, tingled.

When she reached the center, the middle point of the journey, she looked up. Then she raised her arms over her head, the salute Cayenne taught her, as a thank you to Lily Rock. Her heart opened at the thought of her friend.

Blinking away tears, she made a quarter-circle turn and raised her arms again, repeating in her mind, *North. South. East. West.* She slowly eased her arms to her sides. A great peace settled over her body. The tingling stopped. She stared at her shoes planted in the dirt.

Her heart quickened at the sight of a smooth round stone. She bent over to get a closer look. The surface showed a primitive drawing. A hand with a spiral in the center.

"Cay," she whispered. She knew instantly. The stone was a sign. She picked the stone up and turned it over. On the back, she saw one word: friend.

Olivia knew in her heart that she and Cay were connected. If not by physical presence, then by something else. A sense of each other that crossed space and time. She slipped the stone into her pocket and turned to go back the way she'd come.

Taking one step and then the next, she arrived at the entrance of the labyrinth. A crow cawed in the distance. She inhaled the pine-scented air. *I'm home*, she thought. *Not just with Michael but with myself.*

ACKNOWLEDGEMENTS

Acknowledgements

I'd like to thank Christie Stratos for her invaluable editing work. My characters would also like to thank Christie because they feel safe and challenged in her expert hands.

As for Husband, he's the last reader before formatting and publishing. The man has a keen eye for every detail. I can't imagine doing this work without his support and talent.

What about you, dear readers? You and I are partners. I do the writing—that gets the story to the center. But it takes your reading to bring me home. I am grateful, beyond measure, for you.

Keep on reading!
Bonnie
January, 2025

BOOK CLUB DISCUSSION QUESTIONS

Here are some book club discussion questions for Sit. Stay. Play Dead Lily Rock Mystery Book Seven

1. Does Lily Rock's sense of community and loyalty shape the investigation and the interactions among the characters?

2. Janis Jets is quick to suspect Eldred Whitlock of the crime. How does this dynamic affect the investigation and her personal relationship with Olivia?

3. Did you find any parallels between the dogs' personalities and their owners?

4. One of the themes in the book is perception versus reality. How do appearances deceive both the characters and the reader? Were there moments when you were misled by a character's behavior or actions?

5. What techniques or traits in Olivia Greer make her an effective amateur sleuth? Were there moments in her investigation that surprised you?

6. How does the setting of Lily Rock, with its small-town quirks and close-knit community, influence the story? Could you imagine the same mystery taking place in a different environment, such as a big city?

7. How does the Woofstock festival contribute to the story's tone and pace? Did the festive environment contrast with the darker elements of the mystery, or did it enhance them?

8. Were there any clues or red herrings that led you to suspect someone other than the actual culprit?

9. Despite the murder mystery, there are humorous and heartwarming moments, especially involving the dogs. How did these lighter elements affect your reading experience?

10. As Olivia unearths buried secrets, we see how characters hide aspects of their lives. How do these secrets impact the investigation and the relationships among the townspeople?

11. Sit. Stay. Play Dead* is a clever play on words that ties into both the dog festival and the murder mystery. How do you think the title reflects the themes and events of the story?

12. Janis is protective of Tater Tot and takes offense when the dog is snubbed by The Frenchie Connection. How do you think this incident affected her objectivity? Did it make her a more relatable character?

13.How does Olivia manage her friendship with Janis, especially when Janis jumps to conclusions about the suspect? How do their differing personalities complement each other during the investigation?

14. Which scene or chapter did you find most engaging or surprising? Were there any moments that made you laugh, gasp, or reflect?

15. Based on the events of this book, where do you see Olivia Greer and Janis Jets heading in the next installment of the Lily Rock Mystery series? Are there any unanswered questions you'd like to see addressed?

ABOUT THE AUTHOR

Bonnie Hardy, a retired professional turned author, is celebrated for her two enthralling cozy mystery series. The first, set in the picturesque mountain town of Lily Rock, features amateur sleuth Olivia Greer, known for her uncanny ability to draw out confessions from the most unlikely people.

The second series, set in Palm Desert, features the mid-life duo mentalist Rex Redondo and his down to earth next door neighbor doula Vivienne Rose.

Inspired by Agatha Christie, Bonnie's captivating tales of mystery and community masterfully blend fast-paced whodunits with clever sleuthing.

facebook.com/bonniehardywrites.com

instagram.com/bonniehardywrites

bookbub.com/authors/bonnie-hardy

goodreads.com/bonniehardy

ALSO BY BONNIE HARDY

For a full list please go to

bonniehardywrites.com/Books

Welcome to Lily Rock Holiday Mystery Novellas

'Tis the Season

All Aboard for Murder

Wrap it Up!

Lily Rock Mystery Series

Getaway Death

Influenced to Death

Deadly Admission

A Thymely Death

Deadbeat Dad

A Very Tidy Death

Sit. Stay. Play Dead.

Redondo and Rose Neighbors in Crime

A Doula to Die For

Between the Sheets

Sight Unseen

AVAILABLE ON AUDIBLE

Lily Rock Mystery Series

Getaway Death Book One
Influenced to Death Book Two
Deadly Admission Book Three
A Thymely Death Book Three

Redondo and Rose Neighbors in Crime Series

A Doula to Die For Book One
Between the Sheets Book Two

A SNEAK PEAK INTO ANOTHER POPULAR SERIES BY BONNIE HARDY

A Doula To Die For Redondo and Rose Neighbors in Crime
Book One

... Viv drove slowly down her quiet street. She made a left turn into her driveway. The sensor lights came on. Lowering the visor, she touched the garage door opener. As the door slid open she saw the SUV, which occupied half of the tidy garage. *Tamara must be asleep by now.* Viv parked the car inside the garage, noticing that next to the SUV, it looked small and unimposing. She grabbed her phone and purse before exiting the car.

Viv retrieved her doula bag from the back seat before walking to the door to head inside. The knob on the inner garage door turned easily in her hand. *Tamara always forgets to lock this one.*

A quick push of the button and the garage door closed from behind. Viv stepped inside the house. *Ahhh, air conditioning.* She stopped to fully appreciate the cold air against her face, but her skin prickled. In the dark she dropped her bag next to the kitchen counter. "Tamara," she called in a soft voice. *She probably went to bed.*

Calling again, still no one answered. She stopped calling, listening to a sound in the distance. *Sirens...they're close, maybe near my neighborhood.*

Forgetting about Tamara, she hurried to the front of the house. Curtain pushed aside, she stared out to the street. Red lights blinked and darted under the dark sky. The flashes bounced off the large boulders from the landscaping in front of the development.

Two police cars and a paramedic van waited on the other side of the security gate. One enormously tall officer stood in the street, holding what looked like a cell phone to his ear.

Maybe he's calling for the gate code?

Another police vehicle lined up behind the ambulance. Lights blinked and a horn tooted. The officer in the street lowered his cell phone and stepped back as the gate began to rise.

Viv let the curtain drop back over the window.

"'Tamara," she called out, this time in earnest. "You've got to come quick. There are cops in the neighborhood and it looks serious."

When no one answered, Viv decided, *She's probably taken one of her sleeping pills. I'll check in the guest room.*

Made in the USA
Las Vegas, NV
01 February 2025

16935414R00166